Ashes of Death

G.L. Didaleusky

ISBN: 978-1-62420-666-5

Credits
Cover Artist: Designs by Ms G
Editor: Deborah C. Day

Dedication

To Holly whose moral support and analytical opinions mean everything to me.

Chapter One

The sun woke the southeastern horizon of central Florida, bringing early morning light to Clifton Retirement Community in Ocala, Florida. Hungry hawks began their effortless circular flight searching for tiny ground creatures scurrying from their burrows. A prevailing north, cool, late fall breeze touched nature's creatures and people taking advantage of the early morning environment. Two of these people were Mark and Sherry McKinney who walked around the circular road encompassing the retirement community.

Mark peered up at the circling menacing hawk looking for its morning meal, then inhaled deeply. "I love our morning walks. It gets my old circulation going. Plus, it makes the first cup of coffee taste so much better."

"What about the other ten cups or so you drink through the day and evening?"

"It's a necessity to maintain my clear thinking and stamina."

Sherry chuckled. "You've been telling me this story for thirty some years when you were working…which medically I could somewhat understand. But we've been retired for almost two years."

"Yeah, right. I've done more running around with you window shopping, visiting friends and manual labor with all your projects you want me to do around the yard and inside the house. I exert more energy now than when I was working as a sheriff detective."

They had now walked about three-quarters around the community. Up ahead to their left was a row of mailboxes. They stopped in front of mailbox one-four-seven.

"We didn't get the mail yesterday afternoon because we were at Brian and Lucia's house playing cards. We forgot to stop when we got home."

"No big thing. All we normally get are your medical magazines and a variety of advertisements."

Sherry removed advertisement envelopes, flyers and an emergency room medical journal. After graduating from medical school, she did her residency in emergency medicine and practiced as an emergency room physician for thirty-five years. "Your prediction was right on. Must be your detective prowess."

"Hey, Mark, Sherry," yelled a man in his early seventies standing under a carport about forty feet away from them.

Mark turned right toward the man. Thirty percent of Clifton's residence sat at either their kitchen tables, outside carport patios or screened-in porches drinking their coffee or other morning beverages this time of the morning. "Morning, Joe. Another beautiful morning in Florida."

"Sure is." Joe Barrington walked toward them, then stopped when he was about six feet away. A concerned expression flashed across his face. "I'm getting worried about Edna and Carl."

Last time he and Sherry had seen them, about a week ago, the elderly couple were homebound due to Edna's terminal pancreatic cancer and Carl's severe heart failure. Both were frail looking. The couple needed a daily visiting nurse to aid in their care. From Joe's demeaner and statement, Mark assumed the medically compromised couple had gotten worse. "Are they getting worse?"

"No. Not at all. The opposite. Three days ago, they cancelled the visiting nurse. When I talked with the Parkers two days ago, they both acted energetic, as if they were in excellent health."

"Sometimes a few days before terminally ill patients die," Sherry interjected, "there's a period called terminal lucidity, which may last a couple of days to a couple of weeks. It's when a person manifests an endorphin rush. They become energetic and maybe even euphoric...followed by death. Although I never heard of a couple experiencing this medical phenomenon at the same time."

"How were they yesterday?" Mark asked.

"I didn't talk to or see them yesterday. I noticed last night there weren't any lights on inside their house. They normally stay up until about eleven o'clock and are up by six in the morning."

Joe turned around and peered up the street to his left. "As you can see, their home is dark, and it's five minutes past seven. And their car is parked under the carport."

Mark looked at the Parkers' residence, a white and blue-trimmed ranch home two lots down from Joe's house. He knew there could be a few reasons for the couple not following their normal daily habits. Maybe a relative had picked them up and driven the couple to their home for a couple of days. Another scenario could be Mr. Parker called Uber and had them drive to a resort near Disney World or the Universal Studio theme park. This action supported what Sherry said about the couple possibly experiencing terminal lucidity, A chill overwhelmed him as a third scenario streaked across his mind. The couple were lying in bed dead, succumbed to their illnesses. "I think it would be justified to do a wellness check on them. Most people in our community leave a key with a neighbor in case of an emergency. Our neighbor the Kennedys have our door key, and we have their carport side door key."

Joe rubbed his forehead. "Not sure if they gave a door key to either of their neighbors. Although some people hide a spare door key outside in case they lock themselves out of their house."

Mark turned toward Sherry, raised his eyebrows and slightly nodded. She reciprocated with a nod, indicating they should check out Joe's concern about Carl and Edna's welfare. After being married for over thirty years, they understood each other's body gestures. "We'll check it out." After retiring, he had thought his detective work had ended. Not so when you live in a retirement community.

The three of them walked up the carport driveway to the side door. Mark couldn't view inside the house due to the closed mini-blinds so then walked up the three-step stairs to the door. He opened the storm door and looked through a small diamond-shaped window. No lights were on in the kitchen. He knocked on the door. Silence and no movement from inside. He turned the doorknob. Locked.

"I found their door key," Sherry said. "It was under a statue of a cat."

Mark grabbed the key from his wife and unlocked the door. He sighed, expecting the odor of decomposing bodies, an odor he had smelled numerous times as a detective for the Marion County Sheriff Department. They walked inside the kitchen. No odor of death. "Hello…hello. It's Mark McKinney. Are you home?"

No response. The rhythmic clicking of a grandfather clock in the living room filled the air. There were two bedrooms, one at each end of the house. Mark turned around. "Let's check the bedrooms. We'll start with the one here." He led the way past a dimly lit bathroom to his left. He reached for the bathroom light switch and flicked it up. The bright light lit up an unoccupied room. He stepped back and turned to his right. A closed bedroom door stood straight ahead. Mark cautiously opened the door, not sure what to expect. He flipped the light switch upward, lighting up the bedroom. An unoccupied queen-size bed stood to his left. He walked over to the far side of the bed. No one laid on the floor. "One more room to check at the other end of the house." Mark closed the bedroom door. "So far, I'd say Carl and Edna are enjoying themselves with friends or relatives. Or they're by themselves having a wonderful time somewhere."

"I'm sorry I bothered the two of you," Joe apologized.

"No problem. I would've done the same thing."

"We live in an over fifty-five adult community with most of us retired," Sherry interjected. "We have to look out for each other."

Mark peered around the kitchen and saw a few dishes and cups in the sink. There wasn't any food residue on the plates, meaning they were likely rinsed off. A built-in dishwasher sat under the counter to the right. *I wonder why they didn't put the cups and dishes in the dishwasher?* The kitchen counter was clean without anything out of place. To his left was a small, square, wooden kitchen table. Two placemats on the table were positioned in front of two chairs. The living room appeared neat. Again, nothing was out of place. A twelve-foot-long hallway led to a closed master bedroom door. Mark walked several steps toward the closed bedroom door. "Hello. It's Mark." His voice was accentuated due to the confined space of the hallway. No one answered. He slowly opened the bedroom door. Mark turned the ceiling light on from a wall switch to his left, lighting up the bedroom. "Oh my God. What is that?"

Two piles of ashes lay on top of a bed. Each pile of ashes was in the configuration of a human body. No smell of death or burnt flesh lingered in the air. The bedding and mattress, where human ashes lay, showed minimal signs of being burnt. "It looks like spontaneous human combustion," Sherry remarked as she walked up to the foot of the bed, followed by Mark and Joe.

"What's spon...tan...e...? What you just said," Joe asked.

Sherry peered down at the body ashes. "From what I know from reading medical journals, spontaneous human combustion or SHC is the human body burning from the inside at extremely elevated temperatures to the skin, creating an eventual pile of ash. The result is the same as a person being cremated. Although, the body is burnt from the outside to inside the body. Temperatures will reach up to about two thousand degrees Fahrenheit."

Joe raised his eyebrows, showing the upper whites of his eyes. "Holy cow. At that temperature, wouldn't the extreme heat cause the bed and bedroom to go up in flames?"

"You would think so. Not the case. No one really knows why the area surrounding a person doesn't catch on fire. It's a medical phenomenon without proven cause. There have been about two hundred cases of alleged spontaneous human combustion over the past three hundred years. Scientists have theories of how SHC occurs inside the body. There aren't any proven theories. What's interesting, most of the victims had compromised movement either due to obesity or were elderly with decreased mobility."

"Carl and Edna Parker are—I mean were—probably in their late seventies." Mark said. "Both of them had little mobility. They'd definitely fit the profile of a spontaneous human combustion victim." He glanced down at Sherry, who displayed a puzzling expression. "What's wrong?"

"I never heard of two people dying of SHC at about the same time side by side. When we get back to the house, I'll do a medical search on the computer to see if this had happened before."

Mark sniffed. "There's an odd odor in here. Not the odor of decomposing bodies. Something I've never smelled before."

Sherry sniffed deeply through her nose. She then walked forward a few steps and stopped in front of a nightstand next to the bed. She rubbed her finger over the surface. "The top of this nightstand has a greasy residue. From what I've read, this residue is sometimes present after SHC. This weird odor is also sometimes present. There's no scientific explanation for either of these things."

Joe shook his head back and forth, then said, "Man, this sounds like something out of a science fiction book or movie."

Mark brought out his cell phone. "I better call the sheriff's department and inform them what we found." He knew after the detectives did their investigation, the case would be sent to the medical examiner's office, since there wasn't a crime, such as arson leading to two deaths. There was something about the death of Carl and Edna that didn't seem right. It was a gut feeling without any concrete evidence. He needed to discuss these two deaths with Sherry without Joe's presence. "The three of us will need to wait here and give a statement to the sheriff detectives."

Marion County Sheriff deputies arrived within thirty minutes, along with crime scene investigators, then were followed by two detectives. Of course, Mark knew them all. He told Detective Nelson, the lead detective, the circumstances causing them to do a wellness check on Carl and Edna. Sherry told the detective what more than likely had happened to the Parkers.

"Unbelievable," Nelson exclaimed. "Spontaneous human combustion? Heard of it, but never actually seen one."

"Neither have Mark or I."

The detective called the medical examiner's office and told them what they suspected, two spontaneous human combustion deaths. About forty minutes later, the medical examiner, Taylor Evans, arrived with two staff investigators. Seldom did the medical examiner show up at a death scene unless it was a high-profile case. *I guess SHC would be in this category*, thought Mark. "Hey, Doc. Surprised to see you here."

"You got to be kidding me," he responded, gazing down at two piles of human ashes on the bed. "A possible spontaneous human combustion death of two people. I've read about it in medical journals. Some scientists believe SHC occurs from a dangerous accumulation of methane in the body. Other scientists proclaim it's an extreme build-up of static electricity inside the body. Of course, none of these theories can be proven. It's a genuine medical phenomenon and mystery."

Mark heard Joe say to the second detective, Detective Thomas, "As far as I know, Edna and Carl didn't have any children. Edna has a younger sister who lives in Pennsylvania. They don't have any relatives living here in Florida."

"I'm sure the Parkers have an address book somewhere in the house," the detective said. "I'll need to notify the next of kin. Hopefully, the couple also have an estate or living will."

"They have a living will. I have a copy of it since I witnessed and signed the will. It's sort of ironic…they both wanted to be cremated."

Detective Thomas put a small notebook into his shirt pocket. "I appreciate your information."

"Glad to help." Joe turned and said goodbye to Mark and Sherry. He then left the bedroom.

Mark chuckled to himself. Joe was the unofficial informant of several individuals and couples in the community. The retired detective and ER physician stood next to the medical examiner.

The medical investigators obtained pictures of the ashes, bed, nightstands, and dresser. The one nightstand had the mysterious oily residue. Dr. Evans placed samples of the ashes and a sample of the oily substance from the nightstand into specimen containers. Since the mattress was made entirely of memory foam, the technicians cut out the area underneath the ashes, placing the foam and ashes in a plastic body bag. "I'll check for an external accelerant when I get back to the lab. Although, there isn't any obvious accelerant odor around the ashes and bed. There is this unusual smell described in the medical literature. I smelled it when I entered the room."

"Sherry and I also smelled the weird odor when we walked up and stood near the bed. There doesn't seem to be any evidence of foul play in their deaths. No obvious external accelerant poured on their bodies. There aren't any signs of forced entry, a burglary or homicide. How are you going to classify their deaths?"

The detectives walked from across the room, stood near the

medical examiner, Mark and Sherry, listening to what was being said. Detective Nelson answered, "I'd call it 'accidental deaths.'"

Dr. Evans nodded. "I'd add 'By Spontaneous Human Combustion' to give an exact cause of their deaths."

Mark and Sherry stood in the Parkers' driveway and watched the medical examiner's van drive away. The two sheriff deputies and the CSI investigative team had left about thirty minutes earlier. The detectives found the Parkers' address book and living will. Detective Nelson called Edna's sister and let her know of the tragic deaths before he and his partner left the Parkers' residence.

"Never a dull moment in our community," Sherry said. She then removed her eyeglasses and began cleaning them with the bottom of her blue blouse.

"Do you think the Parkers suffered?"

"Not sure if there's been any documented witnesses to spontaneous human combustion." Sherry put her glasses on. "It'll be one of the things I'll check out during my computer search of SHC. In the old days before computers, I would have to go to medical textbooks and journals to look up information. It was a time-consuming process. It's one of the positive things about computer technology."

"I can relate to the advent of computers and their spell check programs. Before their availability, I had to use an electric typewriter to complete an investigation report with a dictionary always next to me." He glanced to his left. A group of people were standing with Joe on the road in front of his home. Joe talked as the people gazed up at him apparently listening to every one of his words. Mark waved at him. He waved back.

"I'm ready for a cup of coffee," Sherry suggested.

"I definitely agree to coffee. I'm way past due for my first cup. I don't want to go through caffeine withdrawal." They headed toward their home six lots in front of them to the left. "I have a gut feeling there's more to the Parkers' SHC incident. I can't put my finger on it." During his career as a detective, he'd have these feelings, which most the time turned out to be significant.

Mark put a small amount of milk, no sugar, in his coffee. As his lips touched the rim of his cup for his first sip of coffee, the kitchen wall phone rang in front of him.

Sherry, who was pouring herself a cup of coffee next to the coffee maker on the kitchen counter, reached to her right and answered the phone. She turned around and faced Mark. "Good morning," she said in a cheerful tone.

Several seconds past when Mark saw a forlorn expression on her face, as she listened to the caller.

"What do you mean, Joe, they won't answer their phone or door. Are you sure they're home?"

A sinking feeling overwhelmed Mark's stomach as a vision of ashes forming the outline of human bodies lying in bed flashed across his mind.

Chapter Two

"I assume you want us to check it out, Joe?" A short pause. "We'll be there in a few minutes." *The morning started off great doing our peaceful walk, like most mornings,* thought Sherry, as she sighed then hung up the phone. She turned back around and faced Mark, who was gulping down his coffee. "Sounds like we may have another couple in the community with spontaneous human combustion."

He placed his empty cup down on the table. "I hope not. But if it is, we're seeing something other than a quirk of medical science." He glanced down at his empty cup. "At least, I was able to drink my first cup of coffee."

Sherry reached into the cupboard and removed a tall plastic cup with a sip lid. She poured coffee into it, then added milk and about four teaspoons of sugar. "Let's check out Gladys and Bill Cummings' house. Joe will be waiting by the carport side door for us. He obtained a key from the next-door neighbor. He was afraid to open the door without us there."

"I don't blame him after we all found the ashes of the Parkers earlier."

They walked up the road passing Joe Barrington's home until they reached the Cummings' driveway, four homes past Joe's house across the road. A grey Chevy Cruz was parked underneath the carport. Sherry recognized that the vehicle belonged to the Cummings. She and Mark correlated people in the community by the vehicle they drove.

Joe sat on the landing, then stood when he saw the community's unofficial detective and medical sleuths. "Thanks for coming."

"Glad to help," Mark said. He reached out and grabbed the door key from Joe, who now stood on the concrete driveway. Mark walked up the steps, opened the storm door, and reached out with the key toward the lock.

Sherry held her breath as her husband placed the key into the lock. Her mind raced with the thought of another couple with spontaneous human combustion. If in fact, they found another couple lying somewhere in the house in a heap of ashes, there might be an evil force, an entity causing these nefarious deaths.

The door suddenly opened, startling Mark, who jump back from the appearance of Bill Cummings holding a revolver pointed at him. "Holy, crap. It's me, Mark McKinney."

Mr. Cummings lowered the gun. "Sorry. I thought you were a home intruder, wanting to rob me and Gladys. I couldn't find my eyeglasses. I saw the fuzzy images of three people standing outside the door. When I heard someone putting a key into the door lock, I grabbed my gun, which I keep in a small box on a shelf next to the door. We had just woken up and I was a little groggy and not completely awake."

Sherry walked up the steps, stood next to Mark on the porch landing, then said, "We were concerned when Joe couldn't get ahold of you and your wife. You didn't answer your phone or respond to his knocking on your door."

"Gladys and I slept in this morning. Besides, we left the bedroom TV on all night which blocked out the sound of the phone ringing and Joe knocking on the side door. Normally one of us turns the TV off. It's reassuring neighbors are looking out for us."

Mark explained to Mr. Cummings what had happened with the Parkers and why Joe was concerned about their well-being. "You can see why we were concerned about you and the missus."

"For sure. I'm so sorry about Edna and Carl. We didn't know them personally, but heard they were gravely ill. May God bless their souls."

Sherry nodded. "Have a good and safe day." They turned around, walked off the porch and headed down the driveway. "I'm glad the Cummings were okay."

Joe reached up and rubbed the back of his neck. "Me too. I guess I was overreactive after experiencing what happened earlier."

"No way to know if they were another case of SHC unless we checked it out." Sherry reached out and gently grabbed Mark's hand as they walked down the road. Most of the people in the retirement community were up and doing their daily routines. A couple of cars passed them. The occupants rolled down their windows to say good morning. Some of the residents were raking fallen leaves from the heavily treed retirement community. You'd think whoever planned out the community, would've cut down on the amount of trees due to the tedious work of raking up fallen leaves by the elderly residents.

Joe stopped in front of his driveway. "Thanks again, you two. I'm sorry I had to bother you."

Mark nodded. "No problem. Talk to you later." They continued walking up the road toward their house.

Sherry gulped down the last of her coffee as they reached the front door of their house. "I'm anxious to get on my computer and see when the last reported case of spontaneous human combustion had occurred, and if there ever had been two people dying side by side of this medical phenomenon."

Mark inserted the door key to the deadbolt lock unlocking the door. "I'd like to know what actually causes people to ignite themselves from inside their bodies. Just think, if someone discovered the how they could devise a perfect killing method." He opened the door, then walked into the living room, followed by Sherry.

"I hope someone with evil intentions doesn't discover its cause." Sherry walked to a small, wooden, rectangular table next to her lounge chair, picked up her laptop computer and remote mouse. She carried them to the kitchen and set it on the kitchen table. She looked at Mark, who was looking inside the refrigerator and asked, "What are you going to make us for breakfast?"

Mark enjoyed making breakfast for the two of them, usually nothing complicated or extravagant. "How about sausage and French toast?"

"Sounds good." She sat down and turned the computer on. A moment later, she typed spontaneous human combustion in Bing's search. A variety of articles showed up on the screen. She began reading. About ten minutes later, she found an article giving a chronological history of SHC. She said, "Spontaneous human combustion was first documented in the sixteen-hundreds…1641 to be exact. This seems odd to me. Had SHC been around prior to the sixteen-hundreds, but was never documented? What conditions inside the human had developed making it favorable for it to occur? There's a lot of unanswered questions."

Mark flipped the sixth French toast on the electric skillet. "Did you find a documented case regarding two people going up in smoke at the same time?"

"No. At least not so far."

The microwaved timer dinged. The precooked sausage links were ready to eat. Mark had already set the table with plates, silverware, and a glass of orange juice for each of them. They ate their breakfast, then put their dishes in the dishwasher. During breakfast, Sherry discussed the different theories of how SHC could develop. All of them sounded possible. Unfortunately, none of them could be proven. It would be difficult to find a human volunteer for the deadly experiment.

Sherry continued her search on spontaneous human combustion. She found out most of the people were between their sixties and eighties. Therefore, nursing homes, assisted living facilities and retirement communities would be breeding grounds for this medical phenomenon. Yet, there were rarely reported cases. Sherry peered up at Mark, who was kneeling in front of their opened refrigerator door, changing a light bulb inside the refrigerator. "For the reported cases to occur around the world for the past three hundred years, the catastrophic event can't be related to a specific race or particular environment. Everything I've read so far, scientists all agree SHC is a human anomaly triggered by an unknown condition."

The darkened refrigerator lit up, displaying its contents. Mark stood as he closed the refrigerator door. "Like we said earlier, we're dealing with a medical mystery regarding the Parkers' deaths." He walked over to a white plastic receptacle at the end of the counter and threw away the dead refrigerator bulb. "One thing bothers me about Edna and Carl, is why they cancelled the visiting nurse. It was as if they knew they'd be dead in a few days. I'd like to look around their house for any evidence supporting this theory."

"I guess a retired detective never loses his inquisitive forte?"

"I'm not any different than you still receiving your medical magazines. You want to know what's happening in medicine and medical science."

"Touché. You'll always be a detective, and I'll always be a doctor. Especially with us living in a retirement community."

They left the house and headed to the Parkers' house. Mark still had the key to the deceased couple's house. Sherry looked around as they walked up the driveway. No one was outside in the immediate area. A moment later, Mark unlocked the carport side door. They walked inside the house. An eerie stillness encompassed their senses, knowing death had visited the elderly couple within the past two days. She sighed, then said, "I feel like we're intruding on Edna and Carl's privacy."

"Welcome to detective work, my dear." Mark looked around. "We need to find something written down about what they were thinking and planning the past several days."

"Also, I'll need to check what medications they were taking. Not that it'll point to what caused their spontaneous human combustion or lucidity. It's a matter of being thorough in our investigation." She already knew from her medical readings there weren't any medications contributing to or causing either of those medical phenomena.

Mark started in the kitchen where a narrow highboy-type dresser with six drawers and a small desk sat along the wall with a window facing the carport. Sherry started in the master bathroom's medicine cabinet. There were over the counter medications such as antacids, eye lubricant drops, toothpaste, and mouthwash. No prescription drugs. She walked into the bedroom. Two cut-out areas on the queen-size bed stood out. Sherry checked inside the drawers of the bedside end tables for medicine vials. None were found. The drawers held a variety of items not relevant to their investigation. *Their medications must be somewhere in the kitchen in one of the cupboards, drawers or in the desk*, thought Sherry. She went to the kitchen. Mark sat at the desk going through a stack of papers and envelops. "I can't find their medications. Did you see any of their pills somewhere in the desk?"

"No. I checked all the desk drawers and found old warranties, household bills, medical bills, brochures, and a variety of miscellaneous items. I'm starting to go through items in the desk. Hopefully, they have a diary."

"I can't believe they don't have any prescription medication." She turned and opened the top drawer in the highboy dresser cabinet next to the desk.

"Maybe they flushed all their medications down the toilet?"

"If both were experiencing terminal lucidity, I could see it. They may have felt they didn't need their medications anymore." Sherry began looking through the drawers. When she got to the third drawer, she found two plastic weekly pill containers. She shook the containers. No sound of pills striking each of the cubicles. Scattered in the drawer were several prescription vials. The label with instructions obstructed the view of the pills inside. She pushed down and twisted the child proof cap. The name on the vial was Edna Parker, and the prescription was for oxycodone, a strong pain pill. She removed the cap. No pills inside the vial. Sherry checked the rest of the vials. All of them were empty. The Parkers had obviously gotten rid of their medications.

"I found something that may be relevant to their deaths," Mark said as he held a sheet of paper.

Sherry turned and faced her husband. "What'd you find?"

"It's a letter from a company called Phoenix Pharmaceutical Research. According to the letter addressed to the Parkers, the company have them in a test group for a drug to supercharge their immune system. Do you think the drug they were taking caused their spontaneous human combustion?"

Sherry furled her eyebrows. "No way to know unless you knew the test results of all the participants in the study." She thought a moment. "Maybe we should investigate the company for this pertinent information and see what they have to say about any side effects to their drug."

"Even if the drug caused the Parkers' deaths, they're not going to release any information to us since we don't have any official credentials to serve a search warrant for their records or drugs. Even if I were still a detective it would be unlikely a judge would sign for a search warrant unless we had concrete evidence. There has to be a connection between the drug and the Parkers' deaths."

Sherry wasn't going to let this stop her from finding out if there was correlation between Edna and Carl's death and Phoenix Pharmaceutical Research experimental drug. She knew there was more than one way to cook a steak.

Mark snapped a picture with his cell phone of the research company's letter to the Parkers. Sherry wrote down the name of Edna and Carl's prescriptions and the doctors who prescribed the medications. "Let's head back to the house. I still feel uncomfortable being in their home."

They put everything back to its original place then left the house. As they walked under the carport toward the road a car pulled up into the driveway. She didn't recognize the car or its driver, a man in his late thirties with a deep brown mustache and medium build. "Do you recognize the guy?"

"No. Never seen him before."

The car stopped, the man got out and walked toward them. "Good morning. Are the Parkers home?"

"No," answered Sherry.

The man leaned to his right and appeared to be staring at the Parkers' parked car under the carport. "Are you sure they aren't at home?"

"No," Mark answered. "What is your business with them?"

The man frowned as he stood a few feet away from them. "I don't think why I'm here is any of your business."

"I didn't mean to be so direct with you. My bluntness comes from my thirty years as a detective."

"My husband didn't mean to offend you. It's because the Parkers died this morning."

"Oh. My God. How did they die?"

Sherry wasn't sure if she should tell the man the truth about their deaths. "They were found dead in their bed this morning. Medical examiner isn't sure what the cause of their deaths is yet." *Partial truth better than a complete lie.*

"If they died around the same time…was it suicide?"

"No. Like we said, the cause of their deaths hasn't been determined." She glanced down at a Manila folder in the man's right hand. "What's your business with them?"

"It's not important now since they're dead."

"Why not?" Mark asked.

"I'm from Stevens Travel Agency. They wanted information on a Caribbean cruise. Have a wonderful day." He turned around, got into his car, then drove away.

Sherry noticed Mark's lip moving without any audible words as he stared at the travel agent's car. "Why are your lips moving?"

"I'm reading his license plate. There something bothering me about this guy."

"What's bothering you?"

"His brash statement when I asked him why he wanted to see the Parkers. A normal response would've been, I'm from a travel agency." He reached down, grabbed her hand, and began walking toward their house. "I have a gut feeling the guy wasn't honest with us. I'm going to ask Ed Young at the sheriff's department to look up the name registered on the car's license plate. Once I get his name, I'll call Stevens Travel Agency to find out if he's a travel agent there."

"You haven't lost your detective thinking and forte."

Thirty minutes later, Mark sat at the kitchen table. He had gotten the name of the alleged travel agent, Fred Cramer. He dialed the travel agency's phone number. He put the phone on speaker so Sherry could hear his conversation.

"Stevens Travel Agency. Can I help you?"

"Can I speak with Fred Cramer?"

Silence for a few seconds, then, "We don't have anyone with this name working here."

"Do you have a travel agent who's in his late thirties with a deep brown mustache and a medium build?"

"We don't have anyone with that description working here either."

"I must've gotten the wrong travel agency. Sorry I bothered you."

Who is this guy pretending to be a travel agent?

Chapter Three

Mark disconnected the call to the travel agency. His intuition had been right about Fred Cramer—the guy wasn't a travel agent. The sound of their fax machine in the den, which was next to the kitchen, began its unique rhythmic sound. "It must be the DMV photo of Cramer. Ed said he'd send it to me."

They both got up from their chair and hurried to the den. Mark picked up the printout. The photo didn't match the guy at the Parkers' driveway. Also, the real Fred Cramer appeared to be in his sixties, whereas the guy in the Parkers' driveway was likely in his late thirties. Mark peered at Cramer's age on the DMV driver license photocopy: sixty-six years old. A paramount question ran through Mark's mind: *What was this guy's actual purpose for showing up at the Parkers' house?* "Maybe this guy worked for Phoenix Pharmaceutical Research and was using Cramer's car? There's a few scenarios of why this mysterious guy was driving a car not registered to him."

"He could've stolen the car. Or maybe the title wasn't transferred to this guy when he bought the car from Cramer. On the other hand, I have a feeling he was from the research company. When you told him you were a detective and after I informed him the Parkers had died, he didn't want his company implicated in their deaths."

He chuckled. "You sound like a detective."

"I'll leave the detective title to you. Although, after being married to you all these years, I'm sure some of your detective prowess has rubbed off onto me."

"I know some of your medical knowledge was planted into my memory cells, listening to medical cases you talked to me about over the past thirty plus years." He looked through the den's window down at their car under the carport. "We need to do three things. First, find out who the guy was in the Parkers' driveway, Second, investigate the research company the Parkers were involved with. And lastly, talk with the real

Fred Cramer." Cramer's address was below his driver license picture, along with a phone number written on the copy paper by Ed.

"Sounds like a good plan to me. How are we going to find out who this mysterious guy is?"

"Before I call Ron Brewer in the computer forensic division at the sheriff's office to help us through his computer magic, I'll call Fred Cramer's phone number and see if he loaned his car to someone today."

"We may find out who exactly the guy in the Parkers' driveway is? Fred Cramer may answer some of our questions. Don't you think?"

"For sure. Although, if we can't get any concrete information on this guy from Cramer, I'm sure Ron will be able to assist us through his computer magic."

"Won't he get in trouble at work helping us?"

"No. He'll help us after working hours. He has a den in his house containing state-of-the-art computers with the capability of finding a needle in a computer haystack."

Mark sat down on a cushioned armchair, as did Sherry in a cushioned chair across from him. He dialed Cramer's phone number. After the fourth ring a male voice recording announced, "Can't come to the phone. Leave a message. I'll get back to you when I can." Mark disconnected the call, not wanting to leave a message. He sighed, shaking his head. "We'll need to go to plan B."

"Drive to the address on Cramer's DMV registration. Right?"

"Exactly."

"I'm starting to get into the swing of detective work."

"I'll give Ron a call." He retrieved the phone number from his cell phone and called Marion County Computer Forensic Division.

"Computer Forensic Division," stated a female. "Can I help you?"

"Can you connect me with Ron Brewer?"

"Who should I say is calling?"

"Detec…Mark McKinney." He still periodically would add detective when introducing himself. It was like his wife. People still added doctor to her name.

"Detective McKinney. How is retirement? It's Sarah Theobald."

"Oh. Ms. Theobald. Sorry, didn't recognize your voice. To answer your question, retirement is great."

"Glad to hear you're enjoying retirement. Let me connect you to Ron."

A click, short pause, then, "Ron Brewer."

"Hi, Ron. It's Mark McKinney."

"Oh, my God. A few minutes ago, we were talking about you. Of how you and our department solved some unique cases."

Mark was amazed how Ron would be able to trace a person and find out detailed information about them through a computer search. Digital forensics incorporates science and engineering by using legal and standard methods to recover digital evidence from computers, cell phones, or cameras. The digital forensic analyst can locate encrypted, deleted, or damage files and data. The evidence found in a criminal or national security investigation can be used in judicial proceedings. The Internet web sites contained a vast number of secrets. All you needed to unlock these secrets was knowing where to find the appropriate computer keys. It's difficult for a person to hide from a computer wizard like Ron. "I need your assistance on finding a person of interest in a mysterious case I'm working on with Sherry."

"I assume you're referring to the two spontaneous human combustion victims. No problem. I'll be glad to help. I leave work at five o'clock. I'll be home about five-twenty. I look forward to seeing you and Sherry. Talk to you then."

Mark cleared his throat. "Word travels fast."

"It does when it's deaths never seen in our forensic department. This is cremation on an entirely different level. When I helped you a few months ago, I thought it was exciting. To help you on this case will be beyond excitement. It'll be pure jubilation. See you this evening. Bye."

Mark and Sherry headed back to the kitchen. He shook his head. "We're not sure if this inquiry has anything to do with the cause of these two deaths contributed to spontaneous human combustion."

"Then again, you're not sure that it doesn't."

They walked into the kitchen. "You're right. We'll see about it this evening."

Sherry walked over to the counter as Mark sat down at the kitchen table. She grabbed the coffee pot and poured herself a cup of coffee.

"Can you get me another cup of coffee?"

"I guess, even though I'll be contributing to the delinquency of a coffee addict."

Mark grinned as he rolled his eyes and shook his head back and forth. After drinking their coffee, they got into their Chrysler 300 and drove to the address on Fred Cramer's DMV registration address. Sherry put the address in a portable GPS device, then placed it on the dashboard holder. He glanced down at 'Arrival Time' on the GPS screen. "We'll be there in sixteen minutes."

Fifteen minutes later, after the GPS device told them to turn four separate times, they were now driving through an area of apartments, single-level duplexes, and two-story townhouses. A moment later the device's female voice synthesizer announced, "You have arrived at your destination."

Mark stopped the car, rolled down his window and stared at the numbers 1666 on the front of a brick townhouse. There weren't any vehicles in the driveway. He hoped they'd find the white Hyundai Elantra driven by the mysterious man at the Parkers' house parked at this address. *Not to be*, thought Mark. They got out of the car and walked up to the front door. Three newspapers wrapped in plastic lay on the six-by-six concrete stoop. A metal mailbox attached to the brick facing to the right of the front door with its lid partially opened due to an overflow of mail caught Mark's attention along with the newspapers. "It appears Fred Cramer isn't home."

"Or he's lying somewhere in the house in a heap of ashes."

A cold chill streaked throughout his body as he peered at the three sixes on the house address plaque. "I hope not." He pushed the doorbell button to the left of the front door. A melodious chime emanated from inside the house. He pushed the button again. No response from inside the house. Mark opened the unlocked metal storm door. He tried to turn the doorknob to a wooden front door. It didn't move. He inhaled deeply through his nose. A pungent odor saturated the ole factory nerve senses in his nose. "I smell death."

Sherry leaned forward on the right side of Mark and sniffed. "No doubt it's the odor of human decomposition."

"I believe we found out why Mr. Cramer hasn't retrieved his newspapers and mail." He got out his cell phone and called 911. Within five minutes, a Marion County Sheriff Deputy pulled up and parked his patrol car on the street in front of the townhouse. A moment later, another deputy parked his vehicle on the street. Mark knew both deputies. He explained to them what he and Sherry smelled coming from inside the house.

They both inhaled deeply through their nose, confirming the distinct odor of death. By now neighbors had congregated in the front of Mr. Cramer's front yard. A deputy was about to break a front window to gain entrance to the house when a woman shouted, "I have a key to the front door. I'm Fred Cramer's next-door neighbor. He gave me a key in case of an emergency."

The deputy retrieved the key and opened the door. The overwhelming death odor caused the deputy to grimace. "Sorry Mark, but you'll have to wait outside."

"No problem." Mark handed the deputy the faxed DMV picture of Fred Cramer. "This is a picture of the man who's supposed to live here." Since he was now a civilian, he didn't have the authority of an active sheriff detective, even though his psyche was still engaged as an investigator. He and Sherry stood on the stoop, waiting for the deputies to return. What would the deputies find? A partially burnt body from SHC, bullet wounds, knife wounds, a beaten body with multiple bruises and boney deformities? Then again, Fred Cramer could've had a fatal heart attack or a stroke. Waiting for an answer generated anxious impatience, a feeling Mark dreaded when he didn't have control of an ominous situation.

"Not yet knowing who the dead victim is or how they died," Sherry stated, "makes me feel helpless and impatient."

It amazed Mark how they sometimes tuned into the same thoughts, a form of mental telepathy. "I definitely have the same sentiment. As you know, patience isn't one of my virtues either."

The woman who gave the deputy Fred Cramer's front door key asked, "You think Fred is dead?"

"Not sure. We'll soon find out. Does Mr. Cramer work?"

"No. He retired a couple of years ago."

"What kind of work did he do?"

"He worked at a research company as the head maintenance man."

"Was the company called Phoenix Pharmaceutical Research?"

She thought a moment. "No. It was Equine Research Company here in Ocala."

Several minutes elapsed when the deputies returned. One of the deputies, Deputy Winters, said, "We found Fred Cramer lying on the floor in the kitchen…deceased. There weren't any signs of a struggle, blunt force trauma, including any wounds from a bullet or knife. We'd classify this as Undetermined Death. The cause of death will be up to the medical examiner." He scratched his forehead. "Did you know the deceased?"

"No. We knew what car he drove."

Both deputies frowned, apparently puzzled by Mark's answer. Deputy Winters turned his attention toward the street. "Detectives Nelson and Thomas just pulled up."

The detectives walked toward them. Detective Nelson shook his head back and forth, then said, "It seems like death follows you two."

"I guess it's our lucky day," Mark replied with a serious expression. Before the detectives asked them twenty questions about why they were here at the deceased man's house, Mark told him about the mysterious man showing up at the Parkers' house this morning driving Fred Cramer's car. He didn't tell the detective who he had talked with at the sheriff's office.

Nelson chuckled. "I'll take over the investigation now. I do appreciate your information. You enjoy your retirement. By the way, can I have the license plate number, so I can do an APB on Cramer's car?"

"Sure." Mark assumed Detective Nelson knew he had contacted someone at the sheriff's office or DMV to obtain the name and address of the owner of the car. A similar incident had occurred a few months ago when two suspicious-looking guys in their twenties were driving around the community peering at the houses and never stopping. Mark called the sheriff's office and asked if they'd check out the license plate number. It turned out the two guys had belonged to a theft ring. As Mark and Sherry were walking away, he heard Detective Thomas say to his partner, "A law enforcement detective never retires, only their working hours change."

Sherry snickered. "Did you hear Detective Thomas?"

"Yeah," he answered, as they walked back to their car in the driveway. "Yeah. There's a lot of truth in his statement. Let's head back home and go back on our computers. I'll check out Phoenix Pharmaceutical Research. You can look up more information on spontaneous human combustion."

~ * ~

Mark headed for the den, as did Sherry. He sat behind the desktop computer, and she turned on her laptop. His home page screen displayed Sherlock Holmes holding a large circular magnifying glass peering down at a table with several small objects. Sherry's laptop screen displayed the side view of a human brain with electroencephalogram waves running horizontally through it. Mark spent an hour researching information on Phoenix Pharmaceutical Research and Equine Research Company. Sherry continued her search for information on spontaneous human combustion.

Mark sat back in his chair. "Equine Research Company deals with the development of food products for horses for the past twenty years. Phoenix has an interesting history. They've been in business for five years and have developed a couple pharmaceutical drugs capable of supercharging the immune system, which potentially can increase the longevity of cancer patients. I can see why Mrs. Parker would be a participant of this research. Not sure where Carl Parker would fall into their research with his heart problem. Unless he had cancer and didn't tell anyone about it." He turned toward Sherry. "So, Mr. Parker didn't take any chemotherapy medication as far as you know?"

"No. He was prescribed medications for his heart."

"Anything more on spontaneous human combustion?"

"A lot of interesting information worth a cup of coffee and a short conversation. Nothing relevant to the Parkers' death other than they will be the first couple dying together of SHC. What I'd like to view would be their medical records from their doctors and what exactly the research company was giving Edna Parker, and possibly her husband, Carl." She turned off her laptop computer.

"I agree. We need more information about Phoenix Pharmaceutical Research and the Parkers, especially when there hasn't been two people dying of spontaneous human combustion at the same time. Hopefully, Ron will find a way to unlock hidden information regarding the research company and the Parkers."

The sun was below the tree line as dusk approached the ebony curtain of night. Mark and Sherry parked their Chrysler 300 car behind Ron Brewer's SUV in his driveway. It was about five-thirty. They got out of the car and stepped into the sixty-five-degree evening air. They stopped at the townhouse's solid mahogany front door. Mark reached to the right to push the doorbell. The door opened before his finger could push the doorbell button.

"Hey, guys. Right on time." A smile lit up his face. "Come on in."

"Thanks," Mark replied, as he and Sherry walked into a small vestibule. "We appreciate you helping us."

"I live for medical mysteries. Can I get y'all something to drink?"

They both declined the offer. Ron escorted them to his computer room up a hallway to the first door on the right. There were three large computer monitors sitting on a counter against the wall in front of them as they stepped into the room. The two end monitors were at about a thirty-degree angle toward the middle monitor making it easy to view the end monitors when sitting in a desk chair at the center computer. A black cord attached the keyboards to a computer tower beneath the counter. Each monitor displayed a different scenario of columns containing numbers, data, and pictures of men and women. To their right was a single window enclosed by a vertical metal security panel preventing outside entry into the computer room. On the short wall next to the door sat a computer printer, scanner and copier on a narrow rectangular table. To their left sat a black futon in the couch position. A ceiling light lit up the room accentuating a hardwood oak floor.

"I didn't notice the futon the last time we were in here," Mark said as he glanced to his right.

"I got it a couple of months ago. It works out great when I'm waiting for an answer from a computer search, which sometimes can take over an hour. It beats sitting in the chair."

Sherry nodded. "It'll work out also for a guest you may have in the room with you."

Ron frowned, followed by blushing. "You mean a female?"

"Oh…oh, no. I didn't mean it in that way. We can sit on the futon while you're doing your computer wizardry. Like the last time we were here, your desk chairs were okay, but sitting on a futon would've been much more comfortable when you and Mark were looking up information for us."

"You're right. The futon would've been more comfortable." His blushing had subsided. He looked at Mark. "So, what do you want me to look up?"

"As you already know, two of our residents succumbed to spontaneous human combustion." He went on and described the situation with the guy in the victim's driveway and Phoenix Pharmaceutical Research. "First, we need you to obtain the employee records of the research company so we can identify the guy we saw in the Parkers' driveway this morning. Our hunch is the guy works for the company."

"No problem," Ron said as he sat down in front of the middle computer monitor, placed his fingers on the keyboard and began typing. Mark and Sherry stood behind him as the monitor rapidly changed data across the screen. Less than a minute past when a collage of facial photographs appeared on the computer monitor's screen. "These are the pictures of Phoenix Pharmaceutical Research employees. See if you recognize the guy in the driveway,"

Mark and Sherry leaned forward peering down at the monitor. A moment later, Mark said, "I don't see him. How about you, Sherry?"

"No. None of these men resemble the man in the driveway."

The screen changed to another set of employee pictures. After a series of employee photographs, Clifton's stealthy sleuths didn't see the mysterious man with the false identification. "This is all their employees," Ron said. "There isn't any feasible way to search in any facial recognition program unless we had a picture of this guy."

"I realize this fact, Ron," Mark responded. "I was hoping he worked for this research company. Unless this guy was an outside contractor. Of course, there's no way of knowing if he fell into this category."

Ron rubbed his lower lip over his upper lip. "I'll go to plan B."

Mark frowned. "What's plan B?"

"Security cameras. They're everywhere today. At street intersections, store fronts…inside and outside apartment buildings and residential homes. The eye-in-the-sky network. The only privacy a person can be sure of is in a bathroom. And there's no guarantee of that either." His fingers glided rapidly over the keyboard. "What time did this guy show up at the Parkers' house this morning?"

Mark looked at Sherry. "About nine o'clock."

"It was two minutes past nine to be exact," Sherry corrected. "I peered at my watch when we walked up to his car in the Parkers' driveway."

Mark raised his eyebrows while rolling his eyes. He knew she would know the precise time the mysterious man appeared. Sherry had always been conscious of time ever since he could remember from the first time they met. She said it was due to her medical background when questioning a patient about their presenting symptoms. *Time is relevant to a sick patient's symptoms,* she would say to him on many occasions.

"What type of car and color?" Ron asked.

"It was a late model, white Hyundai Elantra." Mark answered, peering at the monitor of vehicles passing through an intersection. Sherry also leaned forward, staring at the monitor. "There it is," Mark said. "Can you freeze the frame of the driver?"

"Sure can. I can't get a closer look of the driver." The facial image of the mysterious man was unclear due to a slightly tinted windshield. "I'll check the license plate number." The rear of the car came into view. Ron stopped the video, displaying the vehicle's license plate.

"That's the car. Too bad we couldn't get a good facial image of the guy. What do you think Sherry?"

"I agree. I'm sure it's the mystery man behind the steering wheel who showed up in the Parkers' driveway."

"Ron. Can you follow him and see where he goes?"

"I'm on it."

The white Elantra moved south on Pine Street toward Ocala. The monitor displayed Fred Cramer's car pass through numerous intersections. The car then pulled into the parking lot at Paddock Mall. The mall's security camera showed the man get out of the car, wipe the outside door handle with a cloth, then walk through the mall's north entranceway. The man held his head down toward the ground, making it impossible to get a full facial view. It was as if he knew to avoid security cameras, thought Mark. Once inside the mall, the man proceeded to the south entranceway. Again, he held his head downward avoiding a full facial view. He walked through the vestibule leading to the mall's southside parking lot.

"Where did he go?" Sherry questioned.

Chapter Four

Ron moved his fingertips over the keyboard as he peered at a blank screen on the monitor. "Don't know. The security camera on the southside parking lot isn't working for some reason. No way to know if he got into another vehicle or walked away through the mall's parking lot."

"Something isn't right here," Mark stated. "It can't be a coincidence the security camera didn't work when we were possibly about to identify the mysterious guy, his car or someone planning to pick him up in the southside parking lot. This type of coincidence isn't in my commonsense reasoning process."

"I'll check the three security cameras at traffic light intersections adjacent to the mall." Ron displayed the three different intersection security video camera views on the monitor. The perp didn't show up in any of the security camera footage. "Although, if he sat in the back seat of a vehicle, we'd never see him."

Mark thought a moment. "Can you get the license plate number of the vehicles leaving the mall's parking lot and driving through one of the three exits a couple of minutes past the time this guy walked out of the mall to the parking lot? I know it might be a monumental task for you."

"No problem, detective. I thrive on monumental tasks…as long as I have a computer to do it. What are you going to do with the information?"

"Do tedious leg work to track down the people driving out of the mall based on the registration address of the vehicle's owner's license plate number. There's another choice we have in identifying this elusive guy. Have—"

"Don't tell me," Ron interrupted. "A sketch artist. Right?"

Mark nodded. "You're on the ball, young man."

"I'll call Larry Fortin. He has the computer software and expertise to generate a picture of this guy. I'm sure he'll be glad to help us."

"What happened to Patrick?"

"He accepted the position as a forensic artist for the state police in Tallahassee. Patrick left our department about a month after you retired." Ron called Fortin on his cell phone. "Hi, Larry." Ron gave him the background of why he called. "Great. See you in a bit. Bye." Ron set his phone on the computer table. "He'll be over in about fifteen minutes."

"Great," Mark said as he turned and grinned at Sherry. The hunt for the identity of the mysterious man, who may have had something to do with Fred Cramer's death, created an adrenaline rush, causing a warm sensation to overwhelm his body. One thing was for sure—the perpetrator had possession of Cramer's car, and somehow the perp was connected to Edna and Carl Parker.

Sherry smiled back at him, then said, "You got that gleam in your eyes I've seen a thousand times prior to your retirement when searching for the truth on a puzzling case for the sheriff's department. I'll paraphrase what Detective Thomas said earlier today, '*A detective never retires, only their working hours change*'."

"Does it upset you? I can always—"

"No," she interrupted. "It doesn't upset me. Matter of fact, I'm glad I can now be a part of an investigation and hopefully contribute to solving this mystery."

"I'm glad you asked me to help too," Ron interjected as the monitor's screen displayed an array of vehicles driving through intersections next to the mall.

Mark briefly placed his hand on Ron's shoulder. "You're a vital asset to our investigation."

"Thank you. Does this mean I'm a member of your team?"

Mark chuckled. "Yeah, you are. Unfortunately, it's a nonpaying position without benefits."

"I can live with no pay or benefits." A short pause, then he said, "As long as I can get a home-cooked meal from Dr. McKinney once in a while."

"You sure can," Sherry answered. "You need to find a woman

who can cook for you. Being a bachelor has its disadvantages."

"If I can find someone like you, I'd marry her tomorrow."

Sherry grinned while looking up at Mark, then turned her attention toward Ron. "That's very sweet of you, Ron."

"I better call Detective Thomas and let him know we found Fred Cramer's car," Mark said. "The good news is the forensic lab may find trace elements and even the mysterious man's fingerprints. Although I doubt they'll find any trace evidence from this guy. We saw him wipe the outside door handle. He also likely cleaned the steering wheel and inside door handle." Mark called Detective Thomas on his cell phone. The phone rang three times.

"This is Detective Thomas. Can I help you?"

"This is Mark McKinney. We found Fred Cramer's vehicle. It's parked in the parking lot near the north entrance of the Paddock Mall." Mark didn't think it would be necessary to explain how they happened to discover the car.

"Great. I'm not going to ask how you found the vehicle." A short pause. "Anything else I should know?"

"No. That's all." He thought about asking the detective to let him know if they found any clues such as fingerprints or DNA pointing to their mysterious man. Mark wouldn't have to since they had Ron collaborating with him and Sherry. "Talk to you later."

In less than fifteen minutes, Ron had checked out the license plate numbers matching it with the DMV's registration address of the car owners. There were fourteen addresses. Since it was the beginning of the week and mid-morning, there wasn't much traffic. They agreed if it were the weekend, the amount of traffic would've tripled, prolonging their investigation. On the computer monitor, Ron produced photographs of the driver license photos matching the fourteen vehicle registration names. All the names were male. Unfortunately, none of them matched the guy Mark and Sherry had encountered in the Parkers' driveway this morning. This narrowed their speculation of the mystery man who had entered the mall's south parking lot. They all agreed the unnamed guy either got into someone else's vehicle or walked away from the mall, avoiding any cameras at the mall's south exit.

Ron printed out the address list and handed it to Mark.

The front doorbell rang. "I'd assume it's Larry Fortin," Sherry suggested, glancing down at her watch.

"It could be the pizza delivery guy," Ron said. "I ordered two large pizzas before you guys got here. I should've mentioned it earlier. Hope you don't mind?"

Mark rubbed his tongue on his lower lip, then answered, "Not at all. Sherry and I like pizza."

Ron moved his fingers across the keyboard. The monitor displayed a young man standing at the front door, holding two pizza boxes. "It's him. Why don't you two go into the kitchen? I'll get the pizzas. The plates are in the cupboard to the right of the sink."

Mark and Sherry walked into the kitchen. She retrieved the plates and set them on a rectangular wooden table with six cushioned chairs. Ron walked in and placed the pizza boxes in the center of the table.

A moment later, a man walked into the kitchen. He appeared to be in his late forties with a well-trimmed mustache, short, brown hair with greying around the sides and medium build. Ron announced, "This is Larry Fortin."

"Hi, everyone," Larry said with a solemn expression as he reached out a shook hands with Mark and Sherry.

Mark said, "I appreciate your help, Larry."

"Glad to help."

"Have some pizza with us," Ron suggested, as he opened the pizza carton and removed a slice of pizza.

"No thanks. I already ate. If it's all right with you, I'll set up my program on your desktop computer."

"Sure. We'll be in there shortly."

~ * ~

Mark and Sherry sat on desk chairs on either side of Larry in the computer room. Ron stood behind Larry. "What shape of face did this guy have?" On the screen were numerous facial shapes with a number next to it.

Mark scanned the shapes on the monitor's screen, as his mind visualized the implanted memory of the Fred Cramer impersonator. "I'd say number fifteen."

"I agree," Sherry said. "Number fifteen."

Within thirty minutes, the striking image of the mysterious man stared back at them from the computer screen.

"That's our guy," Mark said assuredly. When Mark was a detective for the sheriff's department, he collaborated with the forensic artist on numerous cases, and was amazed how close they could abstract a composite sketch of a person from a witness's memory. He and Sherry were now the witnesses sitting in the chair in front of the forensic artist.

Sherry agreed it was the guy in the Cramer's driveway. She then added, "It's unbelievable what computers can do today."

Larry nodded. "When I started as a forensic artist, I used pencil and paper to develop a picture of a suspect from a witness. It was tedious but I enjoyed the process from an artistic viewpoint. In today's world of computers, my artistic prowess has been taken over by computer software to develop an image of a suspect. Although, I have to say the end results from a computer program are much more detailed and real looking. I'll print out a few copies."

Ron stood, walked over, and stood in front of the printer as it began printing out copies of the face of the mysterious man. "What are you going to do with the sketch?"

Mark stood, as did Sherry, then answered, "When we interview people from a list generated by Ron, we'll show them the sketch, then check for any change in the person's expression or verbal pattern."

"What do you mean?" Larry asked.

"Through mine and my wife's many years of talking with people, me as a detective and she as an emergency room physician, we've obtained the ability to recognize when people are telling the truth or have something to hide. It's not a hundred percent exact ability."

"You mean like Sherlock Holmes and Dr. Watson?"

Mark, Sherry, and Ron laughed interrupting the seriousness of their situation. "Thanks for the compliment," Mark finally answered. Although he did have good deductive reasoning with an astute observation for miniscule details, and Sherry would give him medical advice on occasions during one of his criminal investigations during his years as a detective. "We appreciate your expertise, Larry. Hopefully, the sketch will help us find this guy."

"Like I said earlier, I'm glad to help in your investigation. I've heard many stories about you when you were a detective for the sheriff's department, and how you solved many difficult criminal cases."

Mark glanced at Ron, knowing he was the one who likely was the instigator of the stories, then brought his attention back to Larry. "It's a team effort. It's getting late and don't want to consume any more of your time."

Ron handed Mark a few copies of the facial composite of the mysterious man. He then turned to Larry. "I'll walk you to the front door."

Larry stood, then nodded. He looked at Mark, then Sherry. "Nice meeting the two of you. If you ever need me again, please call."

"It was great meeting you too," Mark replied. "And yes, we'll give you a call if your expertise is needed again."

"I'll look forward to it."

"Sherry and I are going to stay here. There's something else I'd like you to investigate on your computer."

"Sure. No problem. I'll be right back."

Mark leaned forward and kissed Sherry on the lips. The kiss lasted for at least ten seconds.

"What was that for?"

"For being who you are and for helping me on this investigation. Although, I actually wanted to feel your warm lips against mine."

Ron walked into the computer room and obviously heard Mark's words to his wife, as he blushed. "What did you want me to look up?"

"I'd like you to go back to Phoenix Pharmaceutical Research and find out what drugs are being researched, and the list of people using them. Can you do this?"

"Sure. Although, the facility's computer system has an encrypted security system and a secured computer firewall, I got into the human resource department. I'm sure I can get through to inner workings of the facility. You guys can go home. There's no reason for you to stay. I'll call you when I find something."

"Thanks for your help," Mark said. "We really appreciate it."

"I guess Larry and I will be the on-call guys for the two of you."

"You could say that."

"I'll walk you to the front door."

Mark and Sherry followed a few steps behind Mark from the computer room. "We'll have our work cut out for us tomorrow," Mark said to Sherry, as he glanced down at the image of their suspect. "Are you up for the challenge?"

"Sure am. I'm sure it'll be more exciting, more adventurous than sitting in a folding chair playing Bingo and Bunko at the clubhouse."

"I thought you liked to play those games?" Mark said as they walked into the vestibule.

"I do. Although my brain isn't stimulated like this ominous mystery with a cast of at least one stealthy unknown character and two rare spontaneous human combustion deaths. I look forward to solving this puzzling medical phenomenon."

"You sure put this case in perspective," Ron said as he turned around after opening the front door. "I'm glad I'm part of this unofficial investigative team."

Mark peered seriously at Ron. "We're a clandestine investigative team, not to be publicized. Especially at the sheriff's office or forensic lab."

"No problem. My lips are sealed." Ron pinched the tip of his right thumb and index finger and slid it across his closed lips in the gesture of zipping his lips. "As Larry and I were walking to the front door, I told him not to mention our investigation at work. He said it wouldn't be a problem."

"Great. The fewer people know of our investigation, the better it'll be for us, you and Larry." Mark and Sherry said their goodbyes and left Ron's house. A cloudless night sky displayed a full moon with a scattering of glistening stars as they made their way to the car. The faint odor of pine lingered in the air from the numerous evergreens encompassing Ocala National Forest.

~ * ~

Sherry put her seat belt on as Mark backed out of Ron's driveway. Her thoughts focused on their investigation tomorrow. "What time tomorrow are we going to start checking out the names on the DMV list?"

"First, we'll need a good breakfast to fuel our body for what will be a busy day. Three names on the list are people over sixty-five. During our parents' era, people retired at sixty-five and began receiving social security checks. Today, many people around our age work way beyond the normal retirement of the mid-sixties. We'll still stop at their home addresses and ask whoever answers the door if they know the guy in our composite picture. If they're not home, we'll drive to their workplace."

"Breakfast does sound good." Sherry thought it was smart that Ron also gave them the work address of the fourteen suspects, otherwise their investigative questioning wouldn't start until late afternoon or early evening when most of the people got home from work. As far as retirement, she and Mark had retired the same day, on Friday the thirteenth, almost two years ago. The infamous day created many humorous jokes amongst their friends and co-workers. "Going home and resting also sounds good. This hasn't been a typical day for two retirees."

"No, it hasn't been." He reached over and touched Sherry's thigh. "The good news is we experienced it together."

She loved it when Mark touched her, acknowledging his affection toward her. "We did. Plus, two minds are better than one…since my mind is getting older."

"I like your older mind, especially when it's supporting a beautiful body."

Sherry reached down and gently squeezed his hand. "You still haven't lost your silver tongue. I love it."

They drove along a two-way highway with a heavily treed landscape of the forest surrounding them, as the full moon behind them shined a dim light on the roadway ahead of them like a house's soft glowing nightlight shinning on the home's hallway. An occasional car passed them heading toward the heavenly lit eastern moonlit skyline. Mark decreased the speed of their vehicle from fifty-five to forty-five miles per hour.

Sherry frowned. "Why did you slow down?"

"There are a lot of accidents between vehicles and the wildlife living in these woods deciding to cross the road."

"Never thought about running into wild animals since we live within Ocala's city limits. Although, I have to say the serenity and beauty of the forest around us has a calming effect, instead of potential danger lurking ahead of us." She glanced into the sideview mirror. No vehicle headlights could be seen behind them as their car slowed down. A flash of light resembling a large spark, like a knife striking a flintstone attempting to light a campfire, suddenly appeared to her right about three hundred feet ahead of them. Had lightning struck a tree? A second or two later, a rope-like object began falling toward the ground from the origin of the flash. She shouted, "Power line. Stop the car."

Mark slammed on the brakes. The tires screeched as its rubber tread slid along the concrete surface, bringing their car closer to the electrical line laying across the road in front of them. Sparks emanated from the power line's exposed end. Their seat belts pressed against their bodies prevented Mark from slamming into the steering wheel and Sherry against the dashboard. Their car came to a complete stop, as the car's headlights illuminated a live power line about ten feet in front of them. Mark sighed. "That was close." He reached toward the dash and pushed the car's hazard warning light button. "We better get out of the car before a vehicle behind us crashes into the rear end of the car. I'll get the road flares from the trunk."

Sherry got out of the car and peered behind them down the road. No sight of any vehicle headlights. She turned around and peered up the road. Again, no headlight beams coming toward them. The power line laid across both lanes ending a few feet onto the side of the road. The end of the power line wiggled as sparks projected from the end of the live wire. She peered up at the utility pole to her right. The full moon shined a dim light onto the pole. She squinted and saw the power line had been severed at a junction box near the top of the pole. The evening sky didn't have a cloud in sight. Without clouds it eliminated the possible source of a lightning bolt striking the junction box. There had to be another logical cause for the electrical wire detaching from the junction box. Sherry looked down to her right. There was enough room on the side of the road to drive around the live wire. In less than a minute, they placed warning road flares about two hundred feet in front and behind them along the roadway.

Mark called 911 and told them what had happened. Within six minutes, Marion County Sherriff deputies arrived. Prior to law enforcement arriving, drivers on the west and east end of the road heeded the flare's warning and stopped. The downed lethal power line still needed to be secured and out of harm's way from people and their vehicles. Thirty minutes later, the electric power company arrived in two utility trucks with one of them having a cherry picker attached to it. The moon had moved higher in the eastern horizon, projecting more of its soft glow onto their surroundings.

Sherry and Mark stood next to each other as they watched a linesman standing inside the cherry picker stare intently at the area of the utility pole's junction box where the severed electrical line originated.

The man turned around, shaking his head back and forth, then shouted, "There's a bullet hole in the pole next to the junction box. Someone shot down the power line."

Chapter Five

Twenty minutes later, they pulled up and stopped in their driveway underneath the carport. A motion detector security light above the side door went on, encompassing the driveway with a bright beam of light. Their ride home from being nearly killed by a downed electrical line caused by an unknown assailant with a rifle and malicious intent, who deliberately tried to kill or seriously injure people in their vehicles, brought up unanswered speculative questions. Such as—was the shooting a random act by a crazy person wanting to see people being killed by thousands of electrical volts? Another possibility crossed their minds. The shooter wanted them seriously injured or killed. If this was true, the perpetrator had been following them and knew the make of their car. The perp would know they would be traveling back from Ron Brewer's house. If this scenario was true, the deranged assailant had to be watching them from somewhere in the heavily wooded forest. When the shooter saw them coming up the road, they aimed and shot down the power line, knowing the moonlight would be partially blocking their vision of the road ahead of them and preventing them from seeing the power line lying across the road. Sherry and Mark leaned toward this speculation. Another question followed the assertion. Why? Sherry believed the most logical, feasible explanation would be that the perpetrator didn't want them investigating the mysterious guy at the Parkers' driveway and the SHC couple. Mark agreed with her. Also, there wasn't any way to retrieve the bullet from the wooden utility pole without compromising the integrity of the pole and causing it to fall to the ground.

"I didn't notice anyone following us," Sherry said as she unlatched her seat belt.

"I didn't either," Mark agreed. "I hope we're not becoming paranoid, thinking we're being watched by some clandestine organization or Phoenix Pharmaceutical Research using unscrupulous people to stop our investigation of the Parkers' death and the identity of the guy in the Parkers' driveway. We'll need to be more alert of our surroundings any time we're out of the house."

"I believe we're already doing this."

"Yeah, we are. But now it's an official mandate."

Sherry grinned. His forte of being in charge as a lead detective had never dissipated, which was all right with her. "Okay, detective."

Mark rolled his eyes. "Hopefully, Ron will find something incriminating during his computer search of Phoenix Pharmaceutical Research. Something that'll relate to the Parkers' deaths."

Sherry knew if Ron found something tying the spontaneous human combustion deaths to Phoenix, it would be revolutionary in the world of medical science. They went inside the house. It was nearly eight-thirty. Their normal bedtime was around nine o'clock. Sherry turned the kitchen light on, then gazed around the kitchen. A chill streaked up her spine, causing the hairs in the nap of her neck to stand out. Things seemed to be out of place. "Something isn't right in here. Some of the kitchen drawers aren't completely closed. We better check the house, especially the computer room. I believe someone has been in our house."

"Maybe the intruder is still here." Mark reached toward the left side of his waist with his right hand. "Damn."

Sherry understood his frustration. Normally his Glock would be resting in a belt holster. Since retiring, he didn't carry a gun anymore and apparently learned instinct from his thirty-plus years as a detective kicked in under this moment of potential danger. "Maybe you should start carrying your gun again?"

"I believe I will. It appears things regarding our investigation are becoming dangerous. Stay behind me. We'll check out the house together. We'll go to our bedroom first."

They turned the living room light on. Nothing seemed to be disturbed anywhere in the room. Sherry walked a couple steps behind Mark as they slowly walked down the hallway to their bedroom. They stopped periodically listening for any sounds indicating the intruder was lurking in one of the rooms ahead of them. They stepped into the master bedroom at the end of the hall and stopped. Sherry now stood to the left of Mark and glanced around the room. She immediately saw a few dresser drawers partially opened. "I'm sure someone's been in our bedroom."

Mark reached down to his right, opened the closed nightstand drawer, and removed his holster with the Glock inside. He secured the gun in his right hand, then released the closed safety latch, making the Glock ready for firing.

Across the room to their left stood a partially opened bathroom door. To the right a closed walk-in closet door. Sherry pointed toward the bathroom then the closet gesturing the intruder could be lurking behind one of the doors.

Mark nodded, acknowledging her concerned gesture. He motioned her with his left hand for her to stay put, as he brought his gun up, pointing it out in front of him. The carpeted bedroom floor cushioned his size thirteen shoes from making any sounds as he cautiously walked toward the ajar bathroom door. Mark stopped a couple of feet from the door, reached out, grabbed the doorknob, and quickly pulled the door open as his Glock pointed straight ahead. The light from the bedroom shined into the bathroom. No intruder. He then walked toward the bedroom's closed closet door.

Sherry stared at the closed walk-in closet door with anticipation that an intruder holding a gun might began shooting as Mark opened the door, a door normally kept open to promote air from the bedroom to circulate inside the closet, preventing musty odors from accumulating on the clothes. Her breathing increased, her heart began to pound against her chest wall expecting the worst scenario as her husband grasped the doorknob and turned it slowly. A metal squeaking sound emanated from the doorknob causing an encompassing chill throughout her body.

The door now stood open exposing a six-foot by eight-foot walk-in closet. No one awaited them. Mark sighed as he lowered his gun. He turned around and faced Sherry. "We need to check the other two bedrooms."

The other bedrooms didn't hide the intruder. Whoever was in their house had left before they arrived home. The intruder had checked out every room in the house, leaving signs he or she had been searching for something. Nothing was missing.

"What was the person looking for?" Sherry asked as they walked back to the kitchen. "There were plenty of valuable items they could've taken from the house."

"My hunch is they were focused on what evidence, if any, we obtained on the deaths of the Parkers and possibly what we knew about the mysterious guy in the Parkers' driveway this morning." He put the safety back on his Glock. "They definitely weren't in our house to steal our valuable belongings."

"Should we call the sheriff's department and let them know our house was broken into?"

"No. Not necessary. Whoever was here was a professional. I'm sure they didn't leave any forensic evidence such as a fingerprint or DNA. Besides, nothing is missing. I don't think they'll be back. What we will do is have an alarm system installed in the house. We've talked about it a few times the past several months. I guess this intrusion is the straw that broke the camel's back."

"I haven't heard that cliché in a long time," Sherry said as she walked over to the kitchen light switch and turned the lights out.

"It seemed apropos with the intruder situation."

"I agree. Including us being nearly electrocuted. Why don't we lay in bed and read? Ron said he'd call us tonight."

~ * ~

Mark's cell phone rang on the nightstand next to the bed. Sherry leaned forward and turned right toward Mark. His eyes were closed. She glanced at the clock on the nightstand. It was 10:04 p.m. "Mark, answer the phone," she said putting her book, a mystery/suspense novel called *Strange* down onto her lap. The phone rang again.

His eyes snapped open, then glanced at Sherry, who was sitting next to him. Mark turned to his right, picked up his ringing cell phone. "Hello."

"Hi, Detective McKinney. It's Ron. Hope I didn't wake you?"

"No. We've been waiting for your call. Call me Mark, not Detective. What did you find out about Phoenix? I'll put you on speaker so Sherry can hear what you have to say."

"There's not so good news. The not so good news is I didn't find any evidence of their pharmaceutical products in the research department at Phoenix having anything to do with the Parkers' spontaneous human combustion. There's no mention of spontaneous human combustion in any departmental emails or memos. As far as for Fred Cramer, I searched for any connections between him, the company he worked for, Equine Research Company, and Phoenix. I didn't find any connection between them. It's a dead end."

"The one thing we have left is the mystery man. We know for sure the guy was driving Fred Cramer's car. What we don't know is, why was he at the Parkers' house? Why was he driving Cramer's car? We have to find out the identity of this guy."

"Hopefully, the forensic lab will obtain a fingerprint or DNA from Cramer's car so we can identify this elusive guy."

"I appreciate your help. Talk to you tomorrow." Mark placed the cell phone on the nightstand. He looked at Sherry, who was placing her book on the nightstand next to her. "We don't know any more now than we did this morning regarding Edna and Carl Parkers' deaths or the identity of the mystery guy."

"Maybe one of the persons on the DMV list can be connected to our mystery man? Tomorrow is a new day. Let's get a good night sleep."

"I agree," as he placed his book next to his cell phone, then turned off the light on the nightstand.

Sherry turned off her nightstand lamp, then rolled toward Mark and kissed him goodnight. Her last conscious thought meandered across her mind with the vision of the man in the Parkers' driveway. *Who are you?*

~ * ~

Mark sat at the kitchen table as Sherry reached down and placed scrambled eggs on his plate next to three link sausages and potato tots. "Thanks, Hun." He glanced down at his watch. It was seven-thirty-five. The morning sun peeked through the opened mini blind to his right.

After eating, Mark placed the dirty dishes and silverware into the dishwasher. He wore khaki pants, a light-blue buttoned-down shirt underneath a medium-blue sports coat and laced brown shoes. The sports coat covered his holstered Glock secured to the left side of his belt. Sherry complemented him by wearing cream-colored slacks, light-yellow buttoned blouse, and a medium brown blazer with brown loafer-styled shoes. Mark chuckled to himself.

"Why are you smirking?"

"If we lived in the Northern states in the fall and winter months, we'd be wearing dark-colored clothes, but since we're Floridians this practice doesn't comply."

"There's a reason they call Florida the Sunshine State," Sherry said, as she picked up the DMV list of people they'd be talking with this morning from the kitchen table. "No snow, sleet or ice, mostly sunshine and warmth."

Mark backed the car down the driveway as Sherry brought up the first address saved in the GPS. She had downloaded all the names and their addresses last night into the GPS. She also had a vinyl folder holding the list of the suspects with their home, work address and company name, or just their home address if they were retired. "Who's the first name on the list?"

"Steven Davenport. He's eleven minutes away."

The female voice synthesizer on the GPS announced. "Turn left on to State Road Three Twenty-Six."

Their route to Davenport's residence led them to the east side of Ocala then into the community of Silver Springs. The traffic was heavy as drivers in a variety of trucks, SUVs, and cars hurried toward their place of employment. The morning sun shined its piercing rays through the windshield, prompting him to move the car's visor down to block the blinding rays of the sun. Mark said, "Maybe we'll find this mysterious guy at the first residence?" He knew the odds of that happening were remote, but during his thirty plus years as a detective anything was possible. He knew persistence and sometimes luck were the ingredients needed to solve a difficult case.

"I see optimism hasn't abandoned your drive to find out the truth after retiring from the sheriff's department."

"I guess not since I have a great partner to support me."

"There goes your smooth tongue talking again. You haven't lost that forte. And I hope you never do."

Mark smiled as he slowed the car to fifteen miles per hour. They now drove down a street with residential homes. Up ahead to their right he saw a white van with a sunroof matching the vehicle in the intersection security camera next to Paddock Mall. The image of the van stuck in his mind because the back window was covered with plywood painted white. Plus, Ron had written down the description of each vehicle. "There's Steven Davenport's van up there on the right."

"I see it," Sherry agreed.

A moment later the GPS announced, "You have arrived at your destination."

Mark parked in the street in front of Davenport's house. He and Sherry had rehearsed what they were going to tell each person on the DMV list generated by Ron. Mark pushed the doorbell on the door frame to the left of the front door.

Several seconds passed when the solid wooden front door opened. A man in his late sixties stood in front of them. "Can I help you?"

Mark quickly and inconspicuously scanned the man, searching for any oddities, including the man's general appearance. The man was clean shaven with greying short, brown hair. His clothes were clean with a dime-size red stain on the upper left side of his light-grey pullover shirt. The tips of his fingernails were irregular, probably from biting them. "Are you Steven Davenport?"

"Yes," Davenport answered with a frown.

"We're looking for this man." Mark showed him the composite sketch. The detective peered at him, looking for any expression of uneasiness, shock, or surprise. The man didn't change his blunted affect. "Do you know him?"

"Never seen him before. Are you from the police department?"

"No. We're private investigators." Mark wasn't telling a lie. They were investigating the mystery man's identity.

"Are you going to all the houses on my block?"

Mark didn't want to lie to Davenport. "No. Your vehicle was seen in the area when the man went missing. Your license plate number was written down. Thank you for your time. Have a good day." He and Sherry turned around and walked back to their car.

Sherry got into the car, then closed the door. Once Mark got into the driver seat, she said, "I believe Davenport was telling the truth regarding not knowing our suspect."

"I agree." He started the car. "Who's next on our list?"

Sherry brought up the next name on their list. "Steward Whitfield. It's seven minutes to his house."

An hour passed and the two sleuths had interviewed four more people on the list. Two of the male names on the list weren't home but the wives answered the door. None of them knew or recognized their suspect. All six of the people appeared to be telling the truth. They now stood on the front porch of the seventh name on their list, Phillip Frank. A black Honda Civic was parked in the driveway. They were at the midpoint of the fourteen names on the DMV list.

Mark pushed the doorbell button. The late October southern breeze along with the low seventy-degree temperature felt good against his exposed skin. The front door slowly opened then stopped allowing enough space for a man's head to appear as the remaining part of his body hid behind the door. The man appeared to be in his early seventies and unshaven with a three-to-four-day facial growth. Puzzlement stared back at Mark and Sherry. Mark cleared his throat. "Good morning. Are you Phillip Frank?"

"Yes. Who wants to know?" the man answered harshly.

"We're private investigators. Have you ever seen this man before?" Mark showed him the composite.

"No." The man closed the door.

Sherry appeared stunned as she looked up at Mark. "That went well."

Mark put his index finger to his lips in a gesture of to be quiet. He turned his head, then moved it closer to the front door. His left ear was a couple of inches from the door. A faint voice of another man came from inside the house. The man sounded upset. Mark tried to make out what the man was saying. He picked up part of a question from the man inside, "How did they know…?" The voice fainted completely as they moved further into the house away from the front door.

"What did you hear?"

"Let's get into the car. I'll tell you then." Mark didn't want to take a chance the two people inside the house returned near the front door and would possibly hear his answer to Sherry. Once in the car, Mark answered Sherry's question. "I heard another man inside the house talking to Phillip Frank. I heard part of their conversation. The man said, 'How did they know I was here?'"

"That sounds suspicious. The man talking to Phillip Frank could be our mystery man?"

"Exactly. I'm sure you noticed Phillip Frank's mouth dropped as he peered at the composite of our suspect."

"I did. What can we do now, knowing our suspect was probably standing behind the front door?"

"We go to Plan B."

"What's Plan B?"

"We'll have Ron do a computer search on Mr. Frank, including any social media he participated with, such as Facebook. There could be a photograph of our mystery suspect on one of those social sites. If I still were a detective with the sheriff's department, I'd put a twenty-four-hour surveillance on the house to catch our guy coming outside. Since, I don't have this authority anymore, we go to the resources we have available to us."

Sherry peered down at the DMV list. "We're going to check out the rest of the names, right?"

"Yes. Even though I believe Phillip Frank is associated with our mystery guy. As a detective, you follow up on all your suspects. Otherwise, who's to say there isn't more than one suspect?"

"In other words, determining who participated in a criminal act is a process of elimination regarding suspects."

"Very good. Your mind is tuned in on detective work." Mark started the car.

"Your years of detective work has rubbed off you and onto me."

"I guess that's a good thing." He reached over and touched her thigh. "I'll give Ron a call now." Mark called Ron and explained what he wanted him to do regarding Phillip Frank.

Unbeknownst to Mark and Sherry, two unrecognizable figures images stood behind slightly transparent curtains hanging from a large picture window of Phillip Frank's house.

Chapter Six

Sherry experienced a sudden chill accompanied with the sense someone or something was staring at them as Mark pulled away from the curb. She glanced at Phillip Frank's house but didn't see anything. She then engaged the portable GPS, bringing up the eighth name on their suspects' list. They were directed to Deerbrook Estates. They had found no one at home. The private sleuths asked neighbors on either side of their suspect's house if they had ever seen the man in their composite sketch. Neither neighbor recognized the man. It didn't mean their mystery man didn't get into the eighth suspect's car at the mall, only that the neighbors had never seen him with their neighbor or in the neighborhood.

Sherry and Mark spent another three hours investigating the remaining six suspects. They had stopped at a fast-food restaurant and eaten hamburgers and fries between the eleventh and twelfth suspects. At the end of their search for a relationship between the mystery man and the names on the DMV list, their conclusion still pointed to Phillip Frank having something to do with the disappearance of their mystery man at the mall.

Sherry got into the car after they interrogated the fourteenth suspect at his place of residence. "Detective work is tedious and repetitious, not like what you see on TV as exciting and heart pounding."

"Welcome to the real world of detective drudgery and repetition. We still need to interview three of our suspects at their place of work. Before we do that can you call Ron and ask him to also check to see if any of the fourteen people on our list are somehow associated with Phoenix Pharmaceutical Research via social network or if they're in contact with Phillip Frank or Fred Cramer. We already know none of them actually work for the research company, since we have their work address and name."

"Sure." Sherry closed the vinyl cover of the folder holding the list of the suspects. "You never realize how thorough detective work is until you're part of the investigative team." As a previous emergency room physician, she also had to be thorough when investigating a patient's complaint, including drawing their blood to find any abnormalities and ordering diagnostic studies such an X-ray, CT scan, or ultrasound trying to figure out the cause of the patient's perilous medical condition.

"I'm sure detective work isn't much different than you having to investigate the cause of a patient's medical complaints."

Sherry chuckled as she retrieved her cell phone. "I was thinking the same thing."

"Like we said many times before, after thirty plus years of being together our thoughts sometimes teleport between our brains."

"How true. We do have an element of telepathic connection between each other. Of course, we're not in the same league as was Edgar Casey, who could conjure a clairvoyant connection between himself and another person."

Sherry dialed Ron's cell phone number bypassing the forensic lab's receptionist. The phone rang two times. "Hi, Mark. What's up?"

"This is Sherry. Mark is here with me in the car. I have you on speaker. We need you to do something else this evening on your computer." She told him the needed information.

"I'll add it on my list. No problem. By the way, forensic investigators found the bullet responsible for shooting down the power line. The bullet was mangled but the ballistic forensic people identified the bullet as a 308 Winchester normally used in long-range rifles. I wish I had better news for you."

"Thanks Ron. We'll talk to you later. Bye."

Mark merged onto I-75, reaching the seventy-miles-per-hour speed limit within several seconds. He positioned the car in the center lane as vehicles passed them from the left and right lanes. Mark shook his head and grumbled. "Don't people go the speed limit anymore? Everybody is in such a hurry."

"It's been this way since man sat behind the steering wheel of their car or truck. You notice it more since you're retired and not in a hurry to get things done before having to go back to work."

"Yeah. You're probably right." Mark sped toward their next

destination. The workplace of Chris Mathis, Redding Manufacturing. The mid-afternoon sun shined down on them to their left with medium traffic around them. The sound of an explosion from the front driver-side wheel caused the car to suddenly pull to the left as they crossed over to the left lane and into the pathway of speeding vehicles.

Sherry cringed, anticipating a semi-truck's mammoth weight to slam into them, crushing their car and killing them instantly. She peered at Mark, who grasped the steering wheel, straining to hold the car from rolling over into a deadly barrel roll. He had apparently removed his foot from the accelerator, as their car gradually slowed down. He maneuvered the car to the left side of the road next to the median guardrail. Their car came to a complete stop. Sherry sighed. They had avoided death again. "The Grim Reaper seems to be following us the past two days."

Mark removed his white-knuckled hands from the steering wheel. "It sure seems so, doesn't it?"

They got out of the car and walked over to the front driver side wheel. Sherry stared down at a flat, shredded tire and slightly bent rim. "We'll need to call road service to change the tire."

"No need to. I can change the tire," Mark said as he bent down and examined the mangled tire.

"Maybe when you were younger. Besides, those lug nuts are probably wedged into the bent wheel. It'll take a seasoned road tow man and a power wrench to remove those lug nuts." Sherry knew a lot about car mechanics. Her father had owned a Firestone dealership and was a master mechanic before he retired. She grew up spending time around the daily workings of tire repair, tire replacement, wheel alignments and auto maintenance. She was a certified "powder puff mechanic" due to her upbringing.

"You're right." He removed his cell phone. "I'll call our car insurance's road tow service company."

"Good idea." A flashing blue and red light appeared to her right. A Florida State Police car pulled up onto the median behind them. The distinguished black vehicle sat there for at least a minute. The trooper was more than likely checking the license plate number, making sure it wasn't stolen, involved in a robbery, or some other felonious act. The trooper got out of the car. He appeared to be in his late twenties, as he walked slowly, cautiously up to them. Sherry knew officers had to be prepared for any unexpected actions from people they initially encountered in perilous situations.

"Afternoon, folks," said the trooper as he reached the back of the car. "Having car problems?"

"Yes. Our car tire blew out," Sherry answered as she stepped aside allowing the trooper an unobstructed view of their destroyed tire. "My husband is talking with the towing company right now."

The trooper stared down at the damaged tire. "You're lucky you didn't hit something or roll over."

"I guess someone above was watching over us," Sherry glanced at his name plate attached to the front of his shirt, "Trooper Perkins."

While they waited for the tow truck, Mark showed the trooper the car's registration and his driver's license. The towing company wrecker showed up thirty minutes later. A middle-aged man got out of the truck, walked over, and assessed the mangled front tire. "The best thing to do here is to tow the car to an auto repair garage where they can remove your tire and assess for any frontend damage. From my experience, even if I can change your tire, the spare tire may not fit due to the damage of your wheel housing. What do you want me to do?"

Mark scratched the right side of his scalp. "Tow it to a garage."

The man hooked up the car, lifting the front of their car. When the ravaged tire was about a foot off the ground, a metal object fell from the tire to the ground. The trooper, who had been standing next to Mark and Sherry, stepped forward and picked up the metal object. "Oh, my God. It's a bullet."

"A bullet?" Sherry questioned, as she peered down at the bullet, as did Mark.

"It looks like a 308 Winchester bullet," Mark stated. "It's obviously from a rifle."

"Are you a gun expert?" Trooper Perkins asked with a hint of sarcasm."

"Not exactly. But my thirty years as a detective for Marion County Sheriff Department, I've seen enough of ballistic reports and examination of crime scenes."

"Oh, sorry, Detective McKinney. I didn't know you were one of us."

"Was. I'm retired now."

"I can assume you and your wife didn't see the shooter or realize someone shot at your tire."

"No. We didn't see anything. It'll be important to exam the tire and see where the bullet entered the tire. The angle of entrance into the tire will determine if someone with a rifle shot from a bridge, another vehicle either in front of us or from the side."

"You're absolutely correct," agreed the trooper. "Your accident was caused from a felonious assault toward you and your wife. I'll need to write up this incident and report it to our investigators. Unlikely the shooter was positioned on a bridge since the closest overhead bridge is about ten miles south of here."

Sherry wondered if this was a random shooting, or if she and Mark were the intended victims. This was the second death-defying incident they'd been involved in the past two days. She was now convinced their near-death experiences were intentional and directed at them. The logical conclusion would put the shooter in a vehicle in front of them as they drove down I-75. For the shooter to be positioned from an area next to I-75 would mean they would've had to know their schedule and what time they'd be in the area. This didn't seem feasible. The more logical scenario would be they were being followed, and the perpetrator waited for the opportunistic moment when they were most vulnerable. Diving seventy-miles-per-hour on an expressway fitted this scenario.

Trooper Perkins turned to the tow truck driver. "We'll need the tire and wheel for analysis at our forensic lab in Jacksonville. Can you remove it from the car?"

"I'll try. Let me get my power tool to remove the wheel lugs."

The trooper obtained statements from Mark and Sherry. "I need to call in this shooting. Be right back." Trooper Perkins walked back to his car, then got in.

"I think our shooter was from a vehicle in front of us," Mark suggested. "What do you think?"

"I agree a hundred percent." She then told Mark what she had been thinking a moment ago.

"I agree. Makes the most sense. You're really thinking like a detective. For the shooter to commit this act, he'd have to be in a vehicle where the back window could be lowered. As far as I know there are a few vehicles possessing this capability. Let me Google it." Mark spoke into his cell phone. "What vehicles can you roll down the rear window?"

The female voice synthesizer stated, "Toyota 4Runner, the old Jeep Grand Wagoneer, Toyota Tundra and Sequoia and the Ford Explorer Sport Trac."

Mark turned to Sherry. "Do you remember seeing any of these vehicles in front of us before our tire blew out?"

"I have a tough time recognizing one vehicle from another. They all pretty much look alike today. When I was younger, I could tell you the make, model, and year of a car. But not today. As far as SUVs, I'd have to see the manufacture's logo on the rear or front of the vehicle to know what it was. Besides, I was looking down at the list of our suspects when the car tire blew."

"Same here. But I was looking into the rearview mirror when our tire was shot."

The tow road guy spent about ten minutes removing the tire. Trooper Perkins had the guy put the tire in the trunk of the police car. The trooper then walked over to Mark and Sherry. "I'll have one of our detectives call you and let you know what forensic found out about your tire. It'll take probably a day or two to get any results from forensics."

"I appreciate it," Mark said. "I'm sure your detectives will be talking to us soon. Make sure they call us on my cell phone. We're frequently in and out of our house."

"Sure will. So, you don't have any idea who might wanted to shoot at your car tire?"

"No clue. There's a lot of crazy people out there today."

"That's the truth." The trooper left and headed back to his patrol car.

"You folks ready?" asked the tow truck driver. "Where do you want to take your vehicle?"

"We decided to take it to the Chrysler dealership," Sherry answered. "If there's anything majorly wrong with the car, they'll be able to fix it. Plus, we can get a rental car from them if they can't fix the car today."

~ * ~

There wasn't any damage to the front end of the car. They didn't need a car loaner since their car was finished within an hour. It was twenty minutes past five, too late to talk with the remaining suspects on their DMV list at their workplaces. The sun was below the treetops as early evening blanketed the area. They decided to stop at a restaurant for supper. Mark turned on the headlights as he sat in the Chrysler 300 and pulled out onto Pine Street, turning left. "Ron will be getting home soon and starting his search on the computer for information on Phillip Frank and the other people on our list of suspects. Nothing more we can do today."

"You're right," Sherry agreed. "Let's have a relaxing dinner, even though there's somebody wanting us dead." She thought a moment. "You know, I've been thinking about something. The sheriff's department forensic lab has the bullet that severed the power line last night. The bullet should be compared with the bullet found inside our tire. It would tell us if the bullets came from the same rifle?"

"You mean compare the lands and groove of the two bullets and see if they match?"

"Yes. Exactly."

Mark nodded, "We're dealing with two different law enforcement jurisdictions, the state police and county sheriff department. It's common for the two of them to be working together on a case. We'll need to wait until the official results of the second bullet is completed. Right now, it's speculation the two bullets are from the same rifle."

"Won't we have to tell the two agencies why we think someone is trying to kill us for them to join forces and look into a possible connection of the two shootings?"

Mark turned right off Pine Street and into the parking lot of

Darrell's Restaurant. "To some degree. Even though our investigation isn't against the law, we don't want to tell them about our investigation of the mysterious guy. The best answer we could give them is to say we're not sure who or why someone is trying to harm us. It wouldn't be a lie since we're not one hundred percent sure our working theory is correct." Mark parked the car. He peered around the parking lot, looking for any suspicious individual or individuals. There weren't any people walking or sitting in their vehicles. The restaurant blocked the parking lot on the other side of the building. He and Sherry had to be overcautious, assessing their surroundings and the people in it from now on. They went into the restaurant and ordered dinner. As the waitress brought them their meal, his cell phone rang. He didn't recognize the caller's number. "Hello."

"Is this Mark McKinney?"

"Yes, I am."

"I'm Special Agent Morgan from the Florida Department of Law Enforcement. I'm investigating the shooting incident on I-75 you and your wife we're involved in today. From what Trooper Perkins stated to me, you didn't see the shooter or know who might have wanted to do harm to you and your wife?"

Mark peered at Sherry and nodded. "That's correct, Special Agent Morgan."

"Thank goodness neither you nor your wife were injured according to Trooper Perkin's report. If you happened to think of something about the shooting today, please give me a call."

"Yes, I'll let you know." Mark thought about mentioning the power line incident but decided not to until the results from the FDLE Forensic Laboratory of the bullet involved in the tire shooting was completed, even though he knew it was likely a 308 Winchester bullet. If the bullet officially turned out to be the same caliber of bullet as the one in the power line shooting, he'd mention the I-75 shooting incident with the Marion County Sheriff detective.

"You and your wife take care. Bye."

Mark put his cell phone into his belt holster. "I thought we'd have to meet with the agent tomorrow. But the detective got the trooper's report on our shooting. No need for an interview."

They ate dinner, then headed back to their car when Mark's cell phone rang. He glanced at the caller ID. "It's Ron."

"Maybe he found out something about one of our suspects?" They got into the car.

On the fourth ring, Mark answered the phone, putting it on speaker so Sherry could hear. "Hey Ron. What's up?"

"I discovered vital information on Phillip Frank and our mystery man."

"What did you find out?"

"I'd rather tell you and Sherry here at my house. Plus, there's photographs you'll need to see."

"We'll be there in fifteen minutes. Talk to you then."

Mark left the parking lot and headed to Ron's house near Ocala National Forest.

~ * ~

A Toyota 4Runner with tinted windows sat in the parking lot on the other side of the restaurant, out of view from Mark and Sherry. The vehicle started up, then followed the husband-and-wife sleuths once they left the parking lot and were on the street in front of the restaurant. Two men sat inside. The driver wore a hoodie, making it difficult to completely view his facial features; the passenger wore a baseball cap pulled down, blocking his face, making him unrecognizable.

The 4Runner's rear window was opened about six inches.

Chapter Seven

Night had fallen upon Ocala as headlights lit up the road in front of a range of styles and makes of vehicles. Mark reached to his right and gently grasped Sherry's hand, then said, "From the tone of Ron's voice, he may have identified the mystery man and his relationship with Phillip Frank."

"I agree. It sure sounded like it."

The drive to Ron's house was uneventful, including driving through the area of the earlier downed power line, which caused a mental chill, thinking they could've been electrocuted. Mark pulled up into Ron's driveway, stopped and parked. As Mark was about to ring the front doorbell, Ron's voice projected from a speaker set into a wall to the left of the door, "Hey, guys. Come on in. The door's open." The sound of a deadbolt disengaging filled the air. The two sleuths walked into the house as the deadbolt reengaged, securing the front door from any unwanted intruders. They walked through the vestibule, down the hallway to Ron's computer room.

Ron sat in front of the middle computer with his back to them. "Hey. I wanted to discuss my findings face to face. I hope you don't mind my cloak-and-dagger behavior?"

"Not at all," Mark replied as he and Sherry stood a couple of feet away from Ron.

"I checked all the social media sites, hoping to find our mystery man standing with Phillip Frank. And unbelievable, there it was. I found them together." He moved his chair to the right, allowing Mark and Sherry a clear, unobstructed view of their suspect on the computer's monitor screen.

Mark leaned forward. "It's our mystery man."

"No doubt," Sherry agreed.

Ron turned around and changed the screen to a full facial view of the mystery man. "His name is Henry Baker according to the picture's information of him standing with Phillip Frank. Although, things got strange."

"What do you mean, strange?" Mark asked.

"There's no record of him having a job, credit card, or utility bill. There's many Henry Bakers in Florida, but his face didn't match any of them. I also entered his face into a face recognition data base. Nothing came up. The name this guy used with his photo with Phillip Frank was apparently fictitious. If we could get Henry Baker's fingerprint or DNA, I could try to identify him using these two forensic procedures. Of course, there wouldn't be any guarantee he'd be in any of these databases either."

"It means this mystery man is hiding his identity, which could mean he's either in a witness protection program, an individual who never committed a felony since his face didn't show up in any law enforcement agencies facial identity databases, or he changed his identity for some other reason. Whatever the reason, this guy is connected to Phillip Frank, Fred Cramer, and the Parkers. All we have to do is connect the dots."

Ron chuckled. "You sure know how to become involved in unbelievable, mystery-filled cases. It's not any different than when you were a detective for the sheriff's department."

Mark agreed with Ron's observation. "What did you find out about Phillip Frank?

"He's a sixty-year-old man retired on Social Security Disability due to an on-the-job injury which caused permanent disability from a back injury. He worked as a heavy equipment operator. He has no criminal record."

He turned to Sherry. "We'll have to go back to Phillip Frank's house and talk with him regarding him standing with Henry Baker. We'll show him the photograph." He looked down at Ron. "What about the other names on the DMV list. Did you find any connection between the people on the list?"

"No. There's no connection between any of them to Baker, Frank, the Parkers or Phoenix Pharmaceutical Research."

Mark briefly touched Ron's shoulder. "Thanks for all your help."

"I'll continue to search the internet, including the dark web, for any information on Phillip Frank and Henry Baker."

"Okay. It's too late to go back and talk with Frank. We'll talk with him tomorrow morning."

"I'll get back with you if I find something."

Mark and Sherry left Ron's house. They got into their car. "It's been another trying day for us. We'll go home, have a drink and discuss our plans for tomorrow, which of course, will include our talk with Frank." They again drove by the area of the falling power line without incidence. Once they got home, parked under the carport, and went inside the house, his cell phone rang. He glanced at the caller ID. It was their neighbor, Joe Barrington. "Hi, Joe."

"You're not going to believe this, but I heard they found another couple dead from spontaneous human combustion."

A chill engulfed Mark's entire body as he turned to Sherry. "There's another couple with spontaneous human combustion."

"That's unbelievable." She peered down and shook her head in disbelief.

Mark put the phone on speaker. "Do you have any details?"

"Absolutely. I got a phone call from a friend of mine who lives in a retirement community in Wildwood. They found an elderly couple lying in their bed dead. Their bodies were a pile of ashes."

"When did they find the couple?" Sherry asked.

"Early this afternoon. Their daughter found them. Do you think there's a connection between them and the Parkers?"

"Don't know," Mark answered. "Since there isn't any scientific cause of spontaneous human combustion, it would be hard to say. What's the name of the retirement community and the couple's name?"

"I knew you'd ask me. The couple's names are Margaret and Spencer Watchman. They live at Railroad Crossing retirement community near Wildwood. Are you going to investigate their deaths?"

Mark wasn't surprised by the question. He peered at Sherry and raised his eyebrows. "I'm not a detective anymore. Although, I may call the detective investigating the Parkers' death and let him know. I appreciate you calling and letting me know about the Watchman's deaths."

"Sure enough. Talk to you later. Bye."

Mark put his cell phone away, then looked at Sherry, who was getting out a bottle of Captain Morgan from the cupboard. "What do you think?"

"I'd say it would be statistically unlikely to have four people or two couples succumb to spontaneous human combustion within a two-day period. If I were a gambler, knowing the odds and frequency of SHC, I wouldn't bet a penny, knowing I'd lose the bet. Something is causing this rare medical phenomenon. Like I mentioned yesterday, there are theories, but no concrete proof for the cause of SHC. We thought Phoenix Pharmaceutical Research had something to do with the cause of this phenomenal condition, but as far as we concluded after our investigation, they had nothing to do with it."

"I agree with you," he responded as he removed a bottle of cola from the refrigerator and removed the cap.

"There has to be something causing these cases of spontaneous human combustion."

"I'd like to talk with the medical examiner. Wildwood is still in District Five, and Chief Medical Examiner Taylor Evans will oversee the latest spontaneous human combustion deaths."

"I'm sure he and his medical staff are as astonished as we are regarding the four people dying this way. We can give him a call tomorrow morning. Unless you want to drive to Leesburg and talk with Dr. Evans personally."

Mark chuckled. "Again, you read my mind. I was about to suggest the very thing to you. Also, I know a few of the Lake County sheriff detectives." There were occasions Mark and his department shared information on crimes, especially mysterious deaths, with the other surrounding county sheriff departments.

Sherry poured the rum into the glass. "What about talking with Phillip Frank regarding the photograph with our mystery guy?"

"We need to prioritize. The couple's death in Wildwood today will need investigation first before we go back and talk with Mr. Frank. I'll call Ron and let him know about the couple in Wildwood dying of spontaneous human combustion. We'll need to know all the information regarding this couple, including if they were in contact with Phoenix Pharmaceutical Research, the Parkers or any other similarities connecting them." Mark called Ron. "I need you to do something for us."

"Sure. What is it?"

Mark told him about the deaths in Wildwood and what he wanted from him. "If you can get any information about them, I'd really appreciate it."

"I'll get right on it. The plot thickens, as someone once said."

Mark put his phone away. He poured cola into the glasses containing the rum as they sat down at the kitchen table.

Sherry raised her glass up in front of her and stated, "Here's to us and our nonmundane retirement." They clicked glasses.

"I'll drink to that, my love."

After their second drink, Mark' cell phone rang. He glanced at the caller ID. "It's Ron." He placed his empty glass into the empty sink, then said, "Hi, Ron." He put the phone on speaker.

"I checked out the couple, Margaret and Spencer Watchman. First, there wasn't any connection with Phoenix Pharmaceutical Research. There weren't any similar medical conditions like the Parkers. Martha Watchman had late Alzheimer's. Spencer Watchman suffered from high blood pressure. The one thing all the victims had in common was their ages. All of them were in their seventies."

"Thanks, Ron. Have a good night." He placed the cell phone down on the table. "There doesn't seem to be any connection or significant similarities between the two couples. Tomorrow morning I'll call the medical examiner, Dr. Evans, and see if we can talk with him at his office about the Watchman's deaths."

"It would be great if we can talk to him personally."

As they made their way to the bedroom, Mark thought to himself, *Will tomorrow bring answers, more questions, or more attempts on their lives?*

~ * ~

Mark merged onto south I-75 and headed to Leesburg. The

morning sun shined its piercing rays to his left as he moved the sun visor over to block the blinding light. He had called the medical examiner, Dr. Evans around nine o'clock from the house. The medical examiner agreed to talk with him and Sherry about the couple dying of spontaneous human combustion. The expressway traffic was moderate. Minutes later, they came upon the area where their front driver-side tire had exploded from a bullet fired from the side of the road or from a vehicle with a receding back window in front of them. Mark glanced to his left across the median and the southbound lanes. "We should get the results from the forensic lab in Jacksonville on the trajectory of the bullet sometime today. Like what we said yesterday, the shooter was likely in a vehicle in front of us."

"It's the most logical conclusion to yesterday's shooting," Sherry agreed. "I checked out the terrain on both sides of the expressway. There's no service roads or wooded areas. It's all open land. The shooter would've been easily seen by drivers."

Mark grinned, then said, "Very observant...Dr. Watson."

"Thanks, Sherlock."

The next thirty-plus minutes were uneventful. Mark and Sherry had agreed to keep an eye open for any vehicle in front of them with a rolled down back window. They also peered up at overpasses for a shooter aiming a rifle at them. Mark turned off onto exit 329 from I-75 and headed east on State Road Forty-Four to the Division Five Medical Examiner's Office in Leesburg.

Twenty minutes later, Mark turned off Pine Street and into the parking lot of the medical examiner's office facility. He and Sherry walked up to the reception desk where a woman in her late forties sat.

"Hi. We're here to see Dr. Evans."

The receptionist peered up at Mark and smiled. "Yes. Detective McKinney. Dr. Evans told me to send you and Dr. McKinney to his office. You know where his office is since you've been here before."

Mark couldn't remember the receptionist's name. "Thanks."

"Nice seeing you again."

They left the lobby and entered a long hallway. "I guess you made an impression on the receptionist the times you were here before."

"Probably because I don't have a common-looking face."

She grinned, "Probably."

The odor of formaldehyde permeated Mark's nose as they passed the closed door of the autopsy room to their left. Up ahead to their right, they stopped at a closed door with the name, "Taylor Evans, M.D. Chief Medical Examiner," stenciled on the solid wooden door. Mark knocked.

"Come on in," shouted Dr. Evans.

Mark opened the door. The medical examiner sat behind a large mahogany desk. They walked into the room. He motioned for them to sit down on chairs in front of the desk.

"Please have a seat. After I left your community with two spontaneous human combustion victims yesterday, I didn't expect to see another case."

"That..."

"That makes two of us," Sherry interrupted Mark, then glanced at Dr. Evans. "I should say the three of us."

Dr. Evans grinned as he briefly looked at Sherry, then back to Mark. "Margaret and Spencer Watchman's ashes silhouetted the outline of their bodies as they laid in their bed. Identical to the couple in your community. These deaths are uncanny and unexplainable. I researched quite a few medical computer sites regarding spontaneous human combustion and didn't find a common link between the two couples, other than they were in their seventies with medical problems. Plus, none of their medical conditions or illnesses were the same."

Mark wanted to tell the medical examiner about Ron Brewer last night producing the same conclusion regarding the two couples. "There has to be something causing the spontaneous human combustion."

Dr. Evans nodded. "I agree. So far, I don't have a clue or a piece of evidence pointing to what's causing this medical phenomenon."

Mark's cell phone rang. He glanced at the caller ID. It was Ron. He got up, walked toward the door, and stopped. "Hi, Ron. We're talking with the medical examiner right now. What's up?"

"A few minutes ago, I heard FDLE's lab got the results on your front driver side tire. The bullet's trajectory was from a vehicle driving in front of you. The bullet was a 308 Winchester made specifically for a rifle."

"We pretty much figured that."

"Changing subjects, our trace evidence lab lifted DNA off Fred Cramer's car's driver side head rest. It matched Cramer's DNA. The mystery man who drove the Elantra to the mall didn't lean his head back against the headrest or did he deposit his DNA anywhere else on the car. They ran Cramer's DNA through our nation's DNA database, including the United Kingdom's NDNAD and Interpol databases. No match."

"Another dead end. Other than we know Cramer wasn't a fugitive in the United States or around the world. Thanks for the information." Mark knew it meant Cramer hadn't been arrested for a felony. All individuals convicted of a felon had their DNA taken. Also, their guy hadn't been in the armed forces or law enforcement.

"Sure enough. Talk to you later."

Mark walked back to his chair and sat down. "Sorry."

Dr. Evans sat back in his chair. "Working on another case?"

Should I tell him about the shootings, and that they might be related to the spontaneous human combustion deaths? No. Better not. "Yes."

"I guess a detective never retires, huh?"

Sherry reached over and touched Mark's forearm. "We don't mind. It keeps both our minds active. When you retire, you'll find people will still ask you medical questions or for medical advice."

"Unless when I retire, I move to another area of Florida or to another state and not tell anyone I was a doctor."

"It's an alternative. But you'd probably subscribe to the local newspaper to keep up on what's going on in here."

"Yeah. You're right."

Mark stood, as did Sherry. "We appreciate you talking with us."

Dr. Evans stood. "No problem. It's a medical phenomenon that baffles everyone in the medical field." He came around the desk, then shook their hands. "I'll walk with you down the hallway. I have a meeting to attend."

When Mark and Sherry left the building, he turned to his wife and told her what Ron had said to him on the phone. "The next thing we can do is go back and talk with Phillip Frank. Like we said a couple of times,

Frank lied when he said he didn't recognize the composite sketch of our mystery man, whose alleged name is Henry Baker."

"Maybe this time, he'll come forward and tell us the truth."

Mark merged onto I-75 and headed north toward Ocala. Mark peered at the back end of every vehicle that passed them, anticipating a rolled-down back window. He turned off the expressway to the exit leading them to Mr. Frank's house. A sigh of relief encompassed him, but he knew not to let his guard down about someone wanting to harm them. As a detective, he'd had criminals intimidate him with nefarious words without anyone physically following through with their threats. Twelve minutes later, he turned onto the street Phillip Frank lived on. "Hopefully, this guy will be home." A moment later, his house came into view. A black Honda Civic was parked in the driveway.

"He must be home," Sherry declared. "It's the same car we saw yesterday parked in the driveway."

"You're right." Mark pulled up and stopped behind the Honda Civic. The living rooms opaque curtain was drawn, preventing the late morning sun from entering inside the house. A smaller window on the other side of the front door had its miniblind drawn, blocking the view of peering eyes. *How will Phillip Frank react to the photo of him and our mystery man?*

Chapter Eight

Mark rang the doorbell. He couldn't hear any sound coming from inside the house such as a TV playing, music from a radio, or other electronic devices. Silence filled the air. Was he sleeping? A chill engulfed him as the thought of him lying on the floor dead in a heap of ashes. He pushed the thought of this out of his mind. "He might be home and doesn't want to talk to us. Or he might have left the house with a friend who had a car."

"Could be. Or he's another victim of SHC."

"There's no way of knowing which scenario it is. And hopefully not the latter." He reached out and turned the doorknob. The door was unlocked. He opened the door about a foot and shouted, "Mr. Frank. Are you home?"

No answer. Mark sniffed deeply. No smell of death.

Sherry touched his arm. "He must've left with someone."

"Probably," Mark agreed, as he closed the front door. "He might normally leave the front door unlocked, or he forgot to lock it when he left? There weren't any unusual odors coming from inside the house."

"You mean, body decomposition?"

"Yes. Mr. Cramer lying dead in his kitchen two days ago flashed across my mind."

A loud pounding sound came from inside the house.

"Did you hear that?"

"Yes. It's a thumping sound."

Mark opened the front door and walked into the living room along with Sherry. "Hello. It's Mark McKinney."

The thumping noise was coming from the hallway to their left. A faint male voice said, "Help me, please."

Sherry rushed down the hallway, followed by Mark. At the end of the hallway lying supine halfway out of a doorway was Phillip Frank.

"Mr. Frank, can I help you?"

Mark knew, according to the Good Samaritan Law, Sherry was obligated to help a victim in an emergency without being sued, as long as she didn't exacerbate a medical emergency. An important part of the Hippocratic Oath physicians and other medical professions take stated: Do No Harm.

Sherry stooped a few inches from Phillip's head. "Can you tell me what's wrong, why you're lying on the floor?"

"I became dizzy as I was walking out of the bedroom and the next thing I remember was waking up with extreme pain in my right hip. I can't move my right leg due to the pain."

"When did this happen?"

He glanced at his watch. "About two hours ago."

Sherry stood and stepped over him. She stared down at his hip and leg. "Your right leg is externally rotated and shortened."

"What does that mean?" Phillip asked, then groaned in obvious pain.

"You fractured your right hip."

Mark needed to ask Mr. Frank about Henry Baker before he called EMS. He bent down next to him. "When's the last time you saw Henry Baker?"

Phillip frowned. "I don't know anyone with that name."

Mark showed Frank the photo with Baker standing next to him. "The man standing next to you in the photo."

"Oh. You got me." He groaned in pain reaching toward his right hip.

"You're having a muscle spasm in your leg due to the fracture," Sherry said.

Mark stood, then said, "So you know Henry Baker."

"Unfortunately. We met at a bar in Ocala and played pool together. I've known him for about two months."

"You picked him up at Paddock Mall yesterday, right?"

"I did."

"He was here when me and my wife stood at your front door yesterday."

"Guilty. Got me again. He told me not to say anything about him."

"Where is he now?"

Frank moaned as an apparent muscle spasm overwhelmed him. A moment later, he answered, "Have no idea. All I know is he called someone a few hours ago. I was in the bedroom and heard the front door close. When I started to rush out of the bedroom, I got dizzy then fell to the floor."

"What does the guy do for a living?"

"Henry said he was a hit man for a crime syndicate. Of course, I knew he was fibbing and never pushed to find out what he really did for a living."

"Do you know where he lives?"

"Henry said he stays with a friend in Ocala. Don't know where though."

"Do you have his phone number?"

"Yes. It's in my cell phone. I think my phones in the kitchen."

"I'll get it," Sherry said as she stood from her kneeling position and headed for the kitchen.

"Is there someone you want us to call and let them know what happened to you?" Mark asked.

"Not really. No kids. Wife died a couple of years ago of cancer. Have a brother in Michigan, but he's in a nursing home."

Mark retrieved his cell phone and called 911. "My name is Mark McKinney. We have a man with a right hip fracture."

"How do you know the hip is fractured?" asked the operator with a hint of skepticism in her voice.

"I'm here with my wife, Dr. Sherry McKinney, who's an emergency room doctor. The injured person's name is Phillip Frank." He then gave the dispatcher the address.

"EMS is on the way. Can you stand out front and watch for the paramedics?"

"Yes, ma'am."

Sherry returned with Mr. Franks' cell phone. "Do you want me to look up Henry's phone?"

"Sure. It's in my contacts."

Mark said to Sherry, "I'll be outside waiting for the paramedics."
"Okay."
The operator asked, "Is the patient conscious?"
"Yes. He's talking with my wife."
"I'll stay on the phone until EMS arrives."
Mark walked outside and stood on the front door landing. If what Phillip Frank had told him about Henry Baker was true, there was no way to identify their mystery man since Mr. Frank didn't know where he lived. If Baker's phone number couldn't be traced due to it being a throw-away cell phone, they'd be at another dead end. Criminals normally used untraceable cell phones today. When he went back into the house, he'd ask Frank if Henry Baker drank out of a glass, bottle or can. If he did, he'd obtain the item and obtain a DNA from the forensic lab. Six minutes had passed when Mark saw the fire department's first responders in their red firetruck, followed by the paramedics. Of course, the first responders made sure the site of the emergency was clear of hazards and dangers, making the area around the injured victim safe for the paramedics to assess the victim and perform their life-saving procedures. The EMS dispatcher disconnected her conversation with Mark when the EMS vehicles stopped and parked on the street in front of Phillip Frank's house. As the fire department's first responders walked toward him, Mark recognized the first firefighter, Roger Willis. "Hi, Roger, the victim is in the hallway with Dr. McKinney." Mark knew EMT Willis when he was a detective for the sheriff's department. The EMTs and paramedics also knew Sherry when they showed up in the emergency room with a patient.

"Thanks, Detective McKinney," Roger said with a nod.

Mark hurried inside the house to ask Phillip a question before the emergency team took over the scene. "Mr. Frank, did Henry Baker drink from a glass, bottle or can while he was in your house?"

"I already asked him," Sherry interrupted. "I have three empty beer cans Baker drank from." She raised a gray plastic bag containing the cans. "Plus, I got Henry Baker's cell phone number."

Mark grinned. "Great." She was thinking like a detective. It was no wonder—she had listened to his discussion of forensic evidence collection on many of his cases over the years. Similar to him listening to her medical cases.

The paramedics had now taken over. They assessed his leg and came to the same conclusion as Sherry, a fractured right hip. They concluded his fracture hadn't compromised his circulation or nerves. The paramedics stabilized his right lower leg, put him onto a gurney, started an I.V., obtained vital signs, and put him on oxygen through a nasal canula. "What hospital do you want to go to, Mr. Frank?"

"It doesn't matter to me. As long as the doctors can fix my broken hip."

"Okay. We'll take you to AdventHealth Ocala Hospital in," stated one of the paramedics. They wheeled him down the hallway toward the front door. Mark and Sherry followed from behind. Sherry closed the front door.

A crowd of neighbors had congregated on the front lawn. A woman in her mid-fifties yelled to Phillip, "What happened, Phillip?"

"I broke my frigging hip. Can you believe that? I've never broken a bone in my entire life until today." The paramedics wheeled him down the concrete driveway to the back of their vehicle.

Mark walked up to the woman and two other women standing next to her. "Excuse me, ma'am. Did you happened to see a man walk out of Frank's house a little while ago and get into a vehicle?"

"No."

"I saw a man leave his house about two and a half hours ago," answered a woman in her mid-sixties. "He got into a Toyota 4Runner. I didn't get a good look at the driver due to the heavily tinted windows."

"The vehicle had a trailer hitch with a yellow tennis ball covering the ball mount," added the third woman, who appeared to be in her early sixties.

Mark chuckled to himself. These women probably know the movements of several neighbors around them on a daily basis. "Thanks. Appreciate the information."

"Why did you want to know about someone leaving Phillip's house? Didn't Phillip know?" asked the first woman.

These women likely sit around in their coffee group or other beverage group and discuss the happenings of their immediate neighborhood. He knew he'd have to give her a convincing answer without telling her and the two other women the real reason for the question. "Phillip knew he was leaving but didn't know who picked his friend up."

"That doesn't make—"

"Have a wonderful day, ladies," Mark interrupted. "We have to get going." He and Sherry walked to their car, then got inside.

"I think the lady had twenty more questions to ask you," Sherry said as she glanced over at them while Mark backed out of the driveway.

"I'm sure she did along with her two lady friends." He chuckled. "I'd coin them as the Snoop Sisters."

"Good description of them." Sherry removed a small spiral notebook and flipped it open. "You realize a Toyota 4Runner has a rear window which rolls down. I wrote down the four different vehicles with roll-down rear windows after our shooting incident on I-75."

"I did. And you know I don't believe in coincidences. We're likely dealing with the perpetrator or perpetrators responsible for shooting out our front tire and the power line."

"All we have to do now is find a dark-blue Toyota 4Runner with a yellow tennis ball covering its trailer hitch's ball mount."

"This may be a monumental job for us, but we have a computer wizard by the name of Ron. He may be able to find the vehicle. We'll have him check the traffic light intersection in the area. It may be a long shot, but we have nothing to lose, since there isn't any other way to find this vehicle. I'll also have him check out Henry Baker's cell phone number."

Mark called Ron and gave him the description of the Toyota 4Runner and the area of Phillip Frank's house. He also gave him Baker's cell phone number.

"I'll check on both of these things after work today."

Mark then said, "I, that is, Sherry, retrieved beer cans from our mystery man, Henry Baker, at Phillip Frank's house. We're going to take them to Infinity Forensic Lab to check for Baker's DNA."

"Sounds like you guys been busy today."

"We have been. Retirement's great. Talk to you later." He glanced down at Sherry and winked. She grinned, apparently agreeing with his retirement statement.

Mark turned into the parking lot of the forensic lab. They parked in front of the building, got out of the car, and walked toward the front door of the two-story building.

~ * ~

A black Suburban with heavily tinted windows pulled into the parking lot. The front window was lightly tinted, enabling a fair view of its occupants, two males, one in his late twenties and the other in his late thirties, sitting in the front seats. If Mark and Sherry turned around, they wouldn't recognize the passenger or driver. The two men wore dark suit coats, white shirts without ties. The Suburban stopped behind Mark's car. The driver and passenger peered at Mark and Sherry as they walked into the building.

~ * ~

Sherry and Mark walked into a large vestibule. A woman in her forties sat at a desk directly in front of them. A large logo with an infinity symbol and the name Infinity Forensic Lab encircled the symbol. Two closed doors on either side of the desk were present. Sherry knew the doors led to the different departments of the lab since she and Mark had been here several other times over the past couple of years. They recognized the receptionist, Carol Robbins. "Hi, Ms. Robbins. I have three beer cans needing DNA analysis."

"Sure. I'll call one of the lab technicians." She reached into the desk drawer to her left and removed two sheets of paper with writing on them. "Please fill out your request." She placed the forms on the desk with a pen.

Sherry filled out the forms in less than two minutes. The door to their right opened and in walked a woman in her early thirties wearing a white lab coat with the company's logo and name.

"Hi, Detective McKinney." She glanced at Sherry. "Hi, Doctor

McKinney. Y'all brought us something for analysis?"

"We did, Ms. Page," Sherry answered. "We need the DNA and a DNA genotype from the saliva of a person we're investigating from at least one of these beer cans."

"Sure. That's what they pay me for." The technician picked up the request form from the desk. Sherry handed her the bag of beer cans. "I assume you want this done ASAP?"

"If you could, I'd appreciate it," Mark answered.

"No problem since I don't have any urgent requests. It'll take me about two hours to obtain the DNA results. I'll call you when I have it."

Mark nodded. "Thanks, Ms. Page." He turned to the receptionist. "Bill me as you normally do."

"Sure will," Ms. Robbins replied with a smile.

They walked out of the building to the parking lot, then to their car. A warm fall breeze touched Sherry's face. The sun was in its noon position in the cloudless, blue sky. Sherry opened the passenger side door and slid inside, unaware of a backed-in black Suburban with two men sitting inside of it across the parking lot about six parking spaces away from them to the left, staring at her and Mark. She experienced a chill. Was she coming down with a cold or the flu? No. The chill was different; it was more like someone was staring at her and Mark. She turned to her right, then to her left. No one was in the vehicles next to them. "Let's go to lunch."

"Good idea. Northgate Diner is having breaded porkchops today."

"I can go for that."

Marked backed the car out of their parking space and turned right, away from the black Suburban.

~ * ~

The passenger of the Suburban held his cell phone in front of him in a horizontal position. "They left Infinity Forensic Lab." A long pause as he apparently listened to the person at the other end of the call. "Yes, sir. Talk to you later." He disconnected the call, then turned to the driver. "Continue following them."

"The director doesn't want us to check out yet what Dr. McKinney gave the lab for analysis?"

"No. Since the results will be in the lab's computer frame. Fortunately, most companies and individuals put their data into computers. It's not like Watergate where information was stored in file cabinets. Computers are a godsend for their capabilities, but are they also vulnerable for hackers to break into."

"Isn't that the truth."

The unknown duo left the parking lot, staying at least a quarter of a mile behind the McKinneys. The passenger stared down at the dashboard. A large GPS screen had the streets immediately around them with a red dot in front of them moving north on NW Jacksonville Road.

~ * ~

Sherry still had the feeling someone was watching them. She looked ahead for vehicles with rolldown back windows, including periodically peering into the sideview mirror for vehicles possibly following them.

"I've been glancing at you for the past few minutes. Are you looking for vehicles with roll-down back windows?"

"Yes. But also, I have a feeling someone is watching us, ever since we left the lab." Sherry possessed at time a six sense when it came to people staring at her or when someone was telling a lie to her. It wasn't ESP but an intuition, a feeling she'd had since her teenage years. Most of the time the feeling was true. Although she didn't sense danger prior to their front tire being shot at or prior to the power line being severed by a bullet.

"I believe you. Even though we pretty much know someone is out to do us harm. You having this feeling confirms our belief…we're being watched and followed by someone."

Northgate Diner came into view. Traffic around them was heavy in both directions. Sherry hadn't seen any vehicle following them since they left the lab. Her cell phone rang. She didn't recognize the phone number. "Hello."

"Dr. McKinney?" asked a male with a raspy voice.

"Yes. Can I help you?"

"There'll be more people dying of spontaneous human combustion."

Chapter Nine

A chill ran up Sherry's spine. "Who are you? And how do you know other people will die from spontaneous human combustion?" She looked at Mark, who had pulled into the restaurant's parking lot and parked. He peered back at her, frowning.

"It's not important who I am. All I can tell you is…" The sound of dogs barking interrupted the man's declaration, followed by the sound of his phone's dial tone, disconnecting their conversation.

"He hung up before telling me who he was and how he knows other people will be dying of SHC."

"Call him back," Mark suggested.

Sherry retrieved the last call and dialed the number. She put the phone on speaker. A recording came on and announced: "The number can't be reached at the moment."

Mark said, "If the guy's cell phone was intentionally broken, the phone will be offline, causing the service provider to cut in and make this announcement. I've seen this scenario many times before during my years as a detective. Criminals would use a throwaway phone, then destroy the phone by smashing it with their shoes."

"I wonder what the guy was going to tell me?"

"I'll give the phone number to Ron. He should be able to trace the number to a name and possibly an address." He removed his cell phone from its holder and dialed Ron's number. "Hi, Ron. We need a name and possible address from a person's cell phone number." He gave the number to him. "Thanks. Talk to you later."

"We were seconds away from knowing the cause of these spontaneous human combustion couples. I wonder what it meant by the dogs barking?"

Mark holstered his cell phone. "Maybe he was being chased or walked into a room with dogs inside, such as a dog shelter? We won't know until we get a hold of this guy."

"We now have two mysterious people to identify. There's nothing we can do right now. Let's go eat."

~ * ~

They went into the restaurant, sat at a booth, then ordered the breaded pork chop special with sweet tea. Most of the tables and booths were filled with hungry customers. The murmuring sound of discussions filled the room. The periodical ding of a bell from the kitchen announced another meal ready to be served by the waitresses. They had finished eating their lunch when Mark's cell phone rang. The caller ID read "Ron Brewer." "Hi Ron."

"I traced the cell phone number you gave me. The owner's name is Peter Blankenship. He lives at forty-two, seventy-four Cypress Street in Ocala. He's a divorced sixty-six-year-old retired high school science teacher with two children. He doesn't have a criminal record, not even a traffic ticket."

"Thanks, Ron. Won't you get in trouble at work using their computers?"

"I'm not at work. After talking with you a while ago, I decided to take the afternoon off, using half a business day."

"You didn't have to do that. We could've waited until this evening."

"Yeah, I could have. But it was a slow morning, nothing specific to do. Your two inquiries were much more interesting."

"I appreciate it. You're a valuable team member."

"Does that mean I'll be getting a raise?"

Mark chuckled. "Sherry will owe you two homecooked meals now."

"Great. I'll check out the dark-blue Toyota 4Runner with a yellow tennis ball covering its ball mount. And I'll check out Henry Baker's cell phone number."

"Thanks, Ron. Sherry and I will check out Blankenship. Talk to you soon. Bye." Mark walked up to the front register with Sherry next to him. He paid the bill and grabbed a wrapped peppermint from a dish on the counter.

The parking lot was nearly full, with a few parking spaces left. Mark glanced at a black Suburban across the parking lot to his left, thinking how out of place the vehicle was with the vast number of pickup trucks and smaller cars. When he thought of a black Suburban, he sometimes thought of the TV show, *Criminal Minds*, and their use of this type of vehicle driven by the FBI profilers. The side windows were heavily tinted, preventing him from seeing if anyone was inside the vehicle.

Sherry put the address of Peter Blankenship into the GPS as Mark pulled out of the restaurant's parking lot and turned left onto NW Jacksonville Road. "We'll stay on this road, then turn left onto State Road Twenty-Seven."

"Okay. I know the area of Cypress Street. A few years ago I had to investigate a homicide. The victim was a fifty-two-year-old man. Caught the suspect by identifying him from the sole of his tennis shoes. He had—"

"He had an inversion deformity of his right foot called talipes varus. I remember you telling me about the case."

"Matter of fact, you assisted in my investigation. The perpetrator was caught because of you. You steered me to an orthopedic surgeon, who recognized the wear pattern from the shoe imprint left on the bloody kitchen floor."

"You're right. I did."

Twelve minutes later, the female voice from the GPS announced, "Turn right at the next street, Cypress Street."

Sherry sniffed. "I smell smoke. Wood burning."

"I do too." He turned right onto Cypress Street. Up ahead about a hundred yards, fire trucks with their red flashers warning citizens to stay away and two sheriff cruisers with their blinking blue emergency lights were parked in the street in front of a house to their left. Grey smoke plumed from the house as two firehoses held by firefighters sprayed water on the house. He parked his car along the curb about ten houses away from the emergency vehicles. Small groups of neighbors were scattered throughout yards a safe distance from the burning house. Mark peered at the house number across the street to his left: forty-two fifty-four. Blankenship's address was an even number, meaning his house was on the side of the house fire. They got out of the car and stood on the sidewalk. Mark looked at the house number to his left. He then added two even numbers as he counted houses to the house on fire. "Blankenship's house is on fire by my calculations."

"You're absolutely right. I also counted the house addresses from here to Blankenship's house. I hope he's okay."

"Me too. Let's get closer to the house." They walked up to a sheriff deputy who stood on the sidewalk two doors down from the burning house. The paramedics vehicle was parked behind the deputy's car. The medics weren't treating anyone as they stood at the closed rear door of their vehicle. Mark recognized the deputy. "Hey, Matt."

He turned to his left and stared at Mark. "Detective McKinney. What are you doing here?"

"We came here to talk with Peter Blankenship," Mark answered, then looked at the smoldering remains of a small, one-story concrete-blocked house. "He supposed to be living in the house."

"The neighbors believe he and the dogs are in the house. When I got here, the house was in flames. No way could anyone get into the house. Not sure if the fire started on purpose or if it was an accident. Once the house cools down, the fire department's arson people will determine the cause of the fire."

"Also, if Blankenship is in the house, an autopsy could possibly tell if he died due to the fire or was murdered."

"You're right, Detective. And why would you think this might be a murder scene?"

"Dr. McKinney was talking with him when suddenly the phone went dead. We tried to call him back, but his phone wouldn't accept incoming calls. The situation seemed suspicious to us. I guess it's my ingrained thinking as a homicide detective. It never goes away, even after retirement."

"I can believe that. If it turns out this is a homicide death, I'll let the lead detective know what you told me about your interrupted phone conversation with Blankenship."

"Thanks, Matt. And thanks for the information." Mark and Sherry walked back toward their car. He turned to Sherry. "The dogs barking in the background when you were talking with him must've been his dogs. There may have been an intruder or someone he knew had walked into the house. Doesn't matter which scenario, the house caught fire shortly afterward."

"I agree. If an evil act caused the demise of Blankenship, an autopsy should give us the answer."

"It may give an answer to his death but not who was responsible for it. The detectives in the case would have to interview the immediate neighbors and find out if they saw anyone enter and/or leave the house prior to it going up in flames."

They got into the car and Mark turned their vehicle around by pulling into a driveway across the street. Numerous vehicles were parked on the street, more than what were there when they drove up to the scene. A black Suburban backed out of a driveway, then sped away about several car lengths in front of them. "This is the second black Suburban we've seen today. The first one was parked at Northgate Diner."

"Oh. You noticed the Suburban too," Mark replied.

"I make myself aware of my surroundings. Just as you do. You've always stressed this to me since we've been married. You need to anticipate any potential danger, such as a carjacker or mugger, when you're outside, especially in a parking lot."

"Very true, my love." He reached over and patted her hand. "You listen well. Same as I listen to you about getting a medical checkup every year. And that 'an ounce of prevention is…' We know the rest of this saying. Anyway, it appears we won't know what Peter Blankenship wanted to tell us about future spontaneous human combustion victims. My gut feeling is he was killed, and the house fire was intended to cover up any evidence leading to his killer. What do you think?"

"Probably true, but we'll have to wait until his body is found then autopsied. Assumptions don't always turn out to be correct."

"You're right. Concrete evidence is the proof for assumptions." He stopped at the intersection. "Homicide detectives won't be called in to investigate unless foul play in Blankenship's death is determined." Mark turned right on to State Road Twenty-Seven. "Not much we can do now until we hear from Ron. We'll head home." His cell phone rang. He glanced at the caller I.D. "It's Ron. I'll put him on speaker." A short pause. "Hi, Ron. Hopefully, it's good news."

"Henry Baker's cell phone is a throwaway phone. No way to trace it."

"I was afraid of that."

"As for the Toyota 4Runner, its unexpected news, the vehicle…." The phone went silent with no dial tone.

Mark handed the phone to Sherry. A sinking feeling in the pit of his stomach overwhelmed him. "Call him back." Was it coincident the two cell phone calls today suddenly were disconnected? He wasn't a believer in coincidence.

Sherry called Ron, putting the phone on speaker. The phone rang once, followed by, "The number can't be reached at the moment." A frightened expression appeared on her face. "It's the same announcement as was Blankenship's phone call. My God, I hope Ron's okay."

Mark knew they had to drive to Ron's house as fast as they can. An adrenaline surge overtook him as his heart and breathing increased, He grasped the steering tightly as he pressed down on the accelerator. Within a few seconds he exceeded at least ten miles an hour over the speed limit. "Keep calling him back."

"I will," Sherry replied.

Twenty minutes later, Ron's house came into view. Sherry had called Ron's phone number several times with the same announcement from the cell phone server. The house wasn't on fire and his SUV was parked in the driveway. No other vehicle was present. They got out of the car and hurried to the front door. Mark grabbed the front doorknob and turned. It was locked. He rang the doorbell. No answer. Mark rang the doorbell again. No voice over the speaker telling them to come on in, the door was open. He looked at Sherry with a concerned expression and shook his head. The front door began to open. Mark reached for his Glock and stepped back a couple of steps, expecting the worst scenario, a killer standing on the other side of the door.

The door opened. Ron stood in front of them with a smile and holding a can of soda. He glanced down at Mark's Glock pointed at him. "Hey. Were you expecting someone else?"

"Sorry." He holstered his Glock. "To answer your question. Yes. We couldn't call you back, thinking something terrible had happened to you."

"Nothing happened to me. My phone went dead. My battery had plenty of juice. It could've been a malfunction at the cell tower. It's happened before. I think now I'm going to get a landline phone to avoid this situation again."

"We were worried about you," Sherry said. "That something bad had happened to you. I'm glad you're all right."

"It's nice to know someone cares about me." Ron stepped back. "Come on in. We'll talk in the computer room."

Ron stood next to his computers and faced Mark and Sherry. "The Toyota 4Runner was reported stolen in Pensacola five days ago. I got the license plate number at a traffic light intersection security camera near Phillip Frank's house. Unfortunately, the driver and passenger wore caps and sunglasses." Ron turned around and stepped aside allowing a full view of a computer monitor. "As you can see, the picture of them was impossible to get a clear description."

Mark and Sherry stepped forward and peered down at the monitor screen. "You're right," Mark agreed. "It's impossible to make out any facial features of the two guys in the car. They obviously were aware of security cameras at the intersection since both lowered their heads as they passed under the traffic lights. Also, the driver was wearing driving gloves, making it almost impossible to find any fingerprints on the steering wheel, gear shift, door handles, or anything else inside the vehicle." He paused. "We're not dealing with everyday criminals."

"I agree, they're not amateurs?" Ron said after taking a sip from the can of soda.

"These guys anticipate, especially the driver, that someone may be watching them through security cameras, peering eyes from everyday citizens or from law enforcement authorities. They're definitely aware of their surroundings."

"I agree with your thinking," Sherry said, nodding as she glanced up at Mark.

One of Ron's computers blared out a low-pitched rhythmic beep, causing Mark to stare at a monitor screen to the right of the monitor displaying information about the Toyota 4Runner. "What's that beeping mean?" he asked Ron.

"I had the license plate number plugged into a plate identification program," Ron answered as he sat on a swivel chair in front of the computer and began typing rapidly on its keyboard. "It's the 4Runner."

The monitor screen displayed the vehicle pulling into a park. A sign next to the driveway leading into the park read: TOMS PARK. In the upper right corner of the monitor showed today's date and a time. Mark glanced at his watch. "The time on the monitor was two minutes ago."

"You're right," Ron agreed. "There's a surveillance camera at the park's entrance." He continued typing of the keyboard, then, "There's no cameras inside the park."

Mark crossed his arms, resting them on his lower chest wall. "How far is the park from here?"

Ron rapidly moved his fingers over the keyboard. "It's twenty-one minutes away in normal traffic."

Mark peered down at Sherry, who nodded. "Are you ready?"

"Let's do it," she answered.

"Can I go with you guys? I'll bring my laptop in case you need cyber information."

Mark thought for a moment. "It could be dangerous."

"Probably will be dangerous," added Sherry, "if they're the same guys who shot out our car's tire and the power line the other day."

"I live a boring life. I'd love to add excitement to it. I'll stay out of the way if there's a confrontation."

"All right. You can go." *I hope I don't regret it.*

A couple minutes later, Mark backed out of Ron's driveway and sped towards Toms Park in Ocala.

Chapter Ten

Mark turned onto Magnolia Avenue, heading south toward Toms Park. He peered into the rearview mirror at Ron, who had his opened laptop resting on his knees. "Any vehicle activity at the park's entrance?" Ron had hacked into the security camera earlier and left the site open so he could see what vehicles entered and left the park since the Toyota 4Runner entered Toms Park.

"There haven't been any other vehicles entering or leaving the park. Our two suspects are still in the park. At least their vehicle is still in there."

"They could've left the park on foot." Sherry said, adding to the speculation.

"That's true," Mark said as he approached the entrance to the park. *Abandoning suspect's vehicles seems to be a frequent practice the past couple of days.* Hopefully, they'd find the two guys sitting in their car. Mark had to expect the stealthy perpetrators would be armed as he unsnapped a leather strap securing his Glock to its holster. He sighed as he turned left onto the entranceway gravel road to the park. A large pond was to his right. The water was like a sheet of glass without a noticeable ripple. Up ahead about fifty yards away, he saw one car parked on a graveled parking area. There were a variety of trees encompassing Toms Park except surrounding the pond.

"I don't see anyone walking around the park or sitting near the pond," Sherry stated as she peered through the windshield, then her side window.

"Me neither," Ron agreed.

Mark eased up on the gas pedal, slowing their car to ten-miles-per-hour as suspicious thoughts crossed his mind, causing tension in nearly every muscle in his body. He slowly moved up the gravel road toward the suspect's vehicle. The vehicle's tinted side windows prevented him from seeing inside. Something didn't seem right as he now focused on the vehicle in front of them. He stopped their car about ten yards away from the parked 4Runner. It was standard in law enforcement procedures to stop their vehicle a safe distance from a suspect's vehicle. "You guys stay here."

"Be careful," Sherry pleaded.

"I will. Do not get out of the car." Mark placed his hand on the handle of his holstered Glock. The sound of his leather-soled shoes against the gravel interrupted the surrounding stillness. Not even the sound of chirping birds could be heard. Did nature's winged creatures flee the area, knowing something ominous was about to happen?

Mark stopped a foot away from the 4Runner's front passenger side window. He couldn't see any outline of a passenger, and neither was anyone sitting behind the steering wheel. He then stepped to the window behind the front passenger window and peered inside. No one could be seen. Mark grabbed the door handle and pulled. The door opened. A clicking sound emanated from behind the back seat. He leaned into the vehicle and peered over the back seat at a shoebox size apparatus with wires connected to a counter displaying a red colored number fifty-six decreasing every second. His heart began to race, his breathing increased as beads of sweat cascaded down onto his face from his forehead. It was an explosive device set to go off in less than fifty-two seconds.

Mark quickly exited the 4-Runner and ran toward his car. Thank God he had left the car running. If he had driven to the park alone, he would've likely fumbled for the car keys in one of his pants' pockets, then spent time starting the car. It would've wasted several precious seconds. He jumped into the car, put the car in reverse and sped backwards down the road. "There's a bomb inside the SUV ready to go off in several seconds. Duck down." Two thoughts crossed his mind, getting far enough away so the blast wouldn't affect them, and second, hopefully no one decided to drive into the park behind him.

A moment later, the explosion created a large, brilliant flash with a thunderous boom causing their car to momentarily shake. They were now about a hundred yards away. Mark stopped the car. Sherry and Ron raised their upper torso and peered ahead at the smoke and fire coming from the demolished 4Runner.

Sherry asked, "Was there anyone inside the SUV?"

"No. I saw a timer bomb placed over the area of the gas tank. The explosive device was probably triggered when I opened the rear passenger door. Whoever planted the device wanted the intense fire ball to destroy any trace evidence left inside the vehicle." He reached for his cell phone. "I better call 911." He pushed the three numbers on his cell phone.

"911, what is your emergency?" The female dispatcher's voice was firm and direct.

"This is Mark McKinney. We witnessed a car explosion at Toms Park on Magnolia Avenue."

"Was anybody in the vehicle?"

"No."

"Did anyone in the area get injured?"

"No. As far as we could see, there wasn't anyone in Toms Park at the time of the explosion."

"I'll send the fire department."

"You'll need to send bomb squad investigators."

"How do you know a bomb caused the explosion?"

"I saw the explosive device in the back of the SUV. I'm a previous detective for the sheriff's department."

"I thought your name sounded familiar, Detective. I'll let the sheriff's department know what you saw." She then ended the call.

Mark moved their car to the side of the gravel road onto a grassy section. Several minutes later, Ocala Fire Department trucks arrived and dosed the fire with copious amounts of water. The fire chief walked over to Mark, Sherry, and Ron, who stood in front of their car.

"Hey. Detective McKinney. I understand you're the one who called this car fire in?"

"Yes, I am. And I'm Mark McKinney now. I've been retired for two years."

"I know you're retired. You'll always be detective to me. As I'll likely be called chief by my fellow firemen and law enforcement people after I retire. Do you know who owns the vehicle?"

"Yes. But not who was driving it. The Toyota 4Runner was stolen several days ago in Pensacola. We believe it was the vehicle used in the shooting of the front driver side tire of our car on I-75 two days ago."

"Why would someone want to shoot your tire?"

"Not sure. That's what we were trying to find out. Special Agent Morgan from the Florida Department of Law Enforcement is overseeing the shooting incident on I-75. I assume you'll be notifying the ATF regarding the car bomb."

"Yes. As you know it's normal protocol to ask for their assistance. They have all the technology and certified explosive specialists. We'll have our CSU personnel collect all the pieces of the explosive device, at least as much as they can find and send it to the ATF facility at the Gainesville Satellite Office. Since there wasn't any person or persons inside the 4Runner, sheriff department detectives wouldn't be involved into the investigation."

Mark knew he wouldn't have any difficulty obtaining the results of the explosive device and possibly what malevolent group was responsible since he had Ron, who could obtain the information without any trouble. Many explosive devices had a specific signature of how it was put together and what its components were, which could point to a particular group or organization. Mark believed the bomb was constructed by a pro and not an amateur. What bothered him was whoever placed the explosive device inside the vehicle wanted the individual or individuals inspecting the 4Runner killed or at least severely injured. Another unsettling thought flashed across his mind—the car bomb was targeted toward him and Sherry. *If this is true, how would they have known it would be us to track down the 4Runner?* He thanked the fire chief, who then went back toward the now extinguished vehicle. Mark turned to Sherry and Ron. "I have a feeling our car is bugged, and maybe our cell phones too." He told them what he had been thinking.

"You're probably right," Ron said.

"I agree," Sherry added. "It seemed since we encountered the downed power line the other day, the perpetrators have always been one step ahead of us, knowing where we were going to and coming from."

"I have an electronic device at the house," Ron proclaimed, "that can detect any listening bug. I'll use it to check out the car. Matter of fact, I'll use it to check out my house."

"And our house too," Mark interjected. "We shouldn't say anything relevant to our investigation when we're in our car or our houses until we check them out for listening devices."

They got into their car and drove away from Toms Park.

~ * ~

The black Suburban sat in the parking lot of a veterinarian hospital near Toms Park. The passenger peered at the GPS screen. "They're on the move again. Can you believe it? A car exploding in the park. These guys sure are attracted to danger and death. And I thought our job put us in harm's way. After what happened here, I thought we'd have to introduce ourselves to the McKinneys."

"Not yet, according to our higher-ups. We still need to know what these recent cases of spontaneous human combustion were caused from. There's speculation and theory but no scientific proof. Whoever is trying to kill the McKinneys may have the answer. Hiding in the shadows, so to speak, is the right thing to do at this point."

"Yeah. You're right."

The Suburban left the parking lot and made a right turn onto Magnolia Avenue in the same direction as the McKinneys' car.

~ * ~

The drive to Ron's house was uneventful. Nothing relevant to their investigation was talked about between him and Sherry. Mark knew if any listening device was in the car, it would likely be hidden inside the dashboard. They checked underneath the dashboard with their fingertips for any foreign object. Nothing was felt. Although, a listening device could still be hidden, away from prying fingers and eyes. Mark had continued to periodically glance in his sideview mirror for a vehicle following them on their way to Ron's house. He noticed Sherry had been doing the same thing.

Ron unlocked the front door as Mark and Sherry stood outside near the car. A moment later, Ron returned with a device the size of a small transistor radio. He got into the front driver seat and slowly scanned the front of the dashboard, then underneath it.

Mark leaned into the car from the passenger side and observed Ron's meticulous movement over and under the dashboard. The green light at the top of the electronic bug detector never turned to red, which would've meant a listening device was present.

Ron then scanned underneath the front seats, then the entire back seats. He also scanned each of the car's doors. Ron closed the doors and stood next to Mark and Sherry near the front of the car. "The car is clear of any listening devices."

Mark glanced down at the electronic device Ron was holding by his side. A red light was flashing. "Look at your device. It's blinking red."

Ron raised the device up from his side and the light went to green. He moved the device down to in front of the hood of the car. A red light began to flash. "There's something underneath the hood, in the engine compartment. It can't be a listening device. But it could be…" He turned toward Mark. "Open the hood."

Mark opened the driver-side door, reached down, and pushed a button, unlatching the car's hood. He moved around to the front of the car. Ron had already opened the hood.

Ron moved his device to the left over the engine compartment. The light turned green. "There's nothing here. It's got to be on the other side of this fender housing, inside the wheel well. Many people hide a car's extra ignition key in a magnetic key box there." He then slowly moved his device to the right over the engine. When he got to the right of the engine, the device's light turned red. He moved around to the driver-side wheel well, bent down and reached behind the front fender and removed a small, black device the size of nine-volt battery. "It's magnetized and was attached to the metal wall above the area of the driver side wheel housing."

Mark grunted as he peered down at the device. "It's a GPS tracker. Huh. No wonder we never saw a vehicle following us. They could've been a mile behind us. We never would've seen them."

"Do you think it's the guys who were in the 4Runner?" Sherry asked.

"Could be. Who else would want to know where we were or going to, especially when we left Leesburg and headed north on I-75? They would've known exactly where we were, giving them the opportunity to drive in front of us, then shoot out the front tire."

"And the incident with the downed power line when you and Sherry were driving back home after leaving my house. They also would've known where you were on State Road Forty before they shot down the power line."

"Can you have the GPS device analyzed for prints, then find out where this brand is sold? We may get lucky and find out who the perpetrator or perpetrators are and why they were following us to do us harm."

"I can do that. I have the material and equipment to check the GPS device for prints. If I find a print, I'll put it through AFIS. I have this program set up in one of my computers."

"You never told us that you had a forensic lab in your house," Mark said.

"You never asked me," he replied with a grin. "Beside my computer room, I have a room with several forensic apparatuses. It's sort of a hobby of mine. Some people collect stamps, coins, or butterflies, I collect forensic analysis stuff. Of course, any of my results won't hold up in court since I don't have a state license or certification."

"You amaze me," Sherry said reaching out and momentarily touching his forearm.

"I think I will check my house for any listening devices or spy cameras. Why don't you come into the house and relax while I check out my house? Once I'm done, you can take the bug detector with you and check out your house."

"Sounds great to me," Mark answered. He knew if a listening device were put inside a house or vehicle by law enforcement it would have to have a judge's approval via a warrant with just cause. Without approval by a judge, it was illegal in practically every legal jurisdiction to secretly plant a listening device and leave it hidden to record conversation. The same held true for a GPS being planted on a vehicle by law enforcement. Since none of them had done anything illegal, it was unlikely a law enforcement agency would be responsible. More than likely a criminal enterprise would be involved. Mark and Sherry walked into the house. Before closing the front door, he looked out toward the street for a suspicious vehicle. He chuckled to himself as he thought, *What would a suspicious vehicle look like?* There weren't any cars, trucks or SUVs driving by on the street. Mark closed the door.

Ron checked every room in the house for any spyware. Nothing was found. His house was clean of any type of surveillance devices. He gave the electronic bug detector to Mark. "This is how it works. You'll need to turn off your wireless router near your desktop computer which incorporates your Wi-Fi, including your cordless house phone." Ron reached over to the detector, held by Mark. "Flip this power switch on the detector. You'll need to pay attention to the LEDs on the bug detector. If you see a couple of LEDs flicker, it's a weak signal. In other words, the stronger the signal, the brighter the LED lights and the closer you are to a hidden listening device or a spy camera."

"Thanks, Ron, on how your bug detector works. There are several diverse types of these bug detectors or anti-spy detectors. I've used a similar type in the past."

"I've never seen one of these electronic devices before," Sherry interjected. "You'll never know when I personally may need to use one." A grin appeared as she looked up at Mark and raised her eyebrows.

Mark rolled his eyes. "You'll never have to worry about my fidelity, dear. I'm a man who only needs one woman…a one-woman man."

"That would make a good title for a song," Ron said, nodding. Mark and Sherry chuckled. Ron frowned, apparently not sure why they laughed.

"We'll be heading out," Mark stated. "Let us know if you find anything on or about the GPS device."

"Sure will. And let me know if you find any electronic bugs in your house."

"Will do." Mark and Sherry left the house, got into their car, and headed home. "Whoever planted the GPS on our car will think we're staying at Ron's house. Unless we pass by them, and they see us."

~ * ~

The street in front of Ron's house contained many vehicles parked along the curb for several hundred feet either way. About a hundred yards away a black Suburban was parked along the curb facing Ron's house. The passenger held up a tubular monocular device pointed at Mark and Sherry's Chrysler 300 as it drove away from Ron's townhouse. Earlier they had seen Ron remove their GPS device from inside the front driver side wheel housing. Neither could figure out how the trio had suspected a GPS tracker was planted on their car. They parked their Suburban at the side of the street after Ron got out of Mark's car and was looking inside the engine compartment. They never saw Ron searching inside the car with the bug detector. "They're on the move." He peered down at the dashboard's GPS monitor. "There's no movement on the screen. Our device is still active, meaning it was left behind at Ron Baker's house. We know they won't find our fingerprints on the GPS tractor. And they'll never be able to trace the device to us."

"But they now know they were and are being followed. I'll call this in and find out what we should do now."

Chapter Eleven

Mark parked under the carport. The ride home was uneventful as both had peered in their sideview mirrors, Mark also peered in the rearview mirror for a vehicle following them. Neither of them had seen any suspicious vehicles. They got out of the car and walked to the side door. He turned the device on, then unlocked the door. The air conditioner, which was in a closed area adjacent to the kitchen, hummed, sending its cool air through the floor air vents as they walked inside. Then the sound of a grandfather clock in the living room began to chime. After the fifth melodious chime it stopped, announcing five o'clock.

Mark put his index finger to his lips in a gesture of not to talk. He hurried to the room where their desk computer, router and Wi-Fi sat. He turned the router and Wi-Fi off. Mark then meticulously moved Ron's device throughout the room. No blinking light emanated from the bug detector. He then moved from room to room while he'd checked for a listening bug. "I'm done. The good news is we're not being listened to or observed by a mini spy camera by anyone."

Sherry sighed. "Thank goodness. All we know for sure is that someone wants to know our driving track. Telling them our destination…where we've stopped. I'm sure glad you had phone tap detectors installed on our cell phones a few years ago."

"If I weren't a detective, I probably wouldn't have done it. But since I had gotten court orders to tap phone calls, either cell phones or landline phones, on criminal enterprises, it made me aware we should have phone tap detector software programed into our cell phones. Like I've told you about many times over the years, in today's world of cyber criminals, you can never be too cautious."

The front doorbell rang, startling him and Sherry as they stood in the living room. Mark knew most neighbors came to the carport side door, not the front door. He walked to the front door and peered through the peephole in the center of the door. Standing on the front porch were two clean-shaven men wearing white shirts without ties and dark-blue sports coats. He had no idea who the two men were. He opened the door. "Can I help you?"

"We're not here trying to sell you something." He reached into the inside pocket of his coat, removed a leather folder the size of a wallet, then opened it, displaying an official-looking badge with the letters "F. F. A."

"I've never heard of the F.F.A."

"It's a relatively new federal agency. It stands for Federal Forensic Agency. We investigate unsolved medical death cases in the United States. Our credentials are agents with forensic science background. We'll work in conjunction with the FBI and CDC. Can we come in and talk?"

"Sure." Mark stepped back, allowing the agents entry to the small foyer. "This is my wife, Dr. Sherry McKinney. I'm sure you already knew that."

He nodded. "Yes. Please to meet you both. My name is Ed Cosby." He glanced to his left. "This is Ken Cotton."

"Please come into the living room," Sherry suggested.

She and Mark led them toward the living room. Mark felt his muscles tighten, anticipating he and Sherry had done something wrong regarding their investigation of the four spontaneous human combustion deaths. As far as he believed, they hadn't done anything illegal, or broken any laws, local, state, or federal. They entered the living room. "Have a seat on the couch," Mark said, as he pointed to the couch to his right. Sherry sat on a Queen Anne chair across from the two agents. He sat on the same type of chair a few feet away from hers. A long, low mahogany coffee table with an arrangement of three vases with artificial flowers sticking out of them stood between them. Mark turned his attention to Ed. "What can we do for you?"

"We know about you and your wife…and Ron Baker, looking into the deaths of the four spontaneous human combustion victims. Which of course, is not against the law. What we are concerned about is the possible connection between the two incidents which nearly cost you and Dr.

McKinney severe injury or even death, and the spontaneous human combustion victims. This possible scenario caught our attention. We've already contacted the different law enforcement agencies regarding the four deaths, the power line incident and the deliberate shooting of your car tire on I-75. Then there's the death of Peter Blankenship and his two dogs."

"Oh. They found him in his house?" Mark asked.

"Yes. The medical examiner's autopsy may give us the exact cause of his death, along with his two dogs. We'll then know if his death was due to foul play or an unfortunate accident. You and your wife seemed to be a magnet attracting adverse situations."

"We agree. By the way, do you and Agent Cotton drive a black Suburban?"

"Yes. How did you know that? Did you see us drive up?"

"No. Just a guess. We saw a black Suburban parked at Northgate Diner and the same type of vehicle drive away from Blankenship's house fire. I'm also guessing you planted the GPS device on our car."

Ed frowned. "No. We had nothing to do with that. We had no idea someone planted a GPS tracker on your car. We followed you from a distance where you wouldn't notice us. There wasn't a thought about placing a tracking device on your car."

"When did you start following us?" Sherry asked, as she leaned forward.

"We started following you when you left Northgate Diner. We knew you weren't suspects in felonious activities. No. The opposite. We were hoping you and your wife might lead us to a malicious group possibly responsible for the four people dying of spontaneous human combustion deaths."

"I also assume you attempted to tap our phones?"

"No. We did not for two reasons. You're not suspected criminals. And second, you have spyware on your cell phones which would've detected your conversations were being listened in on."

"True on both things." *They obviously tried to bug our phones but found we had spyware installed on them.*

"Why didn't you approach us at Northgate Diner parking lot or at

Blankenship's house fire and tell us your intentions?" Sherry asked.

"Good question, doctor," Agent Cosby answered. "Like we said earlier, we didn't want to interfere with your investigation. Plus, you can do things in an investigation as private citizens we can't do without court-ordered warrants with justified reasons. Such as checking beer cans for DNA without the person's permission in their private home. Since you now know who we are, we can assist each other, sharing information regarding the spontaneous human combustion deaths."

Mark didn't completely trust these agents. He'd have to do an investigation on their agency. He didn't want to cooperate with the agents at this point. At least not until he could be assured the F.F.A. was concerned about finding the cause of the spontaneous human combustion patients and about his and Sherry's well-being. He still felt suspicious about the agents and believed they had planted the GPS tracker on their car. Something didn't seem right. "There isn't any information to share with you. We have no idea what caused the spontaneous human combustion, or if there was anyone responsible for their deaths. You probably know as much as we do."

"Likely true, Detective McKinney. We don't have anything significant to add to these four deaths. As far as your two incidences with the power line and your tire being shot at, please call me if you uncover who might be responsible for it."

"Will do, agent. I appreciate you coming forward and letting us know who you are. But we don't need your assistance right now. We can take care of ourselves. If you can leave me your card, I'll call you if we find out anything relevant to the deaths of the four S.H.C. victims."

Agent Cosby glanced at his partner and squinted with a nod. He then turned, facing Mark, and said, "I can understand your reasoning for not wanting us directly involved with your investigation. Call us if you need help. We will be available twenty-four-seven. Our agency has a state-of-the-art forensic lab." He stood and handed a business card to Mark. His partner also stood. "We will no longer be following you. Be careful."

"I appreciate your concern," Mark said as he and Sherry stood. "Like I said, we can take care of ourselves."

Agent Cosby and Cotton left the house, got into their black Suburban, and drove away as Mark and Sherry stood on the front porch. Sherry laid her hand on Mark's forearm, then said, "Do you think the agents will back off and not follow our every move during our investigation?"

"I've learned over the years to never take what a person of interest or suspect says as being a hundred percent true. They will lie or hold back crucial bits of information. These two agents may have another agenda. If we hadn't found their GPS tracker, would they have come forward and identified themselves?"

"You believe they had planted the GPS tracker?"

"I do."

Sherry furled her forehead. "They probably would've identified themselves after we had solved the spontaneous combustion deaths and/or after we determined who and why someone was trying to kill us."

"I agree. You're sounding like a detective, which is a good thing." They went back into the house and headed for the kitchen when his cell phone rang. He glanced at the caller I.D. It was Ron. He put the phone on speaker. "Hi, Ron."

"I didn't find any fingerprints on the GPS tracker. As far as the manufacturer, this device is sold around the world. No way to trace who bought it."

Mark sat at the kitchen table with Sherry sitting across from him. "I was about to call you."

"Did you find any listening bugs in your house?"

"No. It was clean. As far as the GPS tracker, we know who planted it." Mark told him about the two agents and who they represent.

"Holy crap. This is becoming like a Tom Clancy thriller novel. We have the Ocala police officers, sheriff detectives, state police detectives and now an agency working with the FBI and CDC."

"I'm assuming you never heard of the Federal Forensic Agency?"

"No. News to me."

"Can you do your computer magic and find out everything about this agency?"

"Sure will. I'll get on it right away. Call you back when I get it."

Mark put his cell phone back into its carrier as Sherry got up from the table and said, "I'll warm up the ziti I made yesterday. Does the ziti sound all right with you?"

"That'll be good. I'll make us a tossed salad to go with it." As he was preparing the salad, his thoughts focused on the guy who called himself Henry Baker and his possible involvement with Fred Cramer's death, his interest with the Parkers, and his relationship with the guy driving the Toyota 4Runner. Baker was the prime suspect in their investigation. They had to find him, for he likely held the answer to these scenarios. What was the....

"Mark," Sherry interrupted, "are you done with the salad?"

"Yes. I'm almost done," he replied as he placed chunks of fresh tomatoes and slices of cucumbers into the salad. *What was the reason Baker or whoever he worked for wanted us dead?*

After eating, putting their dishes and utensils into the dishwasher, they went into the living room. Mark sat in his recliner chair and Sherry sat on the couch, each of them holding a glass containing ice cubes, rum, and cola. "It feels good to relax," Sherry admitted.

"I agree, it sure does. Do you realize if we hadn't gone to check out the Parkers, we probably would've had a peaceful, relaxing past two days, don't you think? The decisions we'd have to make would've been what movie we'd want to see at Ocala Center 6 and where to eat dinner afterwards."

"You're absolutely right. After we're done with our investigation, we'll need to take a vacation, away from our community and from people wanting us to check out something suspicious in the neighborhood."

"I'll second your idea. Plus, we'll need to turn off our cell phones or leave them home on our vacation. That way we'd be guaranteed not to be bothered." His cell phone rang. He glanced at the caller I.D. "It's Ron." He put the phone on speaker. "Hey. What did you find out about F.F.A.?"

"They're for real. The Federal Forensic Agency was established eighteen months ago to work in conjunction with the FBI and CDC. The F.F.A.'s paramount purpose is to investigate nontraumatic suspicious deaths of undetermined cause. They're different from the FBI's Evidence Response Team which investigates a variety of traumatic event such as an explosion, exposure to radiation, chemical, biological, radiological, or nuclear materials. Or from a plane/train crash, or a boat sinking."

"This makes me feel better about the two agents…that they were legitimate."

"I never said the agents were legitimate."

"What are you saying?"

"There are F.F.A. agents with the names Cosby and Cotton. The problem is, according to their personnel records, they're assigned to the San Francisco office. Unless they were recently reassigned to the Gainesville office and weren't posted in their human resource records yet."

"Can you send me the photos of Agents Cosby and Cotton?"

"Sure. I'll send them to your cell phone."

"Thanks. Talk to you after I get their photo. Bye."

Mark disconnected their conversation. A moment later, his cell phone chimed indicating a text message. He went to text message. Two photographs appeared. They weren't the agents who came to their house. He showed Sherry the photos.

Sherry frowned with puzzlement. "Who were the two guys at our house?"

"No idea. I'm sure they left our house thinking we'd never check their photographs, and we'd go on thinking they were agents for the F.F.A. I'll call Ron and let him know of the imposters." Seconds later he called Ron and told him the discrepancy.

"Another piece not fitting into our puzzle," Ron said. "Did any of these guys touch anything I could get a fingerprint from?"

"Good question." He thought a moment. "The one thing they could've touched was the doorbell button. I doubt they left a fingerprint…they're too smart to leave any forensic evidence."

"Yeah. You're probably right."

"Agent Cosby or whatever his real name is gave me his business card with a phone number. I'm sure the number is real. My assumption is they want to find out what we know or who we suspect in the spontaneous human combustion deaths because they're involved and know what caused it. Their ploy to collaborate with us which they believe will give them the upper hand. There's an ancient adage from philosopher Sun Zhu that fits this situation with these two imposters. 'Keep your friends close and your enemies closer.' In other words, keep on top of what your enemies are doing."

"I don't think they'll suspect us knowing they're imposters," Sherry said. "And from what you told me over the years as a sheriff detective, most criminals will use burner cell phones, making it impossible to trace them."

Mark smiled. "You absolutely correct, my dear."

"Where do we go from here?" Ron asked.

"We play along with them and let them believe we think they're Agents Cosby and Cotton. We can use them to our advantage. Even though we didn't find any listening bugs in our vehicles or houses, we still need to be careful what we say to each other when we're in public. They may have enhanced listening devices pointed at us. The advancement of listening devices can pick up a conversation fifty yards away. Don't you agree Ron?"

"No doubt about it. Almost every building or store you walk into today has an eye-in-the-sky surveillance camera in the ceilings. Almost every traffic light street intersection has a camera pointed at you as you drive through, and cameras attached to buildings and homes. Big Brother is watching over you. The next thing will be audio sonar listening in on people's conversations as they walk down the street or in commercial buildings. The fact being this type of technology may already be happening."

"That's a scary thought," Sherry said.

~ * ~

The black Suburban had left the Clifton Retirement Community and headed south on State Road Four Forty-One.

"Do you think they believed we were agents for the Federal Forensic Agency?" asked the man sitting in the front passenger seat, who called himself Agent Cotton.

"I'm sure they did. They'll call the agency and confirm we are agents there. Plus, I gave Detective McKinney my official-looking F.F.A. business card. Our decoy has worked a couple of times before over the past year. No reason it won't work with the McKinneys."

"What are we going to do now?"

"Drive to Infinity Forensic Lab with an official-looking FBI federal subpoena to obtain the three beer cans taken from Phillip Frank's house by the McKinney's and get the results of Henry Baker's DNA. The lab closes at eight o'clock, giving us plenty of time to get these incriminating items."

"I love when we represent ourselves as FBI agents. It gives me a high, seeing people cringe with fear when we pull out our I.D. with the agency's official-looking badge."

Chapter Twelve

Mark and Sherry spent the evening relaxing and playing a card game. The following morning, they ate breakfast and headed for the hospital to check Phillip Frank's condition. A cool morning, fall air and cloudless sky met them as they walked outside to their car under the carport.

"An orthopedic surgeon would've repaired Frank's fractured hip yesterday," Sherry stated. "He'll be alert and out of excruciating pain with discomfort pain at the site of the surgery."

They walked into Phillip's room. He was sitting up in bed. "Hi, Mr. Frank," Mark said. "How are you doing?"

"I guess as good as you could be after the doctor stuck metal pins into my broken hip," he answered with a grumpy old man demeanor. "By the way, I didn't thank you yesterday at my house for calling EMS. I might have lain on the floor who knows how long if you and your wife hadn't shown up."

"Glad we could help. Did Henry Baker happened to call you?" Mark asked as he glanced at Phillip's cell phone sitting on the nightstand next to the bed.

"No. No one called me. I checked the phone before you two showed up."

"Maybe you should call Henry and let him know you're in the hospital?" Mark didn't call his cell phone number, knowing the guy wouldn't answer any questions. Otherwise, when they first talked with Phillip at the front door, Henry would've introduced himself, instead of hiding behind the door.

"Yeah. I probably should give him a call?"

"Plus, I'd like to ask him a couple of questions. But first, let him know you broke your hip."

Phillip reached over and picked up his cell phone, then dialed Baker's number. He held his phone a few inches from his mouth. A puzzled expression emerged. "What the hell? That's strange."

"What's wrong?"

"The operator said the phone number is no longer in use."

Mark knew why but didn't want to tell Phillip. Baker was trying to cover his tracks, and he didn't want his billiard friend or anyone else to be able trace him by using a throw-away cell phone. "Too bad." He glanced down at Sherry. "We're going to get going. I'm glad you're doing okay."

Mark and Sherry left the hospital, got into their car, and headed for Forensic Infinity Lab. The DNA on Henry Baker should have been completed by now based on his previous drop-offs of items at the lab. The elusive suspect might finally be identified if his DNA was in OBIS. The parking lot of the lab was to their left.

"Can't wait to find out who Henry Baker is," Sherry said. "With everything that has happened the past couple of days, somehow this guy is involved."

"I agree," Mark replied as he parked in front of the entrance to the lab building.

He and Sherry walked up to the receptionist, Carol Robbins. "Hi, Ms. Robbins. I'm here to pick up the results from the DNA analysis on the beer cans."

"Sure. Let me check," Carol stated as she typed on the computer keyboard in front of her. "Oh, my," she said as she wrinkled her forehead.

"What's wrong. The results aren't done, yet?"

"No. Federal agents were here yesterday evening with a subpoena and confiscated the DNA results along with the three beer cans."

"Federal agents? Which federal agency?"

"The Federal Bureau of Investigation according to the subpoena."

A sudden frigid wave encompassed Mark's body. Agents Cosby and Cotton flashed across his mind. Mark turned toward Sherry. "The two agents must've left our house yesterday evening and driven directly to the lab." He turned back to the receptionist. "Can you connect me to Silas Benson? I'd like to talk with him." Silas was the CEO of the lab, and Mark hoped he'd validate the subpoena.

"Mr. Benson, I have Detective McKinney standing here. He'd like to talk with you." She handed Mark the phone.

"Hi, Silas."

"Hey, Mark. What can I do for you?"

"I brought in three empty beer cans for analysis of DNA yesterday. A federal agency came to the lab with a federal subpoena yesterday evening and confiscated the cans, including any results of DNA. Can you verify the subpoena was legitimate?"

"My God. I didn't know they were here. I just got here and haven't had a chance to read my memos. You don't think the subpoena was real?"

"No. I believe the agents were imposters."

"Come up to my office."

"We'll be right there."

"We'll? Who's with you?"

"Sherry."

"Sure. It'll be good to see the two of you."

Benson and his wife were members of the Moose Lodge, as were Mark and Sherry. Periodically they'd see each other at Moose Lodge events. A couple minutes later Mark and Sherry walked into the CEO's office. Silas was talking with someone on the phone.

"So, no one in your agency had subpoenaed our DNA results." Several seconds past as Silas apparently was listening to the person at the other end of the call. "Thank you. We'll be contacting our sheriff department on this matter." He placed the phone back on its cradle, then looked up at Mark. "You're right, the subpoena was a fake."

"Can we checkout the security cameras CDs? We might be able to recognize the two imposters."

"You sure can." He stood, then added, "Why would they want the DNA results from the three beer cans?"

"Don't know for sure. Other than they're concerned about anyone knowing the identity of the person who drank from the beer cans at Phillip Frank's house."

The three of them went to a small room down the hallway from the CEO's office. A plate on the door read "Security Room." Four monitors sat on a long table against the far wall. A young man in his late twenties sat at a swivel desk chair. The CEO asked him to retrieve the videos from around seven o'clock last night. A moment later, two men wearing caps with the letters FBI on front of the caps stood in front of the receptionist desk. Their faces were difficult to identify because the brims of their caps were pulled slightly downward. It was obvious to Mark the agents didn't want their face totally visualized on the security cameras, but Mark was sure it was the two guys who came to their house yesterday posing as F.F.A. agents. Security cameras showed them walking down the first-floor hallway and getting into an elevator. They hid their faces by looking downward at the hallway and elevator floor, away from ceiling cameras preventing a full view of their faces. They got off at the second floor. Again, no full view of their faces as the two agents walked into a room.

"None of the lab rooms have security cameras," Silas stated.

"These guys are pros, knowing to avoid the security cameras. More than likely, we won't find any fingerprints on the subpoena."

"How do we know that?" Sherry asked.

"Go back to the security video when the two FBI agents were standing at the front reception desk."

The technician brought up the video on the computer monitor.

"You see one of the agents handing the subpoena to the receptionist. Look how he hands the folded subpoena to her, he didn't touch the surface of the folded paper, only its edges. I'm sure the subpoena had been wiped clean of fingerprints, sweat or skin cells to avoid identification."

The door behind them opened. Ms. Page, the lab technician who received the three beer cans to check for DNA walked into the room. On the way out of the CEO's office earlier, Silas had his secretary call Ms. Page and have her meet them in the security room. "Hi, everyone. Got here as fast as I could."

"I have a question to ask you," Silas said. "How far along were you on obtaining DNA from the beer cans?"

"I hadn't started yet. When I got back to my lab, I had to help another tech complete an analysis on a priority case. I planned to start on Detective McKinney's DNA request first thing this morning. Of course, I couldn't since federal agents yesterday evening seized the three beer cans."

The news devastated Mark as he gazed at the floor, thinking Ms. Page had at least a sample of the DNA from one of the cans. It was becoming disheartening—every time they were close to solving a clue in their investigation, something unexpectedly prevented them from obtaining an answer. Mark thanked everyone for their assistance, especially Silas. As he and Sherry left the building, he said, "I wonder if Henry Baker left his DNA on something else at Phillip Frank's house? Such as a cigarette butt or utensils. I'm going to call Mr. Frank and ask him if Baker smoked or had eaten anything needing a spoon or fork."

"Someone smoked. I smelled the distinct odor of cigarette residue in the house. You should ask Frank when you talk with him."

Mark grinned. "Thank you. Will do, Dr. Watson."

"It's elementary, Mr. Holmes."

Mark pushed the icon on his car key remote, unlocking the car doors. "I think we got that reversed. Anyway, no matter."

Mark and Sherry sat in the car. He dialed Frank's cell phone number. The phone rang twice. "Hello," said a female.

The nurse must've picked up the phone. "Can I talk with Mr. Frank?"

"Who is this?"

"I'm Mark McKinney. My wife and I visited him this morning. I need to ask him something."

"Detective McKinney?"

"Yes. I'm him. At least…"

"Your wife is Dr. Sherry McKinney?"

"Yes."

A short pause prevailed, then, "I'm sorry to inform you but Mr. Frank died about thirty minutes ago. He apparently had a heart attack or a stroke."

A flushing sensation enveloped his body. "Dang. Can't believe it. He seemed fine this morning when we were talking with him."

"I can't say anything more. I wasn't supposed to give out any information regarding a patient due to HIPPA regulations. Your wife will know the possible complications of hip surgery in an elderly patient."

"Thank you. Goodbye." He peered at Sherry. "Phillip Frank died of a heart attack or stroke. The nurse said you'd know why."

"Mr. Frank having a myocardial infarction, pulmonary embolus, or cerebral embolism isn't rare after hip surgery or major trauma. An embolus from the site of the fracture can travel to the heart, lungs and possibly the brain through the vascular system and block the blood flow through any of these anatomical sites. Since Mr. Frank was over sixty-five it increased this probability. Of course, there could've been other circumstances causing his death, such as an underlying heart disease or blood vessel anomalies to name a few. An autopsy should be able to reach a diagnosis and cause of death."

Mark chuckled to himself. If he weren't married to a doctor, he wouldn't have understood fifty percent of what she said. "He could've died of someone's intervention?"

Sherry shook her head back and forth, raised her eyebrows, then answered, "Being a detective with a natural skeptical thinking, it could be a possibility. Again, an autopsy should determine Mr. Frank's death."

"Since we can't ask Mr. Frank permission to enter his house and retrieve any items Henry Baker could've used, I think we'll go to Frank's house and search for these items."

"Wouldn't we be breaking and entering?"

"Not unless Mr. Frank gave us permission. Who's to say he didn't give us permission?" Mark knew Phillip Frank didn't have any children and his one living relative was a brother with senile dementia living in a Michigan nursing home. "No harm, no foul."

"Isn't that a basketball saying?"

"True. But we can loosely apply it to this situation," Mark answered, as he turned the car's ignition key. He drove out of the parking lot and headed for Frank's house. "When we get to the house, we'll have to look for a house key around the front porch. Most people, especially people in the retirement age group, hide a front or back-door key somewhere near the doors."

"Why would we search for a door key? I left the front door unlocked when we left the house behind the paramedics."

"Unbelievable. Even after all our years together, you still amaze me at times."

"I'll take that as a compliment."

"Why did you leave the front door unlocked?"

"Intuition, I guess. I had a feeling I should leave it unlocked."

About fifteen minutes later, Mark noticed a large plume of black smoke off in the distance sky, in the direction of Phillip Frank's house. A sinking feeling in the pit of his stomach developed. "Look at the smoke up ahead to the left."

"Do you think it's Mr. Frank's house?"

"God, I hope not. One house fire in our investigation is enough."

"I agree."

After traveling through six more intersections, Mark turned onto the street Phillip Frank lived on. Up ahead to their left black smoke streaked toward the sky as visible flames streaked out windows. Two fire trucks were parked on the street as fire fighters attached hoses to a fire hydrant four houses down from the raging fire. Mark parked the car several houses away from the firetrucks. They got out and watched two firefighters, holding separate hoses, point a roaring stream of water bursting from its nozzle onto the raging fire. Mark could feel the heat from the intense fire. "Thank God, to our knowledge there isn't anyone or an animal inside the house. Nothing would survive this fire."

Sherry nudged Marks forearm with her elbow. "Including any evidence that would've identified our mystery guy, Henry Baker."

Mark looked around for a black Suburban and the two F.F.A. agent imposters. Neither the vehicle nor imposters could be seen. For the fire to be at this stage, someone would've had started the fire within the past thirty minutes unless a delay technique came into play such as a timer attached to a volatile accelerant igniting the surrounding area in the house. If that was the case, the firebomb could've been placed in the house after the paramedics transported Phillip out of the house yesterday. The fire marshal and the fire inspector's team would hopefully determine the cause of the fire. The possibility the fire was caused by a faulty wire, a short in one of the appliances, cooling system or a careless cigarette was at the bottom of Mark's list for causes of house fires. "There isn't much we can do now." They got into the car, turned around and drove away from the burning house. He continued to glance around, looking for familiar faces such as the fake F.F.A. and FBI agents, or the elusive Henry Baker. None of these perpetrators were seen in the immediate area. His cell phone rang. He pulled over to the curb and stopped. He glanced at the caller I.D. It was Agent Cosby. Mark put the call on speaker. "Yes, Agent Cosby."

"Hey. I got some sad news. Phillip Frank died at the hospital following his hip surgery. I thought you'd want to know."

Mark didn't want to say to the agent he already knew about Frank's unexpected death. It was best to play surprised. The F.F.A. imposter might slip and say what he died from if in fact they were somehow involved in his death. "Wow. What a surprise. Do you know what he died from?"

"Probably a heart attack. Anything new with you and your wife in your investigation?"

He's waiting for me to say the FBI went to Infinity Forensic Lab and confiscated the evidence which would identify the mystery man, Henry Baker. "No. nothing new. We're at a standstill." *He will obviously think we haven't checked up on the DNA results from the forensic lab yet.* "I appreciate you calling and letting me know about Mr. Frank."

"No problem. If you learn anything relevant to the spontaneous human combustion victims, give me a call. And as I said the last time we talked at your house, let me know if you find out who the shooters were of the power line and your car tire."

"Will do, Agent Cosby. Have a good day. Bye." Mark put his cell phone back into its belt holster. This was the second time the guy calling himself Agent Cosby had asked about the two shootings. If they were truly F.F.A. agents, why would they think the two shootings were related to the four SHC victims? Unless they were involved with the shootings or the organization they worked for wanted to know when we get close to solving the mysteries. He turned and told Sherry what he was thinking.

"You're right. All they events are somehow connected. Unlikely these events weren't connected. Whoever is responsible want us to be involved in a tragic accident and not an outright assassination of us, which would draw attention of law enforcement at a federal level."

"It does tell us one thing. We're obviously getting too close to the truth." Mark put the car in drive and pulled away from the curb.

"It's almost noon," Sherry said looking at the car dash clock. "Let's go to lunch."

He raised the right corner of his mouth in a half smirk. "At least this should be an enjoyable event." His cell phone rang. There wasn't anywhere to pull over to take the call.

"I'll answer the call." Sherry grabbed his cell phone from its holster. "It's Ron." She put the phone on speaker. "Hi, Ron."

"Oh. Are you with Mark?"

"Yes. He's driving the car. I got you on speaker."

"I just heard about the autopsy results on the fire victim, Peter Blankenship."

Chapter Thirteen

"What is it?" Mark asked. Blankenship was the one person who more than likely knew if the spontaneous human combustion victims were a freak of nature or initiated by human hands.

"The medical examiner reported there wasn't any smoke residue in Blankenship's lungs, meaning he was dead prior to the fire. There weren't any signs of trauma to his body. As for the cause of the victim's death after completion of the autopsy, it was death of undetermined cause until the results of the toxicology are completed. Toxicology should be done tomorrow."

Sherry cleared her throat. "About ten percent of all autopsies are diagnosed as undetermined death."

"What about the two dogs?" Mark asked. "Had the vet completed the necropsy?"

"Yes. Both of Blankenship's dogs died of smoke inhalation. There weren't any signs of trauma to the dogs. As with their owner, the toxicology report hasn't been completed yet."

Mark sighed as he shook his head in a negative gesture. "Another waiting period for an answer. Hopefully, these tests don't disappear or are taken by the bad guys?"

"Why would you think that?" Ron asked.

Mark told Ron the situation with the three beer cans.

"You got to be kidding me? Whoever these bad guys are they seem to be one step ahead of us. Hold on, I'm hearing some unbelievable news from across the room." About fifteen seconds passed, then, "Two more cases of spontaneous human combustion were reported."

Mark couldn't believe it. He glanced at Sherry, who frowned, then mumbled something. "What do you think?"

Sherry answered, "There has to be a catalytic substance or process causing this phenomenon. There's no other logical explanation. All the known theories, including the 'wick effect', where a candle's wick needs wax to continue its flame. Some scientists believe human fat is the wax, the flammable substance capable of accelerating and spreading the internal fire. The major question is, why had we only seen about thirty cases of spontaneous human combustion in the past three hundred years? And now there's been six cases of this devastating phenomenon the past few days."

"Where did they find them?" Mark asked as he stopped for a traffic signal's red light.

"Belleview. The elderly couple were found sitting together on the couch. The ash silhouette outlined their sitting position according to one of the forensic investigators. The daughter found them a few hours ago when she stopped by her parent's house."

Sherry sighed, as she peered down toward her legs. "Seeing them lying there in ashes had to be a horrifying sight for the daughter."

"Can't imagine it," Ron commented.

"Do you know if they had any medical issues?" Mark asked. "Or if they were obese?"

"I'll find out and call you back."

"Thanks. Talk to you later." Sherry placed Mark's cell phone back into its holster. Mark pulled onto northbound I-75. The traffic was moderate with a sizable percentage of commercial trucks. He couldn't set the cruise control due to the congested traffic as he drove in the center lane of the three-lane expressway. Again, he and Sherry looked around for vehicles with roll down back windows. A semi-truck with a tractor-trailer in front of him was blocking his view, which made him uncomfortable. He'd like to know what lay ahead of him on an expressway or any road, matter-of-factly. Mark peered in his sideview mirror. No vehicle preventing him from getting into the left lane. He pushed down on the accelerator, increasing his speed as he pulled into the fast lane where semi-trucks weren't allowed to stay in for any period. He was travelling about eighty miles per hour, easily passing the vehicle that was blocking his forward view. Without warning, their vehicle began to speed up without him pushing down on the accelerator. He applied pressure to the brake for several seconds to slow down the car. The

Chrysler 300 continued to accelerate. He reached forward and turned the ignition key. It wouldn't move. Beads of sweat cascaded down from his forehead as his breathing and heart rate increased. "What the hell's going on?"

"What's wrong, Mark?" Sherry blurted with panic in her voice.

"I can't slow our car down. The accelerator must be stuck. And the brakes aren't working." He glanced at the speedometer. Ninety miles per hour.

"Turn the engine off," Sherry said anxiously.

"I already tried. It won't turn off."

The vehicle in front of him was about fifty yards away and getting closer. Mark reached down and moved the gear shift to neutral. The engine continued to roar but the forward momentum of the car began to slow down. The car ahead of him got closer. There were vehicles in the center lane making it impossible to merge into the lane. The last option was to cautiously drive to the narrow concrete area adjacent to the guard rail separating the north and south bound traffic. Like he did a couple of days ago when the front driver side tire suddenly began to lose air pressure due to a bullet penetrating the rubber and steel belt, Mark grasped onto the steering wheel firmly as he moved left onto the area adjacent to the median.

He again pressed firmly down on the brake pedal for several seconds. Nothing happened. Mark glanced down at the speedometer, sixty-five miles per hour and slowly dropping. The front and back driver side tires ran over the ribbed caution strips, creating a piercing cry and telling the driver he was leaving the safety of the concrete expressway. Up ahead stood a bridge with a center abutment infringing upon the median, narrowing the space between the left lane and the median concrete strip his car was driving on. The traffic in the left, center and right lanes weren't slowing down as the flow of cars, SUVs and trucks continued its track toward the bridge. Mark glanced down at the speedometer. Forty miles per hour stared back at him. "I'm not sure we'll stop in time before we hit the bridge abutment…brace yourself."

The bridge was getting closer…closer…closer. Mark leaned back, pressing his back against the seat. The final several seconds, he closed his eyes with anticipation of his air bag slamming him in the face when the front of the car crashed into the concrete pillar. He reached over to his right and grasped Sherry's hand.

Clunk! His body moved forward not any more than an inch. The air bag didn't engage against his upper body or face. Mark opened his eyes. He stared at the bridge abutment. The car's engine roared. He leaned forward and turned the ignition key to the off position. The engine stopped. The sound of vehicles passing them were heard. They had avoided another catastrophe. He peered at Sherry. "Are you okay?"

"I'm fine. I was wondering why you couldn't initially turn the engine off with the ignition key."

"Not sure why. I should've been able to turn the key to accessory position, which should've shut down the engine but allowed the steering and brake mechanism to function normally. Putting the car in neutral was plan B if plan A didn't work."

"Thank God, you learned the maneuver at the sheriff's department, and then taught me. Although, I never had to use this knowledge yet. Do you think what happened was a misfortunate malfunction of our car?"

"I'm not so sure. This is the second incident with our car on I-75 in the past two days. I'm starting to wonder if I should avoid I-75 for a while? At least until we find out who's trying to stop us in our investigation. When I was a detective, I never had so many perilous incidences investigating a case." Mark removed the key from the ignition. "We better call a tow truck. Can't take a chance the accelerator won't stick again."

After calling the tow truck company, a Florida Highway Patrol's black-and-white car pulled up behind them with its flashers on. The patrol officer walked up to the driver side window, which Mark had already opened. "You folks having a problem?"

"Yes, we are trooper." Mark explained to the trooper what had happened to their car, then told the trooper a tow truck service had been called.

"I'm glad you two are okay. Can I have…"

Mark handed the trooper his license, registration, and proof of insurance before the trooper finished his request.

"I see you've done this before." He glanced at Mark's driver license. "I thought your car looked familiar Detective McKinney. We got a memo regarding the shooting along with the description of your car, and that you were a retired Marion County Sheriff detective. I-75 seems to be bringing out harrowing events against you and your car."

"We'll be taking alternate roads after today for a while."

The trooper nodded with a smirk. "I'll wait here until the tow truck gets here and secures your car. Y'all have a good and safe day." He handed Mark his driver's license, insurance card and registration.

"Thank you," Mark glanced at his silver name plate attached to his shirt, "Trooper Collins."

Thirty minutes later, a tow truck pulled up behind their car as the trooper diverted left lane traffic to the center and right lane. The driver pulled the Chrysler 300 backwards with cable attached to a winch, enabling the tow truck to safely pull the car about thirty feet away from the bridge abutment. He then drove to the front of the car and lifted the front end of the car onto a T-shaped left. Mark and Sherry got into the cab of the tow truck. Mark waved to the trooper as they pulled onto the expressway, and eventually getting into the right lane.

"Where do you want me to take your car?" Asked the tow truck driver.

"To the dealership," Mark answered.

When they got to the dealership, a male customer service representative, who appeared to be in his late twenties, told Mark they would have a mechanic look at their vehicle right way. Mark and Sherry sat in the service waiting room. After drinking their first cup of coffee, the male service representative walked up to them as they sat in cushioned armchairs facing a TV with no audio, only captions at the bottom of the screen.

"Hi, the mechanics found the problem with your accelerator. It was a broken accelerator link."

"Is it common for the accelerator link to break?"

"Not common, but it does happen. Although, there's more to what caused the linkage to malfunction. Somehow one of the three bolts was missing from the linkage, causing the other two bolts to loosen. When you pushed down on the gas pedal it caused the accelerator linkage cable to advance forward unimpeded once you reached seventy-five miles per hour."

"That's exactly what happened," Mark said, as he visualized the moment on I-75 when he sped up to eighty miles per hour moving from the center lane to the left lane to pass the truck blocking his view of the road straight ahead of him.

"Had someone recently been working on your accelerator linkage?"

"No. Not to my knowledge." Mark had a feeling someone had tampered with his accelerator linkage. But there wasn't any way to prove it. He'd have to have unquestionable evidence that someone tried to sabotage his car for him to contact the Florida Highway Patrol and let them know about someone had sabotaged his car's accelerator linkage."

"Unfortunately, the damage isn't covered under your car warranty. I wish I had better news. Fortunately, no one was hurt. Which is a blessing. Your bill is at the cashier's window. Y'all have a good and safe day." He shook both their hands.

This has to be the saying of the day, Mark thought. "Thank you."

~ * ~

When they were driving away from the dealership, Sherry concentrated on the six cases of SHC and what or who could have been responsible for it occurring. It was against all her medical and scientific reasoning the phenomena were random acts. A mediator with a substance either chemical or a microscopic entity had been introduced to the six victims, causing their demise. Although there were theories of how spontaneous human combustion occurred in humans. The "wick effect" was one, but there are other theories—an extreme build-up of static electricity inside the body, or a dangerous accumulation of methane in the body. Mast cell activation syndrome, a chemical release of substances into fat cells causing heat generation inside the body. None of these theories had ever been scientifically proven. There have been about two hundred cited reports of spontaneous human combustion worldwide over a three-hundred-and-eighty-year period since 1641. That was about fifty people every hundred years. Five victims every ten years. And two and a half deaths every five years.

"You seem to be in deep thought," Mark said as he slowed the car down and stopped for a red light.

"I'm thinking about the six SHC victims. This number of victims is normally seen over a ten-year period throughout the world. I'm not sure how we're going to find out the cause. The death of Blankenship eliminated us from learning the how, who and why of the spontaneous human combustion victims."

The traffic light turned green. Mark continued to drive, and as he passed through the intersection, his cell phone rang. He glanced at the caller I.D., then handed the phone to Sherry. "It's Ron."

"Hi, Ron. We're in the car. I have you on speaker."

"I got more information regarding the couple in Belleview dying of SHC this morning." A short pause. "The man's name is Ralph Clemens, He's seventy-one and a retired clinical psychologist from Lowell Correctional Institution. His wife, Rose Clemens, is seventy and a retired Marion County social worker. Mr. Clemens had high blood pressure and a normal BMI of twenty-four point five. So, he wasn't obese but normal weight. His wife didn't have any medical issues and had a normal weight with a BMI of twenty-two point five. I did a computer check and didn't find any connection between them or the other two couples with spontaneous human combustion. As far as I could find, they didn't know each other, attend the same church or social organization. Although, I did find something interesting after rechecking the three couples."

"What did you find out?" Mark asked as he turned into a gas station and pulled up to a gasoline pump.

"They all had used a microwave oven the evening prior to their deaths. Not sure it means anything. In each of the C.S.I. reports the criminalist mentioned on top of the garbage bags in the kitchen of the first two couples were microwave products—TV dinner cartons and an empty microwave popcorn bag on the couch of the third couple. A lot of people eat microwaved products."

Sherry couldn't think of any link between the microwave and the victims. Even though there hadn't been any theories of spontaneous human combustion and microwaves didn't mean there couldn't be a connection. "I never heard of microwave ovens causing spontaneous human combustion. Plus, there's one problem regarding the theory, Ron. Microwave ovens have been around for a brief period of time, not hundreds of years."

"Somewhat true," Ron said. "I did a little research on the subject of microwave oven. Ninety percent of American households today have one. The first microwave oven appeared in 1947 at a restaurant. It wasn't until 1976 when fourteen percent of homes had a microwave oven due to the fact its size was reduced to fit on a kitchen countertop."

"I was one of the fourteen percent of modern women who owned one," Sherry added. "If these six victims were affected by the microwave which somehow caused their spontaneous human combustion, why only them? Millions of Americans use microwave ovens every day. It's probably a coincidence."

"You know my feelings about coincidence," Mark commented, as he reached out and pushed a button, unlocking the gas cover. "The microwave ovens owned by our three couples might be different. Somehow, we'll need to get them analyzed by our forensic lab. We won't have a problem retrieving the Parkers' microwave oven but the other two will be more difficult to get. This theory may turn out to be for naught but since we don't have any other possible cause for SHC, we'll follow through with this possibility. From all my years as a detective, I've seen bizarre murders and deaths from unlikely causes."

"All we'll need is the Parkers' microwave," Ron suggested. "If the cause of these six deaths were these three microwave ovens, we'll need to examine at least one of them. I know the exact CSI person who can evaluate the microwave. She's an electronic expert and she'll know if there's something unusual about it."

"I figured you'd know who could examine it. Will she come to your house to examine the microwave?"

"Yes. She's been at my house before. We're pretty…anyway, I

know she'll want to help us. I'll give her a call right now. If it's okay, I'll put you on hold."

"No problem. I'll wait."

"It sounds like we're acquiring an unofficial investigative team," Sherry said.

"Okay with me. We can use all the forensic knowledge we can get."

About a minute past when Ron announced, "I'm back, boss. Sorry. I mean Mark. Stephanie said she'd love to help us. She'll be at my house around six-thirty. I'll be home about five-thirty. Once I get the make and model with serial number of the Parkers' microwave, I can check and see where the Parkers purchased their microwave by searching through their credit card purchases over the past five years. If it's not there, I'll increase my search to the past ten years. There's a computer program I have at home that can search for the purchase. I'll also search their bank checking account. A lot of people write down in the memo section at the bottom of the check what was purchased."

"I'll call you back when we get the information off the Parkers' microwave oven," Mark replied, "which should be in less than thirty minutes. We'll be at your house around five-thirty with the microwave oven."

"I'll start on it as soon as I get home. Talk to you later."

Mark filled up the gas tank, got into the car, then said, "We'll go to the Parkers' house and get their microwave oven."

"So…another B & E, huh?"

"Technically yes. But we're following up on their deaths and gathering information which may lead to their cause of death."

"You mean, evidence that'll stand up in a criminal trial."

"You're a fast learner. Someone taught you well."

"A good-looking detective, I know personally." She smiled, then added, "Who at times can be a smooth talker when talking with his wife."

"Guilty as charged," Mark responded as he reached over and tenderly squeezed her hand.

They left the gas station and headed to their subdivision, Clifton Retirement Community. The sun was sinking into the southwestern skyline above the treetops as official sunset would occur at five-thirty p.m. Would this be another dead end, another disappointment in their quest for the cause of the six people dying of spontaneous human combustion?

Chapter Fourteen

Mark pulled into the Parkers' driveway and parked behind the Parkers' car. They got out of the Chrysler 300. Sherry peered around. There weren't any neighbors milling outside within six houses from the Parkers' house on both sides of the street. They walked up the carport driveway toward the side door, to the three-step stairs leading to the small wooden deck and house's side door. Sherry removed the door key from underneath the cat statue. A moment later, she opened the locked door. The kitchen was dimly lit from the late afternoon sun.

"There's the microwave next to the refrigerator," declared Mark as he walked over to it. He reached behind the microwave oven and unplugged it.

Sherry removed a few items off the top, including two different salt and pepper shakers, placing the items on the countertop. "Do you need help carrying the microwave?"

"No. I can manage it," he answered as he turned it around. Taking out a small pen light from his shirt pocket, he shined the light on the small metal plate. "I'll call Ron and give him the information regarding the microwave." He removed his cell phone and called Ron. "Hey. I have the microwave's data." He slowly enunciated the model, make, and serial number. "We'll see you at your house. Bye." Mark grabbed the cord and picked up the microwave. "Ready?"

"I am."

"Get the side door for me, please."

Sherry opened the inside door, then held open the storm door, allowing Mark to pass by her. She locked the side door, then put the key underneath the cat statue on the concrete carport driveway.

"You need to get the car keys out of my right pocket. I guess I should've given the keys to you before I picked up the microwave."

Sherry grinned. "I don't mind getting into your pants…for the car keys."

"Don't make me laugh. It's hard enough to hold this thing."

She reached into his right, front pants pocket and removed the metal ring containing the car keys with the key remote. She pushed the truck lid icon on the remote, opening their car's trunk. Mark placed the microwave oven into the trunk, then closed the trunk lid. Sherry looked up and down the street for prying eyes. No one could be seen. Most people were preparing for the dinner meal or had left for their favorite local restaurant. She and Mark ate out about three to four times a week at various eating places throughout Ocala. There were nearly five hundred and fifty restaurants to choose from in Ocala. Sherry figured they had gone to about three percent of them, or around sixteen eateries. "Let's stop and eat on the way to Ron's house." She glanced at her watch, as she sat in the passenger seat. "We'll have plenty of time to get to his house by five-thirty."

"I am hungry," Mark agreed as he backed out of the driveway and onto the street. "It's been another busy, hair-raising retirement day for us."

"I got to say, we don't have typical retirement days. At least in the past few days, we haven't."

After eating at a restaurant on Silver Springs Boulevard they headed to Ron's house. The sun was now below the tree line, creating shaded areas everywhere as they sped on State Road Forty heading east toward Ocala National Forest, the oldest national forest east of the Mississippi River and the third largest white pine forest in the United States. Ron's house and subdivision was adjacent to The Forest. Mark put the car's headlights on as nature's early dusk began to encompass their surroundings.

Fifteen minutes later, Mark turned left onto a blacktop road leading to Ron's subdivision. In less than two minutes, he pulled up behind Ron's car. "We made it without any downed power lines or tire blowouts."

"Isn't that the truth. I guess we can say this is the epitome of being a defensive driver."

Ron met them at the front door, grabbing the microwave oven

from Mark and carrying it to the room containing various diagnostic apparatuses. He set the microwave down on an empty countertop in the left corner of the room. The countertop ran the length of the three walls in the room, excluding the doorway wall. The brightly lit room displayed an extremely clean microwave oven. "I haven't had a chance to see when and where the microwave oven was purchased." He reached out and opened the microwave's door."

Sherry peered inside. "Pretty darn clean. Don't see any food residue." *It's not like our microwave oven's food-stained walls.*

They went into the computer room. The three computer monitors' screen savers displayed whales jumping out of the ocean water. "Can I order a pizza for you guys?"

Sherry glanced at Mark who slightly moved his head back and forth in a negative response to Ron's question. "No thanks, we already ate something at a restaurant before we got here."

"Okay. We have about an hour before Stephanie gets here. We'll go into the computer room. I'll check and see when this brand and model was manufactured. It'll narrow it down to the year the Parkers could've purchased the microwave oven."

"Sounds like a plan," Mark said.

A moment later, Ron sat in front of the center computer and began tapping on the keyboard as the screen in front of him changed rapidly to different squares of information. "There it is. The microwave oven was manufactured four years ago. So, it's relatively new. I'll have my program scan their credit cards over the past four years and search for the purchase of a microwave oven." Ron then wheeled his chair to the right, stopping in front of the second computer. Ron began typing on the keyboard. "Here, I'll examine their checking account checks in the memo section for the words microwave oven and their savings account for the purchase of one over the past four years. I won't personally stare at every individual check, but my scanning program will do it for me. This may take a while. If you like we can go into the kitchen and get something to drink."

"Sounds good to me," Mark answered as he turned to Sherry. "What about you, babe?"

"Sure,"

They sat at the kitchen table. Mark and Ron had made a cup of coffee, while Sherry drank from a small bottle of water. Ron sipped some of his coffee, then said, "Have you figured out how a microwave oven could've caused spontaneous human combustion in our victims?"

"I've thought about it. There could be two possibilities. The microwaves leaked out from the oven and bombarded its penetrating waves through their skin, changing their body chemistry and/or enzymes. Once this happened a chain reaction occurred creating an internal inferno, a spontaneous human combustion reaction throughout their bodies. This could correlate with the belief of mast cells' spontaneous release over two hundred inflammatory molecules known as mediators, which affect a regulatory protein called UCP-1. The mediator causes adipose oxidization to be released as heat."

"I have no idea what you just said but if this is what the microwave did, why haven't we seen more people die from spontaneous human combustion?"

"That's the million-dollar question. Again, I'm speculating the electromagnetic property in microwave ovens was a catalyst in the spontaneous combustion victims. It may have nothing to do with their deaths. Hopefully, your associate Stephanie can give us an answer after she examines the microwave oven."

The front doorbell rang. "It can't be the pizza delivery guy. I didn't order a pizza." Ron stared at his watch, then stood. "If it's Stephanie, she's thirty minutes early. All be right back." He left the kitchen and headed to the front door.

Sherry got up from the table as did Mark. They put their cups into the dishwasher. A moment later, Ron walked back into the kitchen with a woman in her early thirties wearing a pale-blue sweatshirt with the picture of lightning streaking down from a grey-black cloud.

Underneath the menacing scene the words LIGHT UP MY DAY stood out in bold, red letters. She wore jeans and tennis shoes. She was carrying a large black case with a handle.

"Hey. This is Stephanie Miller."

"I'm Mark. This is my wife, Sherry."

Stephanie set the case down next to her. She glanced at Sherry and smiled, then turned her attention toward Mark. "I heard impressive stories about you, detective. I never got a chance to meet you. You had retired already when I started my position with the forensics lab."

Sherry wondered how many other people, pretty employees at the forensics lab were awed by him. "We brought you here to evaluate a microwave."

"Yeah. Ron told me on the phone you wanted me to check it out for any irregularities. Can you tell me what exactly you're looking for?"

Sherry told her the theory she had come up with regarding the spontaneous human combustion victims.

"Sounds like something out of a science fiction movie. All I know is exposure to elevated levels of microwave radiation can cause cataracts and skin burns. To my knowledge, most microwave oven leaks are too small to create these health risks. Microwave ovens more than nine years old are at risk for leaks. How old is the microwave from the Parkers' kitchen?"

"We know this model started to be manufactured about four years ago. So, it can't be any older than four years old."

Like on cue, a rhythmic beeping sound interrupted their conversation.

Mark turned towards the doorway. "What's that sound?"

"It's my computer. My program must've found when and where the Parkers' microwave oven was purchased. Let's head to the computer room."

Everyone followed Ron to the computer room. The computer screen in front of them displayed red flashing rectangular lines encompassing writing and numbers. Ron sat down in a swivel chair, peered at the monitor screen, then stated, "The microwave was bought three weeks ago at Sam's Electronics here in Ocala. We know the microwave was first manufactured about four years ago. So, it can't be any older than four years old."

"I assume you have the microwave in the other room?" Stephanie asked.

"Yes. Although, I was thinking. If in fact there's a problem with the microwave oven emitting dangerous microwaves or some variant, shouldn't you be protected? Like a lead apron."

"You make a good point, Ron. But if there is a dangerous leak, my head, arms, and lower legs wouldn't be protected. There hasn't been any evidence microwaves can cause spontaneous human combustion. Isn't that right, Dr. McKinney?"

"Yes. It's an assumption the microwave oven had something to do with the six victims dying."

"Can't a pacemaker be affected by the microwaves?" Mark asked.

"In the early days of microwaves and pacemakers, in the nineteen seventies, microwave ovens with their electromagnetic waves could affect cardiac pacemakers, but medical scientists developed shielded circuitry, selective filters, which enhanced the ability of the pacemaker to recognize and reject microwave interference." She wrinkled her forehead. "Do you have a pacemaker, detective?"

"Oh, no. I was wondering about it."

Stephanie picked up her black case. "Why don't we go into the next room and check out the microwave oven. Mark, can you get me a glass of water?"

"Sure. But I can get you something else, like a soda or a cup of coffee if you like?"

"No. The glass of water is for evaluating the microwave oven. I'll explain it to everyone before I start my exam of the microwave oven."

A few moments later, Sherry stood next to Mark as Ron handed Stephanie a glass of water. She grabbed the glass, put it inside the microwave oven, which sat on a counter in the left corner of the room, then closed the door. "I'll need to check for cracks on the hinges. Worn areas or cracks on the door seal or for any dents, breaks in the door and damage to the metal mesh of the door." After checking these areas, she said, "Everything checks out okay, but it doesn't mean there isn't a leakage."

She walked over to her black case which sat on the countertop and removed a gauge of some kind, the size of an ordinary paperback book. "This is called a microwave leakage detector. It will detect high frequency radiation levels emitted from a microwave oven. I attached a clamp to the back of the detector. The clamp will be placed on the door handle allowing the detector to be two inches away from the microwave oven. I'll set the timer on the microwave for one minute. The detector will give us the level of leakage, if any, from the area around the door seals and handle. If the tester displays a measurement of five mW/cm^2 or greater at two inches there will be a cause for concern. I'll turn the microwave on. I'll be in the room for a few seconds."

Sherry peered at the microwave oven with a frown. "What's the glass of water for?"

"Good question. Most people, including me at one time, didn't know you shouldn't turn on a microwave oven without anything inside of it. If you turn on an empty microwave oven, it will expose the magnetron, the element which creates the microwaves, to high power levels that can damage or destroy the microwave oven. The glass of water will lesson this danger, while still leaving enough unaffected microwaves to evaluate for leaks."

"I feel like I'm in a classroom for Electronics one oh one," Mark stated with a grin.

"That makes the two of us," Sherry added, agreeing to his statement. She felt better knowing Stephanie wouldn't be in the room long enough to be in danger if something sinister had been done to the microwave causing the six victims' deaths.

Stephanie walked over to the microwave oven, attached her apparatus to the door handle, then turned it on. A small LED screen on the front of the microwave leakage detector lit up displaying in bold red the equation: 0 over 5mW/cm^2.

She pushed bake on the right side of the microwave oven, then set the microwave oven timer for one minute. "You can all go into the hallway now."

Everyone exited the room, then stood in the hallway.

Stephanie watched everyone leave the room, then turned around and pushed the start button on the microwave oven. The light went on inside as the glass of water began to turn on the Lazy Susan turntable. At the same time, the typical humming sound emanated from the microwave oven. She turned around and sped toward the open doorway twelve feet away from the microwave oven. Stephanie quickly closed the door and stood next to Sherry. Ron and Mark stood behind them in the hallway. "Once we hear the ding from the microwave oven, it'll be safe to enter the room. In a normal situation when testing for leaks in a microwave oven, I'd only have to be about two feet away to avoid any significant electromagnetic effect."

"Why's that?" Sherry inquired.

"The electromagnetic energy in a microwave oven decreases significantly as you move away from the source of radiation. Standing about twenty inches from a microwave oven, the radiation would be one percent of the value measured at two inches from the oven. In this case we're being more cautious due to your hypothesis of it possibly being related to the spontaneous combustion victims."

"If this test shows an elevated level of radiation leaked from the microwave, we'll next have to determine how it could've caused the deaths of these victims. Of course, we'll have to evaluate the other two microwave ovens and see if they'll have comparable results from this test."

The microwave oven dinged, indicating one minute had elapsed. Stephanie opened the door. They were too far away to see the microwave radiation detector results on its LED screen. The light inside the microwave oven was off, as the clock displayed three blue zeros. As they got closer, Stephanie exclaimed, "Oh, my God."

Sherry stared at the microwave radiation detector clamped to the microwave door handle. The LED screen displayed: 0 over $5mW/cm^2$. There wasn't any leakage from the unit. Her theory of the electromagnetic radiation waves from the microwave oven causing the spontaneous human combustion or at least being a catalyst was defunct. "That shoots my theory."

"Scientifically, you're correct. There isn't any electromagnetic radiation leakage from this microwave oven."

Ron walked over to the microwave, bent down, and stared toward the right side of it. "I'll be right back." He hurried out of the room.

Puzzlement showed across Sherry's face. *What was that about?*

A moment later, Ron walked back into the room holding a small square piece of yellow paper. He turned the microwave around, exposing the back of it.

Stephanie frowned. "What are you doing?"

"Checking the serial number and model of this microwave oven. I guess it's my forensic training to be thorough. Besides, when I saw the name of this microwave oven a bit ago, I wanted to check the name from the purchase order. They're not the same. The model and serial numbers are obviously different. This isn't the microwave oven the Parkers bought from Sam's Electronics three weeks ago."

"They must've been switched," Mark concluded. "But when? Before the Parkers died or afterwards? Or they never replaced the new microwave oven with this one?"

"Why can't anything be simple and straightforward in this investigation?" Sherry said, looking up at Mark with a forlorn expression. "We'll need to find the other microwave oven. Maybe it's in the Parkers' house? Or maybe they returned the original one back to Sam's Electronics because it wasn't working?"

Mark shook his head back and forth. "Again, more unanswered questions to our investigation."

Sherry glanced at her watch: six thirty-five. "We need to call Sam's Electronics."

"I wrote their telephone number down," Ron said, "thinking we might have to call them."

"Good thinking," Mark complimented. "Can you call them and asked if the Parkers returned their microwave?"

"Sure." Ron retrieved his cell phone and made the call. Several seconds elapsed. "They closed at six o'clock according to their answering machine."

"Sherry and I will go back to the Parkers' house and see if we can find the microwave oven bought from Sam's Electronics. If we can't find it in their house, we'll need to call or even drive to the electronics store tomorrow morning."

"Give me a call if you need me to check out another microwave oven," Stephanie suggested as she removed the electromagnetic leakage detector from the handle of the microwave oven.

"Sure will," Mark said as he placed his hand on top of Sherry's shoulder. "We really appreciate your help."

"Glad I could help," Stephanie responded as she put the device into her case, then closed the lid. She turned around, holding the black case by its handle. "I have to say this was the most exciting experience I ever had checking out a potentially lethal microwave oven."

Ron grabbed the microwave oven. "Mark, I'll carry this out to your car."

"Thanks Ron, you're a gentleman and a scholar."

"I'll second that," Stephanie agreed as she glanced at Ron with a smile.

Sherry chuckled to herself. *There's obviously chemistry between those two.*

Ron put the microwave into the trunk of the Chrysler 300. Sherry and Mark said goodbye to him and Stephanie. Sherry said to Mark as they drove away from the house, "They make a cute couple, don't you think?"

"Never crossed my mind...but you're right, they do."

"I wonder if we'll find the other microwave oven at the Parkers' house?"

"We'll soon find out."

Chapter Fifteen

Mark pulled up into the Parkers' driveway and stopped. Night's blackened curtain had draped itself over Florida on a moonless sky, accentuating heaven's cluster of sparkling stars. He noticed the house next to them was void of room lights, indicating they had gone to bed early or were out finishing their dinner at a restaurant alone or with friends. Then again, they could be at a friend's house playing cards. The houses across the street were lit up inside with their blinds closed. No obvious prying eyes were upon them, as he removed the microwave from the car's trunk. Sherry closed the trunk lid, shutting out the conspicuous compartment light inside of it. She hurried in front of Mark, retrieved the door key under the cat statue, then opened the side door. Sherry reached to her right and turned the kitchen light on, illuminating an undisturbed room except for an empty space next to the refrigerator. She stepped back and held the storm door open as Mark walked past her. She followed him, closing the doors behind her. "I get an eerie feeling, touching every skin cell in my body, knowing death had engulfed this elderly couple four days ago," she said as she watched Mark return the microwave to the countertop and plug the cord's receptacle into the wall outlet. "There can't be too many places a person could put a microwave oven inside the house. There isn't a basement, garage, or an outside storage shed. I'd guess the microwave would be in one of the closets, in the utility room, or sitting in plain sight in one of the bedrooms."

Mark smirked. "Well, my dear, I believe that would cover everywhere we'd possibly find the microwave oven. Unless they buried it in the backyard."

"You're obviously kidding."

"I am. Although, you never know from the way this investigation is going. I wouldn't eliminate any possibility."

"I agree, a lot of bizarre situations have occurred."

They stayed together searching each of the two bedrooms, including the bedroom closets and the utility room. No microwave oven. Mark sighed as they stood in the kitchen. "This leaves four possibilities: The microwave oven was taken back to the electronics store, the Parkers threw it away, gave it away to someone, or in fact, the microwave caused the death of the Parkers and the killer or killers removed it after their deaths."

"Maybe the guy we met the morning of the Parkers' death was coming to retrieve the tainted microwave," Sherry pointed to the microwave oven on the countertop, "and replaced it with the one on the counter."

"Hum. That's a good possibility. There were a lot of blanks from the intersection security cameras not showing Fred Cramer's car, which could mean our mystery man may have dropped the microwave off somewhere on his way to Paddock Mall's parking lot. He or someone else could've come back to the Parkers' house in the past four days and replaced their microwave oven with this one here."

They left the Parkers' house. After getting back into their car, Sherry asked, "Should we call Ron and let him know we didn't find the other microwave oven inside the Parkers' house?"

"Yes, we should. I'll call him when we get home." He backed out of the driveway and headed down the street to their house. Mark decided to himself, after this investigation concluded, he'd avoid any situation requiring detective pursuance and become a normal retirement recipient. At least for a few months.

"Detective work puts a strain on the body and mind," Sherry said as Mark pulled into their driveway and parked the car under the carport. "And I thought being a doctor was a stressful profession." She released her seat belt. "We're going to make a visit to Sam's Electronics first thing tomorrow morning. Right?"

"Yes. They open at eight o'clock according to Ron."

"If the people of Sam's Electronics are the instigators in the spontaneous combustion event, they'll likely deny everything, including having the Parkers' microwave oven."

"You're right, they'll deny everything. Like we both agreed

during our investigation, we observe suspects' demeaner, their comfortability when interviewing them."

"Good point."

They went into the house and sat down at the kitchen table. Mark called Ron on his cell phone. "Hey, Ron. We didn't find the other microwave oven at the Parkers' house. Can you check to see if the other two couples purchased a microwave oven at Sam's Electronics?"

"Already started on it. As soon as my computer program finds a match, I'll give you a call. I got into the electronics store's computer database. There wasn't any mention of the Parkers returning their microwave oven. They might not had entered the return to their store's inventory. Or like we discussed at my house earlier, they never received the Parkers' microwave oven."

"You're on the ball, my man. Talk to you later. Bye." He told Sherry what Ron said.

"There's no doubt, Ron is a vital part of our team. The way things are going, we should consider getting licensed as a private investigation business…just kidding."

Mark raised his eyebrows, then rolled his eyes. "Unfortunately, if we were licensed, this would be a pro bono investigation towards ourselves. I think we'll stay as we are, retired. Do you want something to drink?"

"How about a rum and cola?"

"That would suit my palate too."

They sat at the kitchen table, sipped their drinks, and discussed the day's events. About an hour later, Mark's cell phone rang. Sherry put her nearly empty glass down on the table. "It's probably Ron."

He glanced at the caller ID. "Yeah, it's him." He put the phone on speaker. "Hi, Ron. What did you find out about the other two couples?"

"The couple in Belleview purchased their microwave oven at a flea market, Market of Marian to be exact, according to a canceled check from Ralph and Rose Clemens' checking account. The other couple, Spencer and Margaret Watchman from Wildwood purchased their microwave over the internet. All the microwaves, including the Parkers, were assorted brands."

"That shoots our connection with Sam's Electronics," Mark said with disappointment in his voice.

"On the contrary."

"What do mean, on the contrary?"

"The person who sold the Clemens' and Watchman's microwave ovens was Timothy Barron."

"Not sure what you're saying?"

"Sam's Electronics is owned by Samuel Barron. They're brothers."

"This is too much of a coincidence. And you know my feelings about coincidence." A sudden tingling sensation wrapped around his neck and upper shoulders as a revelation crossed his mind. Was one of these guys the mystery man he and Sherry met in the Parkers' driveway the morning of their deaths? "Can you send me a photograph of the two brothers?"

"I already checked the Barron brothers' photographs with the composite sketch done by Larry Fortin of the man who called himself Henry Baker. I didn't see any resemblance to our mystery man. I was hoping one of the brothers matched the composite sketch. But I'll still send you their photos. If you want me to?"

"Sure. Go ahead and send it to my phone. Have you checked to see if there's any connection to our other cast of characters in our investigation, such as Fred Cramer, Phillip Frank or Peter Blankenship?"

"Not yet. I'll check them out after I talk with you. If I find anything relevant, I'll call you back. Otherwise, we'll talk tomorrow."

"Have a good night, Ron. And thanks."

"Talk to you later. Bye."

Sherry sipped down the last of her drink, then said, "Is there a way to get the other two microwave ovens and have them examined by Stephanie?"

"It would be great if we could. We'll have to figure out how we could finagle it without an official capacity such as part of the sheriff's department or the CSI's investigative team. There's another way without physically removing the microwave ovens from the victim's houses. Tomorrow morning I'll call the lead detectives in the case and ask them to check the brand, model, and serial number of the microwave ovens. If they're different than the ones purchased by the Barron brothers, we'll know the microwaves were switched after each of the couple's deaths, as it was for the Parkers' microwave oven. Let's sleep on it. You've got the knack of figuring out tough problems in your sleep. Maybe you'll come up with another idea other than mine, which has some flaws. Such as the detectives believing your theory regarding the microwave ovens were possibly the cause of the spontaneous human combustion. They'll ask a lot of questions leading to our conspiracy theory that a terrorist group had participated in the three couple's deaths."

"I don't have to sleep on it. I know what we can do without getting the sheriff detectives involved with our investigation."

"Great. What is it?"

"It seems many people have security cameras on the outside of their homes today, especially in retirement communities. And you said recently the other two couples lived in retirement communities."

"Yeah. They do."

"Why don't we ask the neighbors next to and across the street from the Simmons and Watchman's house if they noticed anyone, other than deputies and CSI personnel, remove anything before or after they were found dead in their houses. When we approach each of the houses, I'll look for outside surveillance cameras. Most of the cameras are connected to WiFi. I'm sure Ron could tap into them and retrieve video surveillance on the day of and after the couple's death. What do you think about my idea?"

"Outstanding, my love. We don't have to check the Parkers' neighbors since we already know no one in our community has surveillance cameras. We'll tell the Watchman's and Clemens' neighbors we're private investigators. Which of course isn't a lie. We're just not licensed, yet. Of course, they don't have to know that bit of information about us. I believe it'll work. I'll hold off from calling the detectives. If your idea doesn't work out, my idea will be Plan B."

"Is there a Plan C?"

"Let's wait until our other two plans fail before we consider something else. Do you want another drink?"

"Sure. This will be our nightcap." She handed Mark her empty glass.

After drinking their rum and cola, the two sleuths made their way into the bedroom. Silence engulfed the darkness except for 9:35 p.m. displayed in red numbers on the rectangular clock sitting on the nightstand to the right of Mark. He kissed Sherry then rolled to his right side, staring at the clock. Mark's thoughts cascaded through his mind on the events of the day as sleep began to absorb his consciousness.

The clock read 2:33 a.m. as Sherry gently shook Mark and repeatedly said, "Mark…Mark…Mark. Wake up."

He felt a rocking sensation and heard Sherry's plea. His eyes snapped open, staring at the clock's time. He quickly rolled on his back as a rush of adrenaline stimulated every nerve ending in his body. "What's wrong?"

"I came up with a Plan C."

He sighed as thoughts of an intruder approaching their bedroom with a loaded gun faded away once he heard Sherry's reason for waking him up from a peaceful sleep. He was used to her producing an answer to a problem or a question in the middle of the night, but normally she'd tell him after he woke up in the morning. "What's Plan C?"

"Contact a family member of the deceased couples and explain to them we're investigating a problem with their particular microwave oven, and that it may be emitting elevated levels of electromagnetic waves which could be harmful to humans or animals. We'll tell them we're representatives for the microwave company. Ron should be able to obtain the names and phone numbers of family members. The relatives wouldn't have to know anything else regarding our real investigation."

"Hmm, this may work. Law enforcement wouldn't have to be involved. Let's switch your Plan C with Plan A. I'll call Ron around six o'clock and tell him our plans. He doesn't have to be at work until eight this morning, which should give him time to check out family members." Mark set the clock alarm for six a.m. He rolled onto his left side and cuddled up to Sherry. Sleep soon overtook his conscious mind as the warmth of their bodies functioned as a euphoric relaxant.

The alarm clock sounded its six a.m. wake-up call. The morning sun lay beneath the southeastern horizon and wouldn't show its light and warmth for another forty plus minutes. Ron sat at the side of the bed, reached over, and turned off the alarm. He felt movement from the mattress on Sherry's side of the bed. "Good morning."

"I'll start the coffee while you call Ron." A burst of light from Sherry's lamp lit up the bedroom.

"Sounds like a plan." He grabbed his cell phone from the nightstand and called Ron.

The phone rang four times, then a groggy male voice said, "Hey, Mark did you 'butt-call' by mistake? The sun isn't up yet."

"Sorry, my man." He then told Ron about Plan C, which was now Plan A. "What do you think? Can you do this before you have to be at work this morning?"

There was a short pause. "I don't work today. It's Saturday."

"Oh, my God. I forgot." Since he and Sherry had retired, every day of the week was nearly the same. The one difference was the congested early morning road traffic on weekends decreased. "Go back to sleep for a while. You can do this for us after you wake up."

"No. That's okay. I'm awake and anxious to contribute to our investigation. I'll call you when I get the information on the two victim's families. By the way, I couldn't find any connection between the Barron brothers and the other people in our investigation."

"I assumed there wasn't any information relevant since you didn't call us back last night. We'll be home until we hear back from you. Talk to you then." Mark went into the kitchen, told her what he said to Ron, and that it was Saturday. She had also forgotten what day it was. He then sat at the kitchen table after getting a cup of coffee. He held his cup of coffee and peered down at the swirling cream at the top slowly blending into the sugarless coffee.

After taking a sip from her coffee, Sherry said, "I'm wondering if the microwave ovens were purposely tampered with by the Barron brothers for some sinister reason, or if they didn't have any knowledge the microwave ovens could cause spontaneous human combustion? What do you think?"

"Could be either or neither possibility. It will depend on who had switched the microwaves, one of them or someone not associated with Sam's Electronics. If we do get permission to remove the microwave ovens, we'll still need to check out the neighbors of the two deceased couples and see if a neighbor saw someone walk into the victim's house carrying a microwave oven, then walk out of the house carrying a microwave oven. Then will need to check if our suspect was picked up on a neighbor's security camera."

"There are a few 'ifs' in these scenarios."

"Welcome to the world of detective work." Mark gulped down a large amount of coffee, then set the cup down on the table. "And we can't forget someone may want us dead or at least prevent us from continuing our investigation."

"I haven't forgotten. Like I've said before, it's made me much more aware of my surroundings."

"We'll call our neighbors in a little while and ask them if they saw anyone coming or leaving with a microwave the early morning hours before the Parkers were found dead or a couple of days afterwards."

Sherry prepared toaster waffles and microwaved sausages, along with a second cup of coffee.

~ * ~

A white four-door Ford Bronco with deeply tinted windows drove slowly by the McKinney's house. The front seat passenger, imposter Agent Cosby, peered out the side window at Mark and Sherry's house. "They're still safe in their house. The living room and kitchen lights are on. A phone call to Ron Brewer around six o'clock a little while ago concerned the Director. Since we can't listen to their conversation due to their tamper-proof cellphones and Ron Brewer's impenetrable computer security system, including his computer firewall, it's impossible to know what they're up to regarding their investigation of the deaths of the three couples."

"I can't understand why we can't tell Detective McKinney and Dr. McKinney what we're up to," said the driver, who had introduced himself to the McKinneys as Agent Cotton. "It would make our job much easier."

"It would. But it's not for us to make that decision. Plus, not having a tracer on their car creates a logistic problem for us. I wonder what they were up to yesterday since we weren't available to check in on them."

"God only knows, other than the Director said Mark and Sherry McKinney had car trouble with the car's accelerator in the afternoon and were at Ron Brewer's house earlier yesterday evening. Like you said a moment ago, we're not sure what the McKinneys are up to lately."

"Putting the mini-spy camera on the magnolia tree at the entrance to the community will make it easy for us to know when they leave. We'll be able to pick up the coming and going of the McKinneys on my laptop's WiFi a quarter of a mile away from the community's entranceway. The marvel of technology today sometimes overwhelms me. Before all the technical spy apparatuses, all we had were high-power binoculars."

The Bronco left Clifton Retirement Community, turned right onto the two-lane blacktop road, and parked a quarter of a mile way near the entrance to a golf course.

~ * ~

Mark and Sherry got dressed and went back to the kitchen. They opened a kitchen drawer and removed the Clifton Retirement Community's list of homeowners with their telephone numbers and addresses. They spent about fifteen minutes calling their immediate neighbors. None of them saw any suspicious activities or strangers coming or going from the Parkers' house since the Parkers' deaths. They then went into the living room and began watching a TV news talk show.

"I hate waiting," Sherry complained as she put the leg rest up in her recliner chair.

"I think it's nice to relax. Besides, this may be the lull before the storm. We'll likely have a busy day ahead of us. And hopefully we'll find answers to our many questions." Mark cell phone rang. He glanced at the caller I.D. "It's Ron."

Chapter Sixteen

"Hi, Ron. What did you find out?"

"Good news. I got phone numbers of family members and relatives of the two spontaneous human combustion couples. Each victim has children living near their deceased parent. I'll text you the names and data to your cell phone after we hang up."

"Great. Thanks, Ron."

"It's part of my job as a member of the McKinney Sleuths Agency."

Mark chuckled. He liked the name. "I guess the next thing you'll want is a T-shirt with the name and a logo printed on it."

"Sounds like a great idea to me. If you want, I'll work on a logo for our agency."

"At this point we should concentrate on our investigation before we consider incorporating and having T-shirts printed. We'll keep in touch and let you know how things work out with Plan A."

"Okay, boss."

Mark ended their conversation and set the cell phone onto the coffee table in front of him. A couple minutes later, his cell phone alerted him a text message had arrived. He read the information to Sherry, who wrote the names, phone numbers and addresses of the deceased couple's family in a small spiral notebook. After writing the information down, they decided to call the Watchman's daughter, Mary Jones, and ask her to meet them at her parents' house regarding a possible dangerous problem with their microwave oven. Mark and Sherry weren't telling a lie. All Mark and Sherry had to do was to check the microwave and make sure it was the microwave oven her parents bought from Sam's Electronics. The daughter lived in the nearby town of Leesburg.

Sherry would make the call, thinking a woman would set the daughter more at ease, and knowing Sherry was a retired physician. She called the number, putting the call on speaker.

The phone rang three times, then: "Hello."

"Mrs. Jones, my name is Sherry McKinney, I'm a retired ER doctor. I'm so sorry to hear about your parent's death. The reason I'm calling…." Sherry explained to Mrs. Jones the detailed theory she had postulated about the microwave oven possibly contributing to her parents' deaths. She didn't tell the daughter about their suspicion that someone had purposely altered the microwave oven to cause SHC. "Could I and my husband, retired Detective Mark McKinney, meet you at your parent's house this morning? Do you have a key to get into your parents' house?"

"Yes, I do," Mary Jones answered. "Why isn't the sheriff department investigating the death of my parents?"

"Spontaneous human combustion deaths aren't ruled as homicides or accidental deaths but diagnosed by the medical examiner as death of unknown cause. This is the reason why the sheriff detectives aren't involved in your parents' deaths. There wasn't a crime committed."

"I see. Sure, I can meet you and your husband at my parents' house about nine thirty this morning. I'll be bringing my husband Wesley with me."

"That'll be great. We'll see you and your husband there." Sherry put her phone into a side pocket in her black purse.

"Smart woman wanting to bring her husband with her. You can never be too safe in today's world. After examining the microwave and seeing if it's the one bought at the flea market from Timothy Barron, we can check out the neighbors for outside security cameras in the front of their houses. I think we'll hold off talking with the neighbors about if they saw anyone carry out a microwave from the Watchman's house if we notice security cameras. If there aren't any cameras, we'll wait and see if there are any security cameras at the Clemens' neighbors in Belleview. If there aren't any cameras or if there isn't any recording of someone walking out of the victim couple's house, then we'll talk to the neighbors. In other words, we'll cross that bridge when we get there."

"Makes more sense."

"Let's get going." Mark removed the house and car keys from one of three hooks on a board shaped like a car, attached to the side of an end kitchen cabinet extending to the floor.

Mark and Sherry approached the front entrance of their retirement community. A magnolia tree stood to the right of the driveway. Sherry looked to her right. "Too bad the white magnolia flower only last a little over a week in the spring."

"Yeah. I love the smell of citrus-honey the flower emits into the air. It brings back the memory when we got married with the arrangement of magnolia flowers throughout the church chapel and the reception center. That's when I learned the ancient Chinese meaning of the magnolia flower. The meaning of the flower depicts you perfectly: a woman's gentleness and her beauty."

"You're such a romantic under your tough-skinned persona."

Mark grinned, as he turned left onto the two-lane blacktop road, then turned right at the traffic light and headed toward I-75. Even though Mark said he wouldn't drive on the expressway until after their investigation had ended, it would take them too long to drive on SR 301 to Wildwood. Unbeknownst to Mark and Sherry, a white, four-door Ford Bronco tailed them with the two imposters. Mark or Sherry would be looking for a black Suburban, not a white Ford Bronco, which stayed about fifty yards away from the unsuspecting sleuths. About thirty minutes later, Mark got off at exit 329 from I-75, then made a left onto State Road Forty-Four, heading east. Several minutes later, he turned right into Railroad Crossing retirement community. "There's the house up ahead on the left," Sherry said as she put her spiral notebook into her blue blazer inside pocket.

Mark pulled behind a small black SUV and stopped. He got out of the car and peered around at the houses across the street and at the homes on either side of the Watchman's house for security cameras. He noticed Sherry was doing the same as she stood next to the car peering around at the houses in their immediate vicinity. Mark's attention stopped at the house across the street to the left. A security camera was attached in front of the house at the front roof's pediment. If the camera had a wide-angle lens, it might include the Watchman's driveway. "See the house across the street to the left?"

"It has a security camera." Sherry retrieved her spiral notebook from her jacket. "I'll write down the address of the house." After she wrote down the address, they walked up to the front door of the Watchman's house.

The front door opened before Mark could push the doorbell. A woman in her early fifties stood in the doorway. The whites of her eyes were reddened and glassy, normally seen during and after a person had been crying. He had seen enough family members and friends of a victim after their loved one had died unexpectedly from a homicide or mysterious death with these symptoms. Behind Mrs. Jones, stood a man several inches taller than her, who also appeared to be in his early fifties with a serious expression. "Hi. I'm Mark McKinney and this is my wife, Sherry."

"Please come in," Mary said, as she and her husband stepped aside. "This is my husband, Wesley."

"So, you think the microwave oven may have caused my in-laws' deaths?" Wesley asked, addressing his question to Mark.

"We're not sure. It's a theory, like I told your wife. We appreciate you letting us examine the microwave oven."

The four of them walked into the kitchen. The microwave oven sat on the counter next to the electric range. Sherry brought out her small spiral notebook, flipped the pages, then stared down at the page.

Mark turned the microwave around, exposing the back. They had already gone over in the car on the way to the Watchman's house that Sherry would write down the serial number, model, and name of the microwave into her notebook.

Sherry leaned forward and wrote down the microwave oven's information. "This isn't the microwave we were looking for with a possible defect." She put the notebook back into the blazers inside pocket. "Sorry you had to drive here."

"So, the microwave didn't cause my mom and dad's deaths?"

"No," Sherry answered. "This microwave didn't cause your parents' deaths. Spontaneous human combustion is a medical phenomenon without any explanation. I'm so sorry for your loss."

Mark and Sherry left the house. They got into their car and backed out of the driveway. "The microwave was switched, I presume?" Mark asked as he drove away from the house.

"Yes. Someone removed the microwave they purchased at the flea market and replaced it with a different one. There wouldn't be any reason to check it for an electromagnetic leak. What's interesting, the replaced microwave oven is identical to the one replaced at the Parkers' house."

"We still have the possibility of identifying the person who removed the original microwave oven and replaced it with a normal one if the neighbor's security camera included the street and the Watchman's driveway. If it does, we might be able to see the vehicle driven by the suspect and the suspect."

Sherry removed her cell phone. "I'll give Ron a call and see if he can get into the surveillance camera's recorder."

"Good. Since the microwave oven in the Watchman's kitchen was exchanged with another one, it's more than likely that Ralph and Rose Clemens' microwave oven was also removed and replaced with another one. I think we'll drive by the Clemens' house and see if there's any surveillance cameras present from their neighbors before we call the Clemens family members."

"That makes more sense than getting family members involved. You're right. We'd probably find the situation with the Clemens' microwave oven as we did with the Parkers and the Watchman's microwave oven." Sherry speed-dialed Ron's phone number, then put the call on speaker.

The phone rang once. "Hey. Good timing. I was about to call you guys. I got the toxicology results on Peter Blankenship. He didn't have any drugs or chemicals in his body which could've caused his death prior to his house burning. The final diagnosis was undetermined cause of death."

"Like I've mentioned before, ten percent of all autopsies have this diagnosis. More than likely, Blankenship died of a deadly heart arrythmia which wouldn't show up on an autopsy."

"What'd you find at the Watchman's?"

"Their microwave oven had been exchanged with a different one," Mark answered, "which is identical to the brand and model of the microwave oven in the Parkers' kitchen. What we want you to do is to see if you can get into a neighbor's surveillance camera's recorder."

"Sure. What's the address?"

Sherry gave Ron the address, then said, "We're going to drive by the Clemens' house in Belleview and check out surveillance cameras. Let us know if you find anything from the Watchman's neighbor's recorder."

"I'll get on it right away. Bye."

"Wouldn't it be great if Ron would be able to retrieve a video on our perpetrator and the vehicle he's driving?" Mark drove by a white Bronco with heavily tinted windows. He glanced toward the vehicle but didn't see anyone inside. He thought about the Google search for vehicles with rolldown rear windows. A moment later, Mark glanced through the sideview mirror and thought he saw the Bronco's brake lights flash. His attention turned toward the stop sign in front of him and Sherry, who was putting the Clemens' address into the GPS device attached to the dashboard. Sherry leaned back against the driver's passenger side front seat. "Our next stop is Belleview and the Clemens' neighborhood. It'll be best to take SR 301 North to Belleview instead of I-75."

"I can go along with an alternative route since we're not in any hurry to get there. And besides, we'll avoid our notorious I-75."

~ * ~

The white Bronco pulled into the Watchman's driveway. The passenger rubbed his nose, then wrote down the license plate number of the car parked in front of them. "Why did they check out the Watchman's house?"

"Don't have any idea. But they're investigating something." He backed out of the driveway, and then sped up the street, making sure he didn't get too far behind the McKinneys.

"We'll find out who the license plate is registered to, then ask the Director what we should do."

"Where do you think they're going now?"

"I'd say they'll be going to the next spontaneous combustion victims in Belleview. That would be my educated guess."

The passenger, who presented himself as Agent Ed Cosby to the McKinneys, said, "I agree with you."

~ * ~

Mark turned right onto SR 301 North. Twenty minutes later, Belleview city limit sign appeared to their right along the side of the road. He methodically had peered up at the rearview and sideview mirror for a black Suburban as they headed north toward Belleview. None was seen. He also peered at major power lines crossing the road, a habit he acquired since the power line incident on their way back home from Ron's house four days ago.

The GPS announced: "Turn right at SE 110th Street."

The retirement community, Peacock Village, will be about a mile on our right," Sherry said staring at the GPS screen. Her cell phone rang. "It's gotta be Ron." She glanced at the phone. "Yep. It's Ron." She put the phone on speaker. "Hi, Ron. Did you access the Watchman's neighbor's recorder?"

"I got through to their recorder…but it didn't show the Watchman's driveway or house. Or the street. The neighbor's video only showed their front yard and driveway. I wish I had better news for you."

"We're disappointed too. Hopefully, we'll find a security camera near the Clemens' house. We're a few minutes from their home. We'll call you back if we locate a security camera. Bye."

Through the GPS's direction, Mark turned right into Peacock Village community.

About a block away, he made a left onto Sparrow Street. "Let's start checking for security cameras now," Mark suggested.

"Okay. Good idea. "I'll check the houses to my right."

"And I'll check the houses on my left." Both of them rolled down their windows as Mark drove slowly down the street.

About thirty seconds later, the GPS announced: "You've arrived at your destination on the right."

Between Mark and Sherry, they had noticed three houses with security cameras, including a house directly across from the Clemens' house. Sherry had written down the addresses in her notebook. "Looks like someone is at the Clemens' house."

Mark turned into the Clemens' driveway to turn around as a woman in her early fifties walked out of the front door. She took two steps, then slipped and fell on her back. "Oh, my God. The woman fell."

"I saw her," Sherry said as she opened the car door. "I better check to see if the woman's okay."

Mark put the car in park, shut off the engine, opened the driver-side door, and walked over to the woman who was now sitting up. Sherry was a step ahead of him.

"Are you all right, ma'am?" Sherry asked standing next to her.

"I'm such a klutz." She reached over, touched her left wrist, and cringed. "Dang. That's sore."

"I'm a doctor. My name is Sherry McKinney. Can I check the wrist?"

"Why sure," she said trying to stand. Mark reached down and helped her stand. "Thank you, sir." She turned to Sherry. "You're the emergency room doctor at ORMC."

"Yes. But I'm retired now."

She turned toward Mark. "Then you must be Detective McKinney."

"I am. And like my wife, I'm also retired." He wrinkled his forehead. "How do you know us?"

"I worked in the kitchen and cafeteria at ORMC for a few years. I knew about Dr. McKinney and that she was married to a sheriff detective. A hospital is like a small town. Words and gossip travel through the hallways."

Sherry grinned. "Yes. It is like a small town." A solemn expression interrupted her grin. "Let me check your wrist." Sherry gently pressed around her wrist, then moved it to various positions. "It doesn't appear to be fractured."

"That's good. I have a lot of work to do. The elderly couple who lived here died yesterday morning. I was hired by the daughter to clean the house, remove food from the refrigerator and the cupboards."

"Hum. I thought most families would do this themselves."

"You'd be surprised how often families hire cleaning service companies or individuals for this task."

"I have a plastic wrap in the car. If you like, I can wrap your wrist which should give you some relief from your sprain. You also might want to take some ibuprofen for any pain and swelling."

"Thank you."

Sherry turned to Mark. "Open the trunk." He pointed, then pushed the trunk icon on the key remote control. The trunk opened. She hurried to the car's trunk, opened a large black medical bag and removed a cellophane-packaged three-inch ACE wrap. She closed the trunk and walked back to the front door, unwrapping the packaged ACE wrap.

"Please come into the house. You can put the ACE wrap on my wrist inside. Don't want to make a spectacle of myself to all the neighbors, who are probably staring at us right now. By the way, my name is Martha Bell."

Mark, Sherry, and Martha walked into the house. Mark normally didn't believe in happenchance, coincidence, but under the present unusual circumstances, coincidence was a positive effect on their investigation, which might give them the opportunity to examine the microwave oven.

Martha led them into the kitchen. She sat down at the kitchen table with her back facing a microwave oven on the counter next to a toaster. Sherry sat to her right and began wrapping Martha's left wrist. While his wife did her good deed, Mark peered at the name of the microwave. It had the same appearance and name as the other two victims' microwave ovens. He looked down at Sherry, who glanced up at him. He tightened his lips and nodded, then said, "They have the same microwave oven and color we have in our kitchen." Mark knew Sherry would know what he meant since their microwave oven was a different brand and color."

"It's probably a popular brand." Sherry completed wrapping Martha's wrist. "Like I said earlier, take some pain medication. And don't do any heavy lifting with your left hand for the next few days. You should also apply some ice on it the next twenty-four hours."

"Thank you, Dr. McKinney."

~ * ~

The white four-door Bronco turned around at the end of the dead-end street and headed back up the street. The Bronco was six houses away from the McKinneys' parked car in the Clemens' driveway. Imposter Cosby peered at McKinney's Chrysler 300. "We need to find out why the detective and his doctor wife have now visited the Clemens' house. Plus, we'll have to check out the owner of the vehicle in front of the McKinneys' car. It's a Florida license plate, making it easier to look up who owns it."

"You need to call the Director and give him what information we have up to now on the McKinney's."

Imposter Cosby got out his cell phone, pushed the speed dial for the Director's number, then glanced in the sideview mirror and saw the McKinney's exit the front door of the Clemens' house. "They're leaving the house. Let's get out of here."

The phone rang twice, followed by a male voice. "What do you have?"

"We got an update on the McKinneys."

~ * ~

Mark and Sherry left the Clemens' house. A white four-door Bronco was about thirty yards up the street, driving away from them. "I think that's the Bronco I saw earlier parked on the street the Watchman's live on." The Bronco sped up heading to the end of the street. The tinted windows prevented him from seeing inside the vehicle, and the vehicle was too far away to get a license plate number.

"It may be a coincident?"

"You know my feelings on coincidence," Mark answered. "I'd never be able to catch them. If in fact they had followed us to the Watchman's house and now to the Clemens' house, I'd guess it was the two guys calling themselves Agent Cosby and Cotton. It's a gut feeling."

"If it wasn't them, maybe it was our mystery man and his accomplice. The ones who blew up the Toyota 4Runner at Toms Park in

Ocala?"

"Either way, we're being followed again."

"I agree."

They got into their car, backed out of the driveway, and headed out of Peacock Village.

Sherry retrieved her cell phone. "I'll call Ron and give him the addresses of the security cameras, and the white Bronco. He can do a DMV search for white four-door Broncos in the tri-county area. We might get lucky this time."

"You're sounding like a detective."

Sherry grinned, as she sat back against the front passenger seat. "Like I said before, I have the best detective to learn from." She got her cell phone out, called Ron, putting the phone on speaker which had become a normal procedure enabling both to hear what was being said.

Chapter Seventeen

Ron's cell phone rang twice. "Hi, guys. What's the good news?"

"Could be great news." Sherry told him about the third microwave oven, gave him the addresses of three surveillance cameras. She then described the suspicious white Bronco that might be following them.

"I'll get right to work on the surveillance cameras, then I'll check out the white Bronco. I presume you didn't get a license plate number of the vehicle?"

"No. It was too far away to read the letters and numbers."

"Maybe I'll be able to visualize the license plate on one of the surveillance camera's recorders. Talk to y'all as soon as I get something."

"Talk to you then, bye." Sherry put her phone away. She looked at Mark. "All we can do now is wait. And patience isn't one of our virtues."

"True," Mark agreed as he stopped for a red light on northbound SR 441/301. "And like we talked about earlier, if nothing significant shows up on the three surveillance cameras and we can't identify the white Bronco's owner, the last thing we can do is go door to door in the Clemens and Watchman's neighborhood and see if anyone saw the microwaves being taken out of their houses by someone."

They drove about twenty minutes before reaching the city limits of Ocala. After passing under the railroad bridge, Sherry said, "Let's stop for lunch. There's a Darrell's restaurant up ahead on the right."

"Good idea, my love. I am getting a little hungry." Mark chuckled to himself. Since retiring, eating out at restaurants had become a popular activity for them and other retirees in their community. Mark had also noticed he'd added a few extra pounds due to this retirement phenomenon. A minute or two later, he pulled into the restaurant's parking lot and parked. He peered toward the highway, looking for a white four-door Bronco. None drove by. They went inside the restaurant and sat down at a booth, giving him an unobstructed view of the parking lot and the highway through the large restaurant's windows encompassing the west, north and south walls. Most of the four-chair tables and booths next to the windows were occupied. They sat at the last empty booth. A murmuring mixture of conversations filled the room.

"What are you going to order?" Sherry asked as she stared down at the plastic menu.

"I'm going to have country fried steak with mashed potatoes covered with white gravy, and a side order of tomato with okra," he answered without looking at the menu. "And a glass of sweet tea."

"Hum. I think I'll get the same."

The waitress came to the table and took their orders.

An elderly couple sat at a two-chair table to Mark's right. They started talking about the death of couples dying of spontaneous human combustion. Mark leaned to his right. Sherry leaned to her left, apparently for the same reason, wanting to hear what the couple had to say about SHC. The man said, "The article stated there wasn't any explanation for the three couples within a few days dying of spontaneous human combustion. It was the first time in recorded history there were these many deaths, especially couples dying at the same time. CDC is now conducting an investigation along with the county and state health departments."

Mark leaned forward and whispered to Sherry, "Sounds like we have competition. More the merrier as far as I'm concerned."

"Maybe we should contact CDC," Sherry whispered leaning forward, "and let them know what we suspect regarding the microwave ovens?"

Mark thought about it for a moment. "Not yet. We'd have to find the three microwave ovens and prove they're the cause of spontaneous human combustion. Knowing what we already know about them being stealthy removed from the homes of the deceased three couples after their deaths, logically points to the microwave ovens involvement of their deaths. Right now, it's circumstantial evidence. We'll need concrete proof."

"Since CDC has joined forces with the county, state health

departments and likely the medical examiner's office, whoever was trying to stop our investigation will probably back off in trying to silence us. What do you think?"

"That would be hopeful thinking. But we still need to be diligent and not let our guard down." Mark leaned back, as did Sherry.

Their conversation changed to small talk and not mentioning their investigation. After eating, Mark paid the bill. During their time in the restaurant, Mark periodically glanced out the window for the white Bronco, which never showed up. He started the car and was about to back out of the parking space when Sherry's cell phone rang. He kept the car in park.

She glanced at the caller I.D. "It's Ron." She put the phone on speaker. "Hi, Ron."

"Got some good news. The security camera across the street from the Clemens' house showed a SUV pull up into the Clemens' driveway at five a.m., four hours before the daughter arrived and discovered her parent's ashes on the couch in the living room yesterday morning. Only the passenger got out of the vehicle. Couldn't get the license plate number due to it being pitch black and no license plate light. Streetlights about thirty yards away on either side of the Clemens' house dimly shined on the SUV in the driveway when it arrived and when it drove away from the house. Although, I did identify the SUV as a late model, dark-colored Ford Escape. As for the one of the occupants of the vehicle, he was a male about six feet tall. Medium build with dark hair. He in fact carried a microwave oven into the house, then came out of the house with a microwave oven, putting it in the back of the SUV. And when the mystery man opened his driver-side door and the back hatch door, the vehicle's dome light didn't go on. They had purposely disabled it, making it impossible to see him or the driver."

"At least our assumption about the microwave ovens being switched was true. We knew the Parkers' microwave oven didn't have any fingerprints after you did a fingerprint analysis on it. Which we said at the time would have to be cleaned meticulously by the Parkers or by the perpetrator. Of course, the perp is our number one suspect. What did you find out about the Bronco?"

"It started off being great news. I got a clear view of the license plate number. I did a DMV search…the plate was a fake. But I did do a DMV search for a late model four-door Ford Bronco. I found eight hundred and twenty-six vehicles. It'll take me awhile to check each of them out. Hopefully, I'll be able to eliminate most of them as our suspect's vehicle by separating the registerer by felon, non-felon, female, male, a few other parameters, and if any of the vehicles were recently stolen, which would likely be our vehicle. I'll call you when I get down to a reasonable number of white four-door Broncos to investigate. As for the Ford Escape, there are three thousand and sixty-two registered the past five years in Marion and surrounding counties. Again, it'll take a while to check it out."

"We're driving to Sam's Electronics in Ocala. And thanks for the information. Talk to you later."

Sherry put the phone back into her coat pocket. "The stature of the guy on the security camera's recorder could be the person who we encountered in the Parkers' driveway Tuesday morning."

"Could be, but so could probably another few thousand guys in the area. If the people in the white Bronco had fake plates, you'd have to believe the vehicle was stolen or untraceable. Like what I've said before, we're dealing with professionals."

Twelve minutes later, they turned into the parking lot of Sam's Electronics. There were several other stores in the L-shaped strip mall, including a beauty shop, restaurant, and a clothing and shoe store. Mark parked across from the electronics store. A melodious ring sounded when Mark opened the front door. He and Sherry walked into a rectangular room filled with numerous electronic devices such as TVs, radios, microwave ovens, toaster ovens, toasters, CB radios and other electronic gadgets. The glassed-in counter about ten feet long was to their right. A man in his late forties with chestnut brown hair and medium build stood behind the counter next to a cash register. "Can I help you folks?"

Mark recognized the man as Samuel Barron from the photo Ron had obtained. He and Sherry walked up to the counter. "I hope so. We're looking for a microwave oven."

"We have several in stock. Do you have one in mind?"

"Yes." Mark gave him the name and model of the Parkers' missing microwave oven from Sherry's notebook. *He should have three used ones.*

Samuel's eyebrows raised showing the upper whites of his eyes as his lower jaw slightly dropped. "Ah…ah, yes we do have this brand and model."

"Great. You see our neighbor has one and we love how it works. Oh, yeah, they said they bought one from you about three weeks ago. You probably remember them…Edna and Carl Parker."

He stared down at the floor, avoiding eye contact with Mark. "Hum. Not sure…they might have bought the microwave oven from my brother."

"Can we see it?" Sherry asked.

"See what?"

"The microwave oven," Mark interjected. *This guy is nervous and hiding something from us.*

"Oh, yeah." He came around the counter and walked to a display of microwave ovens. "This should be the one your neighbor bought from us."

Marked studied the front of it, as if he knew what the Parkers' microwave oven looked like. He and Sherry saw the switched microwave oven, not the original microwave oven. "Can I look at the back of it?"

"Sure," he answered reaching toward the microwave oven.

While Samuel turned the microwave oven around, Mark peered down at the page from Sherry's notebook containing the name and model number of the Parkers' microwave oven. Mark examined the identification plate in front of him. "This microwave isn't the same one the Parkers' bought from you. It's a different model number. Plus, the buttons in the front of the microwave are different."

"Oh. Sorry. We must be out of this particular model."

"Do you have any used refurbished ones we could look at? We really like the Parkers' microwave oven."

"No…no, we don't sell used microwave ovens."

"Don't people bring them in as a trade-in?" Sherry asked.

"Not very often. We strictly sell new electronic products."

"You do fix electronic devices. Don't you?" Mark asked. "Your sign out front says, 'we sell and service electronic devices'."

Again, Samuel avoided eye contact with Mark and Sherry. "We do repair electronic products, including microwave ovens."

Mark handed Sherry her notebook. "Did the Parkers ever bring their microwave oven in for servicing or repair?"

"No. Why would you want to know if the Parkers brought their microwave back to the store?"

"Just curious. That's all. Can you order the brand and model microwave oven our neighbor has?" *You'd think Samuel would know we've been lying to him since we've been using the present tense indicating the Parkers are still alive.*

"Sure. I can order it for you. Come over to the front counter. I'll write out a requisition form."

After Samuel wrote out the requisition, Mark noticed sweat cascading down his face from his forehead. He was convinced the Barron brothers had something to do with the three dead couples, either directly or indirectly. Somehow, he and Sherry had to get access to the tainted microwave ovens. Otherwise, they wouldn't have the evidence to prove their theory. "When do you think you'll be getting it in?"

"About a week," he answered, handing Mark a copy of the requisition. "You folks have a good day."

"You, too." He and Sherry left the store.

"Samuel Barron was obviously lying and hiding something," Sherry said as they walked toward their car.

"No doubt." They got into the car. As Mark pulled away, he glanced at the front glass door of the electronics store. A small sign hung down. It read: Closed. "Somehow, we have to get a hold of the three microwave ovens. To do it legally, I'd have to be an active sheriff detective with a warrant to confiscate them. If I talked with Detective Nelson or Thomas of the Marion County Sheriff Department, they'd have to have undisputable evidence regarding the microwave oven causing the Parkers' deaths. Right now, it's speculation. Since I'm retired, we'd have to break into the store and steal the microwave ovens. The problem with this scenario is we'd be arrested for breaking and entering if we presented the microwaves to the detectives. Like I said, we'd have to prove to them the spontaneous human combustion deaths were caused by the microwave ovens. A problem with that, a judge would likely dismiss our evidence since we obtained it illegally. We'll have to think this all out before we resort to a felonious act."

"What do you want to do now?"

"Let's drive to Ron's house and discuss what we suspect of Samuel and his brother's involvement in the three couple's deaths, especially after talking with Samuel. There isn't anything more we can do until Ron completes his inquiry of the white four-door Bronco and the Ford Escape." Mark turned left onto Pine Street and headed north. The traffic was heavy. "We now have to look out now for a dark-colored Ford Escape, a white four-door Bronco and the black Suburban."

"You realize how many vehicles today, especially SUVs, look the same unless you are directly behind them and can read the vehicle's emblem on the trunk."

"True. It's not like when we were younger and could tell a Chevy from a Ford, Dodge or Plymouth." Mark turned right onto Silver Springs Boulevard and headed towards Ron's house. The afternoon sun was behind as they approached Ron's house, which was about a mile away. Ocala National Forest with its white pines and variety of deciduous trees surrounded him and Sherry. The sun's rays highlighted the utility pole and the power line crossing the road, a downed power line that could've electrocuted them if they had run over it four days ago. He peered up at the utility pole, then the menacing power line.

"Mark, watch out," screamed Sherry.

Mark looked straight ahead as a black bear with a cub following behind are in the middle of the road, slowly meandering to the other side of the road. He slammed on the brakes, stopping about fifteen yards away. The mama bear gazed up at them as she and her cub made their way to the shoulder of the road. Mark's heart raced as his grasp on the steering wheel relaxed. "That was close."

"This part of the road has to be jinxed toward us," Sherry complained.

"I wonder why the bear and its cub decided to cross in the middle of the day?"

"Maybe they were trying to get away from the Skunk Ape?" Sherry conjectured, as she watched the bear and her cub disappear into the forest.

"The Skunk Ape is an urban myth," Mark said, as he lifted his foot off the brake and applied pressure on the accelerator moving slowly forward.

Sherry put her window down and sniffed, "I think I smell a skunk."

Mark rolled his eyes, while shaking his head back and forth. "Next thing you're going to say you see a half man, half ape peering at us from between the trees to our right."

"You know what? I think I can see…." She chuckled, then said, "Must be my imagination is working overtime."

A few minutes later, Mark drove down the street leading to Ron's house. No one he could see behind him followed them into the subdivision. He peered up to his right and saw Ron's vehicle parked in his driveway. A moment later, he pulled up behind Ron's vehicle and stopped.

They walked up to the front door, and like before, Ron's voice over the intercom said, "Come on in. The door is open."

Mark and Sherry walked inside. When they both were in the vestibule, the front door lock clanked securing the deadbolt. They walked down the hallway, then entered the computer room where Ron sat in his swivel chair in front of the middle computer screen displaying a rapid change of photos and inscription. The computer to his left displayed the same rapid sequence of picture and inscriptions. The computer to the right displayed the front door and driveway. "We probably should've called you and let you know we were coming over?"

He turned around and faced them. "Hey. No problem. I like pleasant surprises."

"We finished up talking with Samuel Barron," Mark said, "and didn't have any other thing to do or people to see. I assume you haven't got a hit on either vehicle?"

"No. Not yet. Can I get you guys something to drink?"

Mark turned and looked at Sherry. She shook her head in a negative gesture. "No, we're fine." He then went in detail their conversation the Samuel Barron. "We feel the three microwave ovens are in the store's backroom. I thought about asking him if we could look around in his back room where they service electronic products, especially the three missing microwave ovens. Of course, I didn't. Besides, we didn't have any legal rights to search for them."

"Hmph!" Ron uttered. "You're right. We'd need a search warrant. No way we could get one, or fake FBI badges and IDs."

Sherry cleared her throat. "Didn't our two FBI imposters use a fake warrant, IDs, and apparel to obtain the three beer cans from Infinity Forensic Lab yesterday?"

"True, they did," Mark answered. "No way we could obtain those illegal items. We'll have to think about another plan to confiscate the three microwave ovens at Sam's Electronics."

"You know, I thought of something," Ron said. "We really don't know if the three microwave ovens are at the electronics store. Do they have surveillance cameras?"

"Yes," Mark replied. "We need to check their surveillance camera recorder. I saw the eye-in-the-sky surveillance dome in the store's ceiling. They probably have cameras outside in front and behind the store. Why didn't we think of that before? I guess my senility is setting in."

"Where does it leave me?" Ron asked. "I'm still a young man. I should've thought of it when we found out the Barron brothers had sold the three microwave ovens, and that they may have taken them out of the three couples' houses after the couples' spontaneous human combustion. After one of my searches is completed, I'll try to get into Sam's Electronics surveillance system."

"That'll be great. Finally, we may have the evidence the Barron brothers are involved with the tainted microwave ovens."

The computer to Ron's left began to flash. He looked over at it. "The white Bronco search is finished."

Ron scooted his chair to the other computer, followed by Mark and Sherry. The three of them stared at the computer screen.

Chapter Eighteen

The computer screen displayed a column of eleven Broncos with the vehicles' VIN number, registration name, address, and phone number for each one. More important, Ron's search program got into each of the Bronco's GPS systems and brought up the pings from the satellite towers within the area of the Watchman and Clemens' houses around the time Mark and Sherry were near the victims' houses. One vehicle matched those coordinates and time. Mark stared at the name Christopher Larson. "We finally got a name of one of our perps." His voice was filled with elation.

The monitor changed to Ron's driveway and a white Bronco pulling up and stopping behind Mark's vehicle. "It's the vehicle that was following us," Sherry exclaimed.

"Oh, my God." Mark reached for his Glock. "This could mean trouble."

Two men got out of the Bronco and walked toward the front door.

Sherry leaned forward toward the monitor. "It's the two men who came to our house two days ago calling themselves Agent Cosby and Cotton."

"You're absolutely right. It's them."

A frightened expression crossed Ron's face. "What should we do?"

Mark removed his hand from the holstered Glock. "Find out what they want."

The monitor showed imposter Cosby about to push the doorbell button. Ron pushed a key on the computer keyboard, then said, "Can I help you with something?"

Imposter Cosby brought his arm down to his side. "We need to talk with you and the McKinney's."

"About what?" Mark interjected.

"Oh, Detective McKinney. We haven't been upfront or honest with you all."

"We already know you aren't Agent Cosby of F.F.A. nor is Agent Cotton. Or matter of fact agents of the FBI."

"You're right we aren't from these federal agencies. If you'll let us in, I'll explain everything to you. We're not here to harm you. Nor have we ever had intentions of harming any of you."

Mark didn't trust the two imposters. He was skeptical of taking their word. "Are either of you armed?"

"No. We're not carrying any weapons." They opened their jackets exposing the front of them, then raised their jackets as they turned around to expose their backside. They turned back around. "See, we're clean."

"We'll be right there to let you in."

Ron turned off the microphone, so the two mystery guys couldn't hear them. "Do you think it's wise to let them in?"

"I figure if they wanted us dead, they would've done it at our house two days ago. After watching their demeaner and not being armed, I'd like to know who they are, and who they represent."

"I'll unlock the front door when you get into the vestibule. Take them into the living room. I'll meet you there."

Mark and Sherry walked into the vestibule. The familiar click sounded, unlocking the front door. Mark removed his Glock and lowered it to his side in case the two mystery guys had sinister intentions. He took a deep breath, then sighed as he opened the door. Sherry stood behind him, placing her hand on his back.

The two imposters nodded their heads and walked into the vestibule. "Thanks for letting us in," said imposter Cosby. "There's a lot to tell you." He glanced down at the gun held by Mark. "Like I said, we mean you no harm."

Mark put the Glock back into its holster, as he stared at him with a stern expression. "We'll go into the living room and talk." He walked up to a closed wooden sliding door and opened it, sliding the panels into wall channels on each side. The room opened into a Victorian décor with an ornate glass chandelier in the center of the ceiling, a tri-tone leather Victorian love seat, two matching armchairs on either side, a full-length

Victorian-style leather sofa with two dark mahogany end tables with Tiffany-styled lamps sitting on top of the tables. A large burgundy and tan colored Persian rug lay in the center of the room on top of a wooden slat hardwood floor. "I never expected a living room like this from Ron."

"What did you expect?" Ron said, as he walked into the room.

Mark turned around. "Let's say something more modern looking."

Sherry stood with her hands on her hips, nodding. "I have to say, Ron, the room décor is quite eloquent. I love it."

"Thank you." He glanced at the two precarious visitors. "Have a seat, everyone."

Mark and Sherry sat on the love seat. Ron sat next to them on the armed chair to the right. The two guests sat across from them on the couch.

"Is one of you Christopher Larson?" Mark asked.

"Yes. That's me?" answered imposter Cosby. "And this is Jeff Simmons. These are our real names. Let's get right to the point. We are agents of a clandestine federal agency who investigates unexplained deaths in the United States. We at times must take on roles from other federal agencies, such as the Federal Forensic Agency and the FBI to protect our anonymity. Sorry for the deception. We were following orders."

Mark uncrossed his arms from against his chest wall. *So apparently they're not the bad guys.* "Why didn't you tell us who you were the first time we met?"

"Reasonable question," Larson answered. "Again, we maintain our anonymity during our investigations to gain information on unsolved deaths by taking on the roles of other federal agencies. We're able to open more doors that way. It's like during an interrogation of a criminal suspect, law enforcement can lie to them to gain information."

"So, your agency is like a chameleon. Instead of changing colors, you change identities."

Larson nodded. "Good way to put it."

"What is the name of your agency?"

"Can't tell you, Detective McKinney. We're a covert organization under federal auspices. If we told you, we'd have to either kill you or you'd have to join our agency."

A cold wave rushed over Mark as he reached for his Glock in the holster on his belt. He abruptly stopped, realizing the agents didn't have any weapons on them. And he also assumed the agent was kidding them with his austere comment about killing them. He then grinned. "So, since you have no intention of killing us, and we're unlikely to join your clandestine agency, what do you want from us?"

"You're very perceptive, Detective," Jeff answered. "Of course, we'd never do harm to you, your wife, or Mr. Brewer. We're the good guys, like the three of you are. Who we represent is irrelevant. And like Jeff said, we are a covert federal agency. Maybe down the road, we'll be able to tell you. What we previously told you when we were at your house a couple of days ago holds true. We're concerned about the three couples succumbing to spontaneous human combustion. Added to our concerns about the six deaths, there were three incidences that could've killed the two of you...the power line across the road, your tire being shot at on I-75, and your car's accelerator being stuck on the expressway. We now know there's a connection between those deadly situations and the spontaneous human combustion cases."

"We already figured that out," Mark said. "The problem is, we don't know who it is." He paused, then asked, "Are you saying you know who the perpetrators are?"

"Yes. At the beginning of our investigation, we were trying to determine how three couples suddenly died of spontaneous human combustion within a few days of each other. We initially sent an agent to the Parkers' house..."

"You mean the guy impersonating a travel agent?" Mark interrupted.

"Yes. He's one of our agents. You caught him by surprise. He didn't expect anyone was at the Parkers' house, since the sheriff detective, deputies, and medical examiner people had left earlier."

The pursuit of the mystery man flashed across Mark's mind like a sped-up CD video. Things regarding the clandestine agent started to make sense to him. "I'm assuming he ditched Fred Cramer's car at the mall because he knew I'd trace the license plate number back to Cramer?"

"Yes. True."

"Was Cramer a member of your agency?"

"No," Jeff answered. "Mr. Cramer didn't have any knowledge of our agent's true identity."

"If Henry Baker wasn't the agent's real name, what is his name?"

"Privileged information since he's undercover."

"What do you mean he's undercover?"

"All I can tell you is he has infiltrated an organization responsible for the deaths of the three couples. You and your team had likely discovered the mechanism causing the three episodes of spontaneous human combustion. Up to now in our investigation, we didn't have a clue of how they caused this medical phenomenon. Since you've been a target of the organization, we assumed you were getting close in solving the medical phenomenon, and they were trying to stop your investigative inquiries by either seriously injuring or killing the two of you. It's why we were keeping an eye on you and your wife. Of course, that went for naught when you discovered us following you. We tried to deceive you by telling you we were agents of the Federal Forensic Agency. Once you and your team's prowess uncovered our deception, we had no choice but to come here and tell you all who we really are and our intentions."

Mark leaned forward. "Why didn't your undercover agent inform you of the microwave's possible involvement of the deaths of the three couples?"

"Good question. We haven't heard from him since he left the Parkers' house. He normally calls every few days informing us of their activities. They may have found out his identity as a federal agent, or he was unable to call us. God only knows if he's dead or alive. We knew nothing about the microwave ovens. We also didn't know about Sam's Electronics involvement."

"That's what we were about to find out before your got here," Ron explained. "I'm going to try to access the electronics store's surveillance security system and see if they're carrying in the microwave ovens from the three dead couples' homes. We're hoping there's security cameras in their work area in the back of the store."

"We're still not a hundred percent positive the microwave ovens have anything to do with the couples' deaths," Sherry stated as she reached over placing her hand on Mark's knee.

"We'd like to stay and find out...if you don't mind?"

Mark pursed his lips, turned his head toward Ron, who nodded. He then leaned back, glancing down at Sherry, who peered back at him and nodded. Mark next turned his attention to the two agents. "Sure. You and Agent Simmons can stay. But there's a few more questions I'd like to ask you."

"More than happy to ease your mind about us," Agent Larson agreed.

"I'm going into the computer room and start my search on Sam's Electronics," Ron said as he stood. "If you like, you can get yourselves a cup of coffee or a soda from the refrigerator in the kitchen?" He then left the living room.

"I could go for a cup of coffee." He turned to Sherry. "What about you, Hun?"

"A soda sounds good to me."

"What about you, agents? We can talk in the kitchen while having our drinks."

"Coffee would be great. Thanks." Larson answered.

Agent Simmons nodded, agreeing with his partner. "Although, a soda sounds better."

The four of them walked through the dining room and into the kitchen. Mark got Sherry a root beer soda from the refrigerator, then handed Agent Simmons a cream soda. He made himself and Agent Larson a cup of coffee from the Keurig coffee maker. The four of them sat down at the kitchen table. Mark still had a feeling of skepticism toward the two agents from a clandestine federal agency. He'd heard of branches of the federal government involved with covert operations which didn't go through approval by the House of Representatives or the Senate. They could originate from the Executive Branch or directly from the President. Apparently the two agents sitting at the kitchen table represented one of these covert agencies. "You and Agent Simmons still haven't told us who this organization is who's trying to kill me and my wife?"

Agent Larson sipped some of his coffee, then clasped his cup with his left hand. "They're a homegrown terrorist group who call themselves Scorpios Justice. Their purpose is to create fear by introducing clusters of unexplained deaths throughout the United States."

"They're like a serial killer."

"That's one way to put it."

"Are you saying there have been other cases of spontaneous human combustion other than our three couples?"

"No. These are the only deaths, so far. Our undercover agent, who you call Henry Baker, infiltrated Scorpios Justice about two months ago."

Mark thought a moment. "That was about the time Phillip Frank met Baker at the pool hall."

"You're right. No wonder you have the reputation of solving difficult homicide cases when you were a detective at the sheriff's department. I'm sure your next question will be, 'Was Frank a Scorpios Justice member?' The answer is no. He befriended Baker and they were good friends. It was unfortunate Mr. Frank died of a massive stroke. Apparently, the clot formed in the area of his hip fracture and then travelled to his brain, causing a massive stroke."

"That's what I thought when we heard about his death at the hospital," Sherry said. "It's not an uncommon event after an older person fractures a hip."

"The two of you definitely make a good investigative team," Agent Simmons stated with a grin.

Mark gulped a large amount of his coffee, then said, "I have another question. Was Peter Blankenship a member of Scorpios Justice? And was he killed because he was about to tell us about his organization's demonic plan regarding the spontaneous human combustion deaths?"

"Again, you're right on the ball," Larson answered. "That's our assumption also. You now know pretty much what we know about the characters involved in our investigation."

"There's one more thing I'd like to know," Mark inquired. "You removed the three beer cans from Infinity Forensic Lab because you didn't want your undercover man being exposed as a federal agent. Am I right?"

"You're absolutely correct, detective."

Mark's cell phone rang. He glanced at the caller I.D. It was Ron. "Hey, Ron. Did you find something?"

"Yes. Have everyone come in the computer room. You won't believe what I brought up on Sam's Electronic surveillance cameras."

"We'll be right there."

He announced to everyone in the kitchen, "Let's go to the computer room. Ron has something to show us."

Everyone got up and hurried to the computer room. Mark walked into the room with Sherry behind him, followed by Agent Larson and Simmons.

Ron sat in front of the middle computer, blocking what was on the monitor screen. "I want you to see the back entrance to Sam's Electronics." The screen displayed a still frame of the front end of a white van at a back door of a building. "There are two security cameras outside, one at the front entrance and one in the back entrance to the electronic store. Two inside cameras directed at the front register and one wide-angle of the entire store. No cameras in the backroom where apparently they repair electronic products brought in by customers to fix. I saw security video of different electronic devices, including microwave ovens, coming and leaving the store through the front and back entrances. Apparently, employees and vendors are supposed to use the back door of the store. The security cameras have motion detectors, going on when someone is within ten feet of the entrances or when in the store. Which makes my job easier not having to stare at an inactive screen. I saw you and Sherry today at the store. Then at twelve thirty-eight this afternoon I saw this scene." Ron pushed a key on the computer keyboard activating the video of the still view of the white van.

"That was about the time when Sherry and I left the store."

A white van with a sunroof drove up from the bottom of the screen and stopped a few feet from the back door of the electronic store. Plywood painted white covered the two back windows of the van.

Mark had seen the van before during their investigation of vehicles at the intersections near the mall around the time the undercover agent dropped Cramer's car in the mall's parking lot. *What was the name of the van's owner?* A man in his late sixties with greying hair came around from the driver side of the van, opened the back door of the van. Mark looked at Sherry. "He's the guy…"

"Steven Davenport," Sherry interjected. "The guy we interviewed with the red stain on his shirt. We both thought he had nothing to do with our mystery man calling himself Henry Baker," she then peered at Agent Simmons, "who we now know is one of your agents."

A man shuffled himself from the back of van onto the ground. The man had his hands tied with zip-cuffs behind his back. His mouth was duct taped. *It's the agent we met in the Parkers' driveway. It's why Samuel Barron turned the closed sign on when we left the store.* "Isn't the handcuffed guy your agent?" Mark asked staring down at the monitor.

"It is," Larson replied. "They must've found out he was a government agent or someone who was a threat to them."

Behind the agent was another man, he wasn't cuffed. "That's Timothy Barron, Samuel's brother," Mark said. "He has the same height and build of the guy in the surveillance video carrying a microwave in and out of the Watchman's house the morning of them dying of spontaneous human combustion. He probably drove the late model, dark-colored Ford Escape."

Timothy walked to the back door of the store and unlocked the door. The three of them walked into the store.

Agent Larson turned to Simmons. "We gotta call the director and let him know what we saw on the surveillance footage."

"The van is still at the back of the store," Ron stated. "And no one came in or out of the back door since the three of them went inside. They're still in the store."

Chapter Nineteen

Simmons brought out his cell phone and pushed a couple of areas on the touch screen. A few seconds passed, then, "We found Agent Richards." He told the person at the other end of the call what they saw on the surveillance video, followed by a long pause as he apparently listened to the person at the other end of the call. Then, "Yes, sir. Agent Simmons and I will take care of it. Bye." He put his cell phone away inside his jacket pocket. "The Director is going to contact the FBI and have their agents obtain a warrant to search the store and arrest the three people inside the store for kidnapping Agent Richards. The FBI's forensic team will be there too. Knowing what you told us about the microwave ovens possibly being responsible for the spontaneous human combustion deaths, the warrant will include confiscating microwave ovens in the store's work area in the back of the store. We now have just cause to arrest them, thanks to you, your wife, and Ron. The three of you make an effective team."

"We're glad we could help," Mark said, "even without knowing the name of the agency you and Agent Simmons represent." Even if Agent Larson and Simmons hadn't come into the picture of their investigation, the electronic store's security video of a handcuffed guy being shuttled into the store, Mark would've called the FBI due to their mystery man being restrained against his will, which would be kidnapping in any law enforcement agency. "So, your undercover agent's last name is Richards."

"Humm. I guess I let the cat out of the bag. Yes. His last name is Richards." Simmons looked at his partner. "Are you ready? We're going to meet the FBI agents, along with their forensic team in the parking lot of Paddock Mall. From there, we'll discuss our plan in rescuing Agent Richards."

"We may not have found Agent Richards if it wasn't for the three of you," Larson claimed. "I hope he's still alive."

The agents left Ron's house, got into their vehicle and headed toward Paddock Mall, as Mark and Sherry watched them drive away. Sherry said, "I wish we could go with them and find out how the microwaves caused the spontaneous human combustion."

"We'll probably read about it in the newspaper. Or the government will suppress the cause of the spontaneous human combustion to the public and use it in covet operation against an enemy of the state. If you're a believer of a government coverup at Area 51 regarding extraterrestrial beings crash landing in a field in Nevada, then you'll assume the cause of the three couple's deaths will never be revealed publicly."

"Hey, guys. Come here," Ron shouted.

Mark and Sherry hurried to the computer room. Ron sat in front of a computer. Mark asked, "What's up?"

"I decided to do a computer search on Davenport. He had an honorable discharge from the army twenty years ago. Guess what his specialty was?"

"No idea," Mark answered. "But I got a feeling it was relevant."

"A special forces sniper."

"Oh, my God. He's got to be our shooter of the power line and the front tire of our car." Davenport's unobtrusive demeanor when they interviewed him at the front door of his house came from his military background, training him as an unshakable and mentally focused marksman. "It now confirms from everything revealed by Agent Larson and Simmons that we were getting too close to discovering their organization. Our investigation is now coming to a close."

Sherry turned and stared up at Mark. "It seems so anticlimactic now that we're at the end of our investigation. Don't you think?"

Mark reached out and placed his hand on top of Sherry's shoulder. "You're experiencing what sometimes detectives feel at the end of an investigation."

Sherry sighed. "But on the other hand, I'm glad we're finished."

"We're not done yet," Ron announced, as he now sat in front of the other computer. "Timothy Barron walked out of the back door of the electronic store."

Mark and Sherry stared at the monitor screen. Barron opened the back door of the van, then walked back into the store. Davenport walked out of the store's back door carrying a microwave oven. He placed it inside the van, pushing it forward into the van. He then went back into the store. Barron walked out of the back door carrying a microwave oven and put it into the back of the van. Davenport carried the third microwave oven and put it next to the other two. The perpetrators went back into the store, closing the back door.

"I got a feeling the three microwave ovens we're seeing put into the van were taken out of the three deceased couple's homes," Mark surmised. "I think they're going to get rid of them."

"Why do you think that?" Ron asked.

"They restrained Agent Richards, believing he's a threat to their operation. It only makes sense they need to get rid of the incriminating evidence tying them to the three couple's deaths. The perps must believe they're about to be arrested soon by the authorities. They could be taking the microwave ovens to another location, or they're going to destroy them. Whatever we're seeing here, we must notify Agent Larson or Simmons." Mark pulled out his wallet and searched for Agent Larson's business card given to him when the agents were at his house two days ago. "Where is the card?" He removed everything from the wallet, examining every item. He sighed, shook his head, displaying an expression of disgust. "I could've sworn I put his business card in my wallet."

"Since we don't know the name of his agency," Ron said, "there's no way to contact him. If we contact the FBI, they're not going to confirm the existence of Agent Larson and Simmons or their agency, or will they tell us their agency was about to raid Sam's Electronics."

"You're right. There is one thing we can do."

Sherry peered up at Mark. "Drive to Paddock Mall and tell them what we saw on the security video."

"That's it." Mark turned to Ron, "Stay here and continue monitoring the van. If they leave, call me. Then follow them if you can by hacking into the intersection cameras."

"I can do that."

Mark and Sherry got into their car and headed toward Paddock Mall. The traffic was light going west on State Road Forty. He periodically pushed the car to seventy miles per hour as traffic allowed. Once they reached Silver Springs commercial district, he decreased his speed to five to ten miles over the posted speed limit. "Ron hasn't called," Mark said. "The van must not have moved yet."

"That's good news," Sherry agreed.

Mark focused on the traffic ahead of him moving from lane to lane, avoiding any slow vehicles. Luck was on their side since he had to exceed the speed limit since leaving Ron's house without encountering law enforcement speed traps. Up ahead to his left he saw the Paddock Mall sign. The strip mall of Sam's Electronics was about a quarter of a mile up to his right on College Boulevard. Mark turned left onto the entranceway to the mall. "We're almost there."

"Like you said the other day," Sherry said, "we need to go somewhere on vacation and not tell anyone where we're going."

"Amen to that, my love." He turned left onto the circle drive encompassing the mall. The two of them peered around the north parking lot which was about twenty-five-percent full. FBI vehicles and Agent Larson and Simmons' white Bronco were nowhere in sight. They continued their track around the mall's three remaining parking lots. No agents in the east or south parking lot. They now headed for the last parking lot.

"Our luck," Sherry said. "They're in the west parking lot. We should've started to the right when we first pulled into the mall."

A moment later, they turned into the west parking lot. "They're not here. I know Agent Simmons said Paddock Mall."

"Maybe they were here and already left?"

Mark retrieved his cell phone. "I'll call Ron and see if the FBI and the two agents are at the electronic store." The phone rang once. "Hey, Ron. We're here at Paddock Mall. The agents aren't here. Are they at the electronic store?"

"No. There isn't any movement at the front or back door."

"This doesn't make any sense. I wonder…"

"Wait a minute," Ron interrupted. "The back door opened.

Davenport is coming out. He's carrying a closed cardboard box. He set the box down on the ground behind the van and is opening the van's rear door. Timothy Barron is behind him carrying what appears to be a box of files and papers. Davenport put the box inside the van. Barron is putting his box next to the other box in the van. He now closed the rear door of the van. Barron is saying something to Davenport. Barron went back into the store, closing the back door. Davenport is going around to the driver side of the van. I believe he's going to be leaving."

"I can't believe the FBI and the two agents aren't there yet," Mark said. "I need you to follow Davenport using intersection security cameras."

"Sure can. I'll go to the other computer." Ron rolled his chair to the other computer and began typing on the keyboard. "I'll keep you on speaker phone."

"We'll head in the direction of the electronic store." Mark then turned to Sherry. "Something isn't making sense here, with not finding the FBI agents and Agent Simmons and Larson."

"Maybe they're on their way to the electronic store?"

"That could be a possibility." Mark said with skepticism. He had a "gut" feeling there was a different reason the mall's parking lots were void of law enforcement agencies. Had Agent Simmons and Larson deceived them again? What he and Sherry knew for sure was that the white van carrying three microwave ovens left the electronic store with an unknown destination. Second, the mystery man, Agent Richards, was being held against his will inside Sam's Electronics. "Any image of the van or the FBI and the other agents yet?"

"No," Ron replied.

Mark stopped at the mall's traffic light intersection with College Boulevard in front of him, running to his right and left. Saturday afternoon traffic was heavy with a variety of vehicles speeding through the intersection. He peered to his left at the variety of vehicles, while Sherry scrutinized the vehicles to her right. No sight of the white van or the FBI and Agent Simmons and Larson.

"The white van turned right at the strip mall's traffic light," Ron announced. "It's heading away from you toward I-75."

About a minute past and the traffic light changed to green. Mark turned left then sped forward, heading toward the white van.

"Boss. The FBI's two black Suburbans and Agent Simmons' vehicle pulled into the mini-mall's parking lot and parked in front of Sam's Electronics. It looks like one of the Suburbans is going around to the back of the store."

"For some reason they changed location where to meet. It really doesn't matter, since now we're sure Agent Larson and Simmons are legitimate."

"Should we go back and tell them about the white van carrying three microwaves?" Sherry asked.

"No. We may lose sight of the van if it turns down one of the side roads and into the countryside where there aren't any intersection traffic light cameras."

"He's right," Ron agreed. "Once Davenport leaves the commercial district, there won't be any intersection security cameras to follow him."

Mark passed under I-75. Numerous vehicles were on the road as they stopped for a traffic light near Sam's Club and several other businesses. "Can you see where the van is now?"

"It's about a mile ahead of you. Still heading west."

Mark reached down with his right hand and touched the handle of his Glock secured in its holster. He might have to use it, depending if Davenport decided to use force against him and Sherry once they confronted the ex-military sharpshooter. The evidence that could convict the group of domestic terrorism and six senseless deaths lay in the back of the van. The traffic became more congested as they headed west on State Road Two Hundred.

"Hold on," Ron said, "two FBI agents are at the back door of the electronic store, and two FBI agents, along with Agent Larson and Simmons are at the front door. One of the FBI agents is pounding on the front door. The surveillance camera inside the store isn't showing the Barron brothers. There aren't any cameras in the back work area of the store. Wait a minute. One of the agents cut a hole through the glass door and is now reaching through the hole. He unlocked the door. There going into the store with guns drawn. The FBI agents at the back door also have their guns drawn, apparently waiting for any bad guys. This is like a thriller movie playing on the monitor in front of me."

"What about Davenport?"

"He hasn't turned yet. You're still about a mile behind him."

"I wish I had my detective car with the emergency headlights and siren. We'd be able to weave through this traffic and make headway." Right after he made the comment, the light changed green and the road ahead of him had little traffic. The next traffic light appeared to be about a mile away. Mark floored the Chrysler 300's V8 engine and sped up the road at seventy miles per hour.

"You're about a half a mile away from Davenport. His red light changed to green."

"I can see the white van now."

"He turned right at the road past the traffic light."

As Mark was about two hundred feet from the green-lit traffic light, it turned amber, then red. He slammed on the brakes, stopping at the vertical white line across the road. "Dang. Almost made it through the light." About a hundred yards ahead on the right was the road Davenport had turned onto. Mark was tempted to drive through the red light if the traffic cleared to his left and right. No such luck as a stream of vehicles crossed in front of him. The traffic light changed to amber, then green. He pushed down on the accelerator and sped forward. A moment later, he turned right at the next road, the road Davenport had turned on to.

The black-topped, two-lane road at the beginning had a few commercial businesses but after driving about a minute, open fields, and grove of trees filled the surroundings. They were in a countryside setting with an occasional house taking up small areas of nature's beauty. The road meandered through a slightly hilly terrain.

"You're on your own now," Ron announced. "No more intersection eye-in-the-sky surveillance cameras."

"What's happening at the electronic store?" Sherry asked.

"They brought out Samuel and Timothy Barron in handcuffs from the backroom of the store. Agent Richards appeared to be okay. He walked out of the backroom on his own talking with Agent Simmons and

Larson as they walked toward the front door of the store. The two FBI agents at the back door were let in by another FBI agent. I'm sure they'll confiscate and take pictures of everything in the work area. Unfortunately, the agents won't find any incriminating evidence because it's more than likely in the van."

"Keep in touch," Mark requested. "We'll call you after we catch up and stop Davenport." Mark traveled about forty-five miles per hour due to the hilly, meandering road with its hidden driveways. The sun was behind them above the treetops as shadows from trees lay across the road.

"It's nearing sunset which means creatures will be coming out of the woods and fields wanting to cross the road," Sherry said, peering slightly to her right through the windshield, then through the side window.

"That's all we would need, an animal suddenly crossing the road in front of us." He let up on the gas pedal, and thought they'd never catch up with the van at this pace.

"I see the van up ahead of us," Sherry exclaimed as they crested a hilly rise in the road.

"It sure is. Can't believe it." He estimated they were about fifty yards away from Davenport and the van. And they were getting closer. They had seen two vehicles in the other lane going in the opposite direction. Mark took a deep breath and let it out slowly. He wondered if Davenport knew what car they drove, and if he realized he was being followed?

"How are we going to confront this guy?" Sherry asked as she now stared at the road straight ahead of them.

"We'll stay back where we are, about fifty yards away. I don't want to spook him. We need to know where he is going. When Davenport stops, wherever that is, I'll decide if I should confront him." The road leveled out for about a quarter of a mile. Up ahead was a traffic light and State Road Forty. "Even if there's an intersection surveillance camera, which I doubt, since we're in the country, we'll be able to see which way he'll turn."

The van stopped, then turned left, heading west on State Road Forty.

"Where could he possibly be going?" Sherry questioned. "There's ranches and houses on large acreages out here. There were commercial businesses on State Road Forty going west, two gas stations, a Hispanic grocery store, and few small businesses on either side of the highway. We've driven down this road many times going to Brian and Lucia's house."

"You're right, we have." He thought a moment, then, "There is a county dump out here near Dunnellon. It would be an ideal area to discard the microwave ovens, never to be seen again."

"Now I know how Agent Simmons and Larson felt tailing us. Not knowing for sure where we were going."

Mark stopped for a red light at an intersection with a gas station and a Hispanic grocery store. A moment later, the traffic light turned green. He sped forward, then saw the van ahead of him, about a hundred yards away. The two-lane paved road was slightly hilly, like the road they had been driving on previously. The sun was low in the south-western horizon slightly to their left. Clouds hung low in the southwestern skyline, obscuring the sun's brilliant beam of light. Dusk was drawing its grey-ebony curtain. In about thirty minutes, vehicles would be putting on their headlights to light up the road ahead of them and warning other vehicles they were behind them or heading toward them in the oncoming lane. Ten minutes went by and Mark was now about fifty yards away, when the van's break lights went on, indicating the van was slowing down either because a vehicle in front was going slower, or Davenport was slowing down to make a turn. The van turned right, either into someone's driveway or onto a side road. "He's turned." As they got closer, Mark saw a street sign. Davenport had turned onto a black-topped road. "This isn't the road to the county dump."

"Where is he going?" Sherry questioned.

Chapter Twenty

The van descended a crest in the road, causing it to disappear. Mark slowed down, not wanting to get too close and create suspicion. When they reached the crest of the hill, the white van had turned right into a driveway about fifty yards long, which made a circle in front of a ranch-styled house. A car was parked in front of the house. The sun was now below the treetops creating a grayish hue over the countryside. "Write down the address, then call Ron and ask him to find out who lives at that address." Mark turned around at a driveway to the right about a hundred yards up the road, then parked along the side of the road where he could see the back of the van.

"Hi, Ron." She put the cell phone on speaker. "We followed Davenport to a house. We'd like to know who lives there?" She gave him the address.

"Oh, my God. Are you sure you gave me the correct address?"

"Yes. I'm sure. Why do you ask?"

"Stephanie lives there!"

Mark's vision of Ron's girlfriend, Stephanie, raced across his mind with the one event involving her during their investigation. She had evaluated the Parkers' microwave oven, knowing it was innocuous. She acted convincingly during the testing procedure. "She must be part of the evil organization calling themselves Scorpios Justice. How long has she worked for the forensic department?"

"About six months…I can't believe she's part of Scorpios Justice. What are you going to do?"

Mark's cell phone beeped, indicating someone was calling him. "Ron, I have an incoming call. I'll call you back." He pushed the answer icon, followed by speaker, then said, "Hello."

"Detective McKinney. This is Agent Larson. We're at the electronic store. Agent Richards is safe. The white van isn't at the back door."

"I know. We saw the van leave and followed it. It's at a house on a road off West State Road Forty."

"Why didn't you call me?"

"I couldn't find your cell phone number. We drove to Paddock Mall to inform you about three microwave ovens being put into the back of the van."

"Didn't you have Agent Larson's phone number in the Recent Calls section in your cell phone? I know he called you yesterday afternoon regarding Phillip Frank's sudden death."

"Not sure why it didn't register on Recent Calls. Anyway, we're parked on the road near the house the van's driver, Steven Davenport, stopped at. We know the owner of the house, Stephanie Miller. She's an electronic analyst for the Marion County Sheriff Department's Forensic Lab."

"Are you saying she's a part of Scorpios Justice?"

"We're assuming she is. Why else would Davenport drive to her house? Since she's an electronics expert, it makes sense he'd take the three microwave ovens to her house for disposal or to disassemble the microwave components."

"I'll let the FBI know what you told me about Stephanie Miller. Stay where you're at and don't encounter Davenport or Miller. We'll have a search warrant for the van and Miller's house and premises when we get there. We may now get an answer to the six spontaneous human combustion victims. What's the address?"

Mark gave him the address. "I'd say the Miller house is about forty minutes away from the electronics store. What if Davenport and/or Miller leave the house?"

"Follow them. You seemed to be efficient at following suspects without being detected. We'll be there shortly."

Mark set the phone on the car's counsel.

"I guess we're on a stakeout," Sherry said as she looked around the counsel. "So, where's the thermos of coffee? On TV, you normally see the detectives drinking coffee when they're on a stakeout."

Mark chuckled. "That's true on TV detective programs. But in real life you sit and observe your target with occasional small talk between you and your partner. If you drink coffee, what do you think happens shortly afterwards?"

Sherry smirked. "Oh…yeah. You're right. Unless you're towing a portable outhouse, or you're close to a restaurant, a gas station, where do you go to pee?"

"Exactly, my love." His cell phone rang. He glanced at the caller ID. It was Ron. "Hey, Ron. I was about to call you, and let you know what we were going to do regarding Davenport and Stephanie."

"What are you going to do?"

"The FBI agents, plus Agent Larson and Simmons are coming with a search warrant in about forty minutes. Sherry and I are parked on the road near Stephanie's house."

"After you told me about Stephanie being involved with the terrorist group, I dug into her life history. She has an impeccable history without any mention of her being involved with any radical groups, organizations, or individuals. As you know, to be hired for the sheriff's department, you must go through an FBI evaluation for any criminal blemish. So, it's hard to believe she's involved with this evil organization."

"We'll have to wait and see what explanation she gives regarding the three microwave ovens to law enforcement people." Mark knew there wasn't any other feasible explanation for Davenport to visit Stephanie, especially with him leaving Sam's Electronics with three microwave ovens likely contributing to the spontaneous human combustion deaths. Right now, it was circumstantial evidence, her being involved with this group. A confession, incriminating evidence, or collaboration from another member of Scorpios Justice could seal her fate as a criminal who would likely spend the rest of her life in prison. She could also get the death penalty.

Thirty-eight minutes passed and night had encompassed the countryside. Security lights attached to poles lit up sections of peoples' front yards in front and behind Mark and Sherry. There weren't any streetlights in the countryside community. Three sets of vehicle headlights approached them. "It must be the FBI agents, and Agent

Larson and Simmons," Sherry suggested.

"I'd say so." Mark turned his headlights on low beam, then turned them on and off rapidly two times. The leading vehicle reciprocated with two quick blinks from its headlights, acknowledging Mark's gesture and presence. Mark turned the car on and drove forward, meeting the caravan of vehicles about thirty yards beyond Stephanie's driveway. He rolled down his window, as did Agent Simmons and Larson's driver side window.

"I assume no one left?" Simmons asked in his distinct raspy voice.

"No. Both vehicles are still parked in front of the house." A security light shined down on the van and a small compact car. "Where's Agent Richards?"

"He's at the hospital being evaluated. He was roughed up a little. It's a precautionary measure. Thanks for asking about him." He turned to Agent Larson and said something to him. He then turned toward Mark. "You can follow behind the second FBI Suburban onto the property. Unfortunately, you all can't intervene during the arrest, or during the forensic search of Miller's house."

"I know, we're civilian observers. We won't get in the way."

A moment later, Mark followed the FBI's second vehicle down the driveway and stopped several feet behind the Suburban. He and Sherry got out of their car, walked up to the back of Agent Simmons and Larson's car, then stopped. An FBI agent with his gun drawn headed to the back of the house. A wide beam of light from his flashlight shined his way. Agent Simmons and Larson stood a step back and to the right of an FBI agent as he knocked on the door and yelled, "This is the FBI. We have a warrant to search your house and the white van." The agent moved to his left a step away from directly standing in front of the door. All three of them had their guns drawn, hanging them next to their bodies.

Mark knew in situations where law enforcement approached a home with a warrant, lethal force might be standing behind the front door. The agent yelled the command again. Would a hail of bullets penetrate through the wooden front door striking anyone standing directly in front of the door? A light above the door went on, illuminating the three agents.

The solid front door opened.

Stephanie stood in the doorway with a forlorn expression and slouching shoulders.

The sound of gunfire ignited the still evening air. One shot followed by three rapid shots rang out from behind the house. The FBI agent raised his Glock and pointed it at Stephanie. "Get on your knees and put your hands behind your head with your fingers locked together."

She slowly got onto her knees and locked her fingers as commanded by the FBI agent.

Agent Larson ran to the back of the house with both hands gripping his gun in front of him.

Mark removed the Glock from its holster. "Step behind the agents' car." His detective-trained reflex was to run toward the gunshots. But his job now was to protect the woman he loved from any danger. He turned around, hearing footsteps behind him.

Two FBI forensic agents, who were examining the white van, hurried cautiously toward them while gripping their guns with two hands in the ready to shoot position. "Where did the shots come from?" asked one of the agents, who appeared to be in his early thirties.

"From behind the house. One of your agents was behind the house when we heard the four shots. Agent Larson went to investigate a moment ago. Your other agent as you see," he pointed toward the front door, "has restrained the female, Stephanie Miller."

"Thanks, Detective McKinney." He turned to the other agent. "You check out the back of the house. I'll help Terry with the female suspect." They both left, leaving Mark and Sherry standing next to the rear of Agent Simmons and Larson's car.

Sherry placed her hand on Mark's back. "I hope no one is dead...especially the FBI agent." Empathy and concern touched each word.

An eerie silence hung in the air, not knowing what had taken place behind the house. Mark continued to grasp onto his Glock, not knowing what to expect as he prepared for any adverse situation that might suddenly arise. A beam of light pointed down at the ground came around the left side of the house. Three silhouette figures walking side by side with the person on the right holding a flashlight came into view, as the front porch light revealed three figures. The center person, Davenport, had been handcuffed in the front. A large red spot on his shirt showed up over the area of his anterior, right shoulder, which likely was a blood stain from a gunshot wound, thought Mark.

"It looks like Davenport has been shot," Sherry said. "I'll get my medical bag out of the trunk." She grabbed the car keys from Mark, then hurried to their car.

The FBI agent sat Davenport on a small wooden bench next to the front door of the house. "Where's the other agent?" Mark inquired.

"Agent Davis went through the back door and into the house," answered the agent.

Sherry came back with her black medical bag and proceeded to bandage the gunshot wound to the right shoulder. Mark stood next to her and observed. He had already holstered his Glock. He looked at the FBI agent. "How did the shooting go down?"

"You asked that question like a detective, which of course, I know you had been. Anyway, I see no problem telling you what happened. I came around to the back of Stephanie Miller's house with my gun drawn. The back porch light came on when Davenport came out of the house, likely due to a motion light near the back door. He had a gun in his right hand. I told him, 'FBI, put your gun down.' He raised his gun and fired one shot at me as he tried to flee to his left. I returned fire with three shots, the last bullet hitting him in the right shoulder and causing him to drop his gun. Agent Larson came around the corner of the house and helped me handcuff the suspect, defusing the lethal situation."

Mark grinned. The FBI agent had described the incident perfectly as if he were writing a shooting incident report, which he'd have to do when he got back to the FBI office. Mark looked down at Sherry. She completed bandaging Davenport.

"You're lucky," Sherry said to Davenport. "The bullet was a through and through missing any vital vessels or structures."

"Lucky would've been if I had gotten away."

"Thanks, doc, for treating him," said the FBI agent.

"He'll need antibiotics to prevent any infection," Sherry recommended.

"According to the FBI gunshot protocol, I'll have to call the EMS operator once I get Davenport secured in the back seat of my car. I'm glad his medical condition isn't life-threatening."

Sherry began to walk back to their car, carrying her medical bag.

"I'll walk with you," Mark said. He turned to the agent. "I'll help you put Davenport into your car."

"Thank you. I'd appreciate the help." The agent, along with Mark, escorted Davenport to the back seat of his FBI car. Mark leaned into the car and fastened the seat belt to the suspect. The agent secured the handcuff's chain inside a locked ring attached to the floor. He closed the car door, then looked at Sherry, who had returned from putting her medical bag in the car trunk. "I'll let the paramedics know he'll need antibiotics according to you."

"That'll be a good idea. We don't want anything bad to happen to him."

Mark and Sherry walked back to the house while the FBI agent stood by the car and called EMS. Sherry reached out and touched Mark's forearm. "I'd like to know how the microwave ovens caused the spontaneous human combustion."

"That makes two of us," replied Mark.

He heard the agent behind him say to the 911 operator, "This Special Agent Thompson from the FBI, we'll need the paramedics to assess and transport a gunshot victim to the emergency room." As he and Sherry got closer to the house, the agent's voice was fading, and he was unable to hear what the agent was saying to the operator.

Sherry and Mark now stood by the opened front door of the house. Mark saw Stephanie sitting in a living room chair, hands cuffed behind her. They then sat on the bench next to the front door. Mark's cell phone rang. He peered at the caller ID. "Hey, Ron."

"Did they arrest Stephanie? And did she confess being a part of the three couples' deaths?"

"Don't know. The federal agents haven't said anything to me. We're sitting on the bench next to the front door. Stephanie is inside the house handcuffed and sitting in the living room. I don't have any other information. Oh, yeah." He then told him about the shooting incident between the FBI agent and Davenport.

Ron sighed. "It doesn't look good for Stephanie."

"No, it doesn't, my friend."

"Let me know if you find anything else out regarding her and the couples' deaths."

"Sure will, Ron. Talk to you later. Bye." Mark put his phone away.

They watched the forensic agents bring out three normal-appearing microwave ovens. It didn't appear they were taken apart.

Flashing emergency lights could be seen to their left coming down the road. The EMS vehicle turned right into Miller's driveway and stopped behind their Chrysler 300. Agent Thompson met them next to his car. He removed Davenport from the back seat and escorted him to the back of the EMS vehicle. The agent got into the back of the vehicle with the shooter. Fifteen minutes later, the vehicle left. Mark overheard the FBI agents say they'd have the paramedics take Davenport to West Marion Community hospital.

It took about an hour to search the house and remove potential incriminating evidence. Several cardboard boxes were removed from the house, probably including the two boxes seen being removed from the electronic store. Mark found out from Agent Simmons that the microwaves and the other evidence would be taken to the FBI lab in Quantico, Virginia. Since kidnapping of a federal agent occurred by a terrorist group, the investigation was taken over by the FBI. Mark, sitting on the bench with Sherry, leaned toward her and whispered in her ear, "Like we mentioned before, we may never find out how the microwave ovens played a part in the deaths of the three couples. Which would be a shame since we were the ones…that is you were the one…that produced the theory of the microwaves causing the spontaneous human combustion deaths."

"I agree, it would be a shame. But even if we don't find out, at least we stopped this group from causing any more deaths of innocent people. That's a positive consolation."

"You're right. At least we stopped any more deaths."

Agent Larson brought Stephanie out of the house handcuffed.

Mark heard the FBI agent read Stephanie the Miranda Rights before he brought her outside. She looked at him, then Sherry with a disdained expression, followed by a smirk. Mark thought to himself, *Evil can be hidden behind a kind and seemingly caring person.*

Chapter Twenty-One

Two weeks later

A warm breeze blew over the light-blue water covering pearl-white sand of a Cancun beachside resort. The breeze touched the bare skin of Mark and Sherry, who lay on lounge chairs covered by large beach umbrellas blocking the radiant sun rays. Mark reached over and touched Sherry's warm, soft forearm skin. "We definitely earned this vacation after what we went through a couple of weeks ago."

"We sure do deserve it," she replied, then sipped some of her liquor-spiked fruit drink. "I feel sad for Ron regarding his friend Stephanie being an evil, deceitful woman who fooled us all. One good thing came about for Ron, he got two of my homecooked meals we promised him."

"Yeah. He sure enjoyed your cooking." His cell phone rang. He peered at the caller ID. "It's Agent Larson. He knows we went on vacation and didn't want to be bothered."

"I have a feeling it's good news."

Mark put the phone on speaker. "Hey, Agent Larson. What's up?"

"Something I'm sure you and Sherry would want to know. FBI Forensic Division at Quantico found out how the microwave oven contributed to the spontaneous human combustion deaths."

"Oh, my God. That's great," Sherry exclaimed.

"There's one stipulation. You can not divulge this information to anyone. If you do, you will be prosecuted and spend at least ten years in a federal prison. Do you still want to know?"

Mark looked at Sherry, who nodded affirmatively. "Yes, we do."

"Okay. Unfortunately…I can't reveal it over the phone due to security reasons. You never know who might be listening on our unsecured phone lines. When the two of you return from your vacation next week, I'll come to your house. There's also something else I need to discuss when I talk with you and Sherry at your house. Until then, have a wonderful time on your vacation. Bye."

Sherry experienced an overwhelming wave of disappointment. She wanted to know the information now, not when they got back home next week. It was obvious the information regarding the cause of the three couples' spontaneous combustion deaths wouldn't be in any newspaper or news broadcasting station, such as radio or TV. She thought this would happen. The government would keep the cause of SHC a secret. Although, she could understand the government's position, since if another terrorist group or a deranged individual obtained Stephanie Miller's blueprint for producing spontaneous human combustion, they could duplicate the process, bringing havoc and death. One thing did make her feel good. She and Mark were responsible, along with Ron who had originally mentioned the fact the three couples all ate microwave food prior to their deaths, for pursuing her presumptive theory. She shared her thoughts with Mark.

"Yeah. You right. We can now enjoy our vacation, knowing we'll have an answer to the spontaneous human combustion deaths." He sipped more of his drink. "I wonder what the other thing Agent Larson wants to discuss with us?"

"Not sure."

~ * ~

Mark retrieved his car keys from his pocket as they walked up to their car in the Extended Stay parking lot at Gainesville International Airport. He pushed the icon on the remote attached to his key ring and opened the car doors. After putting their luggage into the car's trunk, they sped home. Late Monday morning traffic on the roadways heading south was congested. His cell phone rang. He handed the phone to Sherry.

Sherry looked at the caller ID. "It's Agent Larson." She put the phone on speaker. "Morning, agent."

"How was your flight?"

"Uneventful. A smooth ride home." On their way to Cancun last week, the plane had hit a period of severe air disturbance. Which the agent likely already knew about, since he knew they were driving home from the airport. The watchful eye of federal investigative agencies today had the eye-in-the-sky satellites observing select citizens, properties, or whatever they needed to see.

"Glad to hear the flight was uneventful, doctor. Agent Simmons and I will meet you at your house at one o'clock. If the time will be okay with you?"

"That'll be fine. We'll see you then." Sherry disconnected the call and set the phone down into the counsel's cup holder.

The fifty-minute ride home seemed longer to Sherry and Mark, as he turned left from State Road Four Forty-One at the traffic light and headed east on NW Seventy-Seventh Street. They were three minutes from their house. Sherry glanced at the clock on the dashboard: 12:35 pm. In twenty-five minutes, the agents would be arriving at their house. She'd had a wonderful time with Mark in Cancun, and another memorable chapter in her life with Mark. Soon she'd learn how the three couples had died from spontaneous human combustion, a revelation the world could not know about, especially evil entities.

Mark put the house key into the front door lock, turning the key to the right, unlocking the door. He opened the door and walked inside. A flashing red light emanated from a security pad next to the front door on the wall. He pushed seven-seven-four-four on the security pad. A green light appeared. Sherry and Mark would normally check around the house, making sure everything was where it was supposed to be after an unknown intruder entered their house a few weeks ago. Before they went on vacation, they had installed a failsafe home security system.

They put the suitcases in their bedroom and began unpacking. After putting everything away, they walked into the kitchen.

The front doorbell chimed.

Sherry glanced at her watch, as she stood between the kitchen and the living room. It was almost one o'clock. She looked at Mark who was standing near the refrigerator opening a bottle of water. "It's got to be the agents."

Mark put the water bottle down on the counter, went to the front door, and opened it. Agent Simmons and Larson stood on the landing, both wearing casual clothes and jackets. Simmons displayed a serious expression while Larson had a friendly smile. "Come on in, gentleman."

"How was your vacation?" Larson asked.

"It was good. Can I get the two of you a water, pop or coffee?"

Both declined Mark's offer.

"We're anxious to hear about the cause of the spontaneous human combustion," Sherry said. She wanted to get right to the point for their visit. "Please have a seat on the couch." The agents sat on the couch, while Sherry and Mark sat on cushioned armchairs across from them.

Agent Simmons brought out a sheet of paper from his jacket pocket and unfolded it. "Three microwave ovens were inspected and analyzed by forensic scientist at the FBI Quantico Forensic Laboratory to determine if they were the cause of six cases of spontaneous human combustion. I brought the forensic scientists' report. There was no way I could summarize what was on the report. Most of the analysis is in medical terms I never heard of. We were instructed by our director to read the report to you." He glanced at Agent Larson, then back toward Sherry. He got up and handed the report to Sherry. "We're not going to tell the director I had you read the report. Who's going know besides the four of us anyway?"

Mark slid his chair next to Sherry's. They both stared down at the report.

The three microwave ovens were inspected. Several small openings an eighth of an inch diameter on the facing next to the door allowed the leakage of electromagnetic radiation. Microwave ovens use electromagnetic waves which penetrate food or liquids causing some molecules to vibrate. This vibration generates heat throughout the food or liquid substance. The electromagnetic wave frequency was altered on each of the microwaves. The frequency had an effect on anyone within twenty feet of its electromagnetic radiation. The altered electromagnetic radiation caused a dramatic increase of UCP-1, a regulatory protein inside the body, which caused adipose oxidation to be released as internal body heat. The internal body temperature increased to three thousand degrees Fahrenheit. This extreme temperature caused every cell in the six victims' bodies to turn to ash, creating the ideal condition for spontaneous human combustion. According to Stephanie Miller's notes, they chose elderly couples as their victims because they wouldn't have any children living in their homes. The Barron brothers asked the couples if they had any children living with them due to safety reasons before selling them the microwave ovens. It would draw too much media attention if an entire family of children and parents died of spontaneous human combustion. The last entry in her notes stated their group was going to sell their deadly microwave oven technology alteration to other terrorist cells throughout the world.

Sherry leaned back after reading the FBI report, as did Mark. "Thank God, they didn't have a chance of selling their microwave technology."

"We're assuming they haven't. The Barron brothers, Steven Davenport, and Ms. Miller lawyered up. Because of you, Mark, and Ron, we have enough evidence to put them in prison for the rest of their lives. And maybe even the death penalty."

"You mentioned on the phone to us when we were in Cancun about something else you wanted to discuss with us," Sherry said, not having a clue to what he wanted to discuss with them.

"Yes. You're correct," Agent Simmons answered as he stood, walked over to Sherry and retrieved the FBI forensic report from her. He then sat backdown on the couch. "We gave the two of you FBI information because of your honesty and integrity. By the way, we also talked with Ron Brewer regarding him helping in the investigation. He will not discuss anything that happened during the investigation, or the reason for the arrest of Stephanie Miller."

"Sherry and I wondered about that," Mark said.

"Anyway, we want to know if you decide to investigate another criminal or medical mystery. We'd like to be involved. And if we're investigating a case in your area, we'd like to contact you for your assistance."

"You mean like a subcontractor?"

"That would describe your assistance. The agency would pay the two of you for your assistance. And of course, you can decline our request for help."

Sherry looked at Mark, then back toward the agents. "We appreciate your offer and confidence in us. Right now, we don't want to make any decision on your offer."

"I can understand that. The offer will be open if you decide to accept." Simmons and Larson stood, as did Sherry and Mark. The agents then left the house.

"I sensed you agreed with me regarding the Agent Simmons' offer?"

"Your innate feeling was correct, as usual. Right now, we don't want to commit to any criminal or medical mysteries. We're retired. Let someone else do it."

Sherry's cell phone rang. She looked at the caller ID. It was Joe Barrington, their neighbor. She put her phone on speaker. "Hi, Joe."

"How was your vacation?"

"Relaxing."

"Great. The reason I called, besides asking about your time in Cancun, I was talking with Myrtle Smith. She's complaining about feeling fuzzy, unable to focus her eyes. Do you think…"

"Have her call her doctor. Mark and I are leaving for an appointment right now. Talk to you later. Bye."

"What appointment?" Mark questioned.

"Northgate Diner for their spaghetti dinner special."

Frozen Death

Something is causing people to freeze to death in Florida during ninety-degree weather. Ancient Indian lore holds the answer to these mysterious medical aberrations. A newly constructed Florida male prison sits on ancient hallowed grounds called Forbidden Hill. Soon after the prison opens, two male inmates freeze to death without exposure to frigid temperatures. John Randall, a widowed prison doctor, meets Lena Windmaker, a single, off-duty sheriff detective at a local library. Their initial platonic relationship soon kindles into a more amorous one. They hide a personal secret that could bring them together or destroy them. They uncover articles in local, post-Civil war newspapers describing residence succumbing to Frozen Death. John and Lena race to discover a cause before it chooses other victims.

Chapter One

"Dr. Randall!"

He pivoted around and saw Nurse Jones, a middle-aged overweight woman, standing in the hallway outside the infirmary. "What's the matter?"

"Inmate Armstrong is shaking all over." She paused to catch-her-breath. "He's saying over and over, 'I'm going to die.'"

The small hairs on the back of John's neck stood straight out. He had only examined Armstrong a few minutes ago. What could have gone wrong with him in that short period? John raced into the hallway between the infirmary and the nursing station. He looked to his right through glass panels. Armstrong lay in bed. His entire body shook as if an electrical current pulsated through it. Nurse Rollins stood next to him. He rushed into the six-bed ward and heard Armstrong shouting, "I'm going to die. I'm going to die. I'm going to die..." His unemotional words sounded like someone reading the ingredients off a soup can.

Rollins, a male nurse in his early thirties, removed a thermometer.

"What's his temperature?" John asked, reaching down and placing the back of his hand on top of Armstrong's left forearm. The skin felt cool and dry.

"Ninety-four degrees."

Armstrong kept repeating, "I'm going to die. I'm going to die. I'm going to die…"

"You're not going to die!" John interrupted. "Try to stay calm." Armstrong stopped his chanting. His uncontrollable shaking continued. He turned toward Rollins. "Did you get a blood pressure and pulse?"

"It was normal. Blood pressure was a hundred and twenty over sixty-eight and a pulse of seventy-two before he started to tremble."

John tried to grab Armstrong's wrist to take a pulse, but his violent shaking made it difficult. He removed a stethoscope from his lab coat, placing it over the left side of Armstrong's chest. The heart gaited at about sixty beats a minute. John removed the stethoscope, flipping it around his neck. "His vital signs are dropping. His skin is cool and dry. There's uncontrollable shivering. You'd think he just stepped out of a walk-in freezer."

"He hasn't been out of our sight for the past hour and a half," said Jones.

"What's important now is to raise his vital signs. Jones, get the crash cart from the trauma room. Rollins, call EMS."

"What diagnosis do I give them?"

"Possible heart attack." John knew if Armstrong's vital signs continued to drop, a heart attack would occur.

Jones and Rollins ran out of the room.

John turned off the air conditioning to the infirmary. He grabbed blankets off the other beds, placing them over Armstrong's shivering body. He next placed a thermometer on a dry forehead. The temperature read ninety degrees. It dropped four degrees in less than ten minutes.

Armstrong stopped shaking. His body lay still with eyes and mouth closed.

John reached down and shook a cold, lifeless arm. "Armstrong! Open your eyes!"

No response; his eyes remained closed.

A squealing sound of two pieces of metal rubbing together behind him caused him to spin around toward the infirmary door. Nurse Jones rushed toward him with the crash cart. "Put it over here," he said pointing toward the head of Armstrong's bed. "Start an IV and open it all the way."

"Okay," she said slightly out of breath.

John placed a blood pressure cuff around Armstrong's upper right arm. He squeezed the bulb several times, raising the dial up to two hundred. His fingers opened the valve, deflating the cuff. Armstrong's pressure had dropped to eighty-four over fifty--much too low for a young robust man. John uncoiled the tubing attached to a nasal cannula from the top of the portable oxygen tank, placing its prongs into Armstrong's nose. He turned the oxygen on to two liters.

He next attached self-adhesive electrodes across Armstrong's chest wall. A moment later, he turned on the EKG machine.

Beep...Beep...Beep from the EKG machine engulfed the room. John stared at a slow heart rate of thirty-six flashing in the upper right corner of the monitor.

Rollins ran into the infirmary. "Dr. Randall, I called EMS. It'll take them awhile before they get here."

"Why's that?"

"All their EMTs and Paramedics are tied-up at a multiple car accident on I-75."

"Damn! What can go wrong next?" He reached into the top drawer of the crash cart, removing a needled-syringe filled with atropine--a drug to increase the heart rate. He pierced the needle through the IV's plastic portal and pushed the drug into the IV line. He looked up at the monitor. A heart rate of 36 continued. "Jones, take his blood pressure. He leaned over and listened for chest sounds with his stethoscope while looking for movement of the chest. Both were present. "No need to intubate, yet."

"Blood pressure is sixty systolic," said Jones.

John picked up the thermometer, placing it onto Armstrong's forehead. A few seconds, he removed it. "Eighty-six degrees. It had dropped another four degrees. Why are the vital signs dropping so fast?"

John injected another vial of atropine into the IV line. "Be the one." The monitor displayed 32, then 34…36…38…." It's working! His heart rate is increasing."

"Great," said Rollins, turning and high-fiving Jones.

John took Armstrong's blood pressure. "Eighty over fifty-four. We did it."

"I'll take his temperature," said Jones, placing the thermometer on Armstrong's forehead. "It's dropped to eighty degrees!"

John rubbed the back of his head. "What the hell is going on?"

A piercing sound screamed from the cardiac monitor. John stared at the monitor. "He's in Ventricular Fibrillation! Rollins, give me the paddles. Turn the defibrillator on two hundred. Jones, start CPR."

A moment later, Rollins handed John the paddles. He reached over Armstrong, placing the paddles on a bare chest. "Stand clear!" Armstrong's body jerked. The monitor still showed V-Fib. "Turn it up to three hundred."

"Ready," said Rollins.

"Stand clear!" Armstrong's body jerked. The monitor continued to show V-Fib.

"Three hundred and fifty."

"Ready."

"Stand clear!" Armstrong's body lurched upwards. Again, John saw no change on the monitor.

"Rollins, give me the laryngoscope." In less than thirty seconds, John intubated Armstrong. "Jones, start bagging him. Rollins, take over chest compressions."

Over the next twenty minutes, John injected other cardiac drugs into the IV line.

"Stop CPR." The straight line moved across the monitor.

"Should we continue CPR?" Jones asked.

"No…," John's shoulders slumped,"…we've done everything we can for him."

Jones removed the endotracheal tube. "What caused his death?"

Sweat dripped off John's face. His saturated shirt clung to his skin. He slowly moved his tongue over his upper lip then over his lower lip. He stared down at a lifeless body. "Armstrong froze to death."

Other Books by the Author
at
Rogue Phoenix Press

The Strange Horizon

The Strange Horizon ranges from stories less than a hundred words to over four thousand words. There isn't any profanity, gore or sexual innuendo in any of the short stories. The genre varies from mystery, suspense, contemporary, horror, science fiction and fantasy. You may smile, chuckle, express a tear or two, feel a sudden chill or feel a warmth at the end of the story. Emotions are in the mind of the reader and the heart cuddles or rejects those emotions.

Strange Appearance

Two hairless teenage bodies are found dead with ritual-type death masks on their faces in Ocala National Forest. Robert Jenson, a fourth year medical student and Cynthia Davidson, a pathologist's assistant, join together to solve these unexplained mysterious deaths. Clandestine members of a secluded satanic cult adjacent to the national forest cross their paths. Shortly afterwards, Robert and Cynthia face deadly situations jeopardizing their own lives as they soon discover someone doesn't want them to know the truth behind the teenagers' deaths. Robert and Cynthia's initial platonic relationship evolves to amorous feelings and needs complicating their investigation. Evil touches the two medical sleuths. And they don't realize it until it's almost too late.